THE
GUEST
HOUSE

Also by Bonnie Traymore:

Killer Motives
Little Loose Ends
The Stepfamily
Head Case

THE
GUEST
HOUSE

A PSYCHOLOGICAL THRILLER

SILICON VALLEY SERIES

BONNIE TRAYMORE

First Edition
Pathways Publishing
Honolulu, HI

Cover and Interior Design by FormattedBooks

Paperback ISBN 979-8-218-33018-7

Library of Congress Control Number: 2024902906

For Erica

Contents

PART ONE

PROLOGUE

One thing I've realized over the years is that not everyone has what it takes to do what's needed when the time comes. If you want something done right, you need to be prepared to do it yourself. I'm committed to reaching my goals, whatever the costs.

If I could achieve them without spilling any blood, of course, that would be my preference. I have killed before though, and I'll do it again if that's what it takes to succeed.

But only if I have no choice. That's what separates me from the crazies. I get no pleasure out of harming people. In fact, it leaves me feeling very empty. But I won't stop until I get what I need. And I'll eliminate anyone who stands in my way.

ONE

Allie

I'm half awake when I feel a thud reverberate through my apartment and shake the bed. I spring up, and my heart is immediately in my throat.

Is this what an earthquake feels like?

Grabbing my phone, I check to see if there's an alert. It's 3:17 in the morning, and there's nothing of concern on my phone, but maybe it takes a while to get the word out. I'm new to California, so I have no idea what an earthquake feels like or if anyone even bats an eye at something like this.

I hold still for a few minutes, and I don't feel any more shaking. I reach for my speech processor on the nightstand. I'm deaf, and without my cochlear implant I hear nothing. Now I'm concerned there might be an intruder or some other threat lurking outside my door.

The small guest house I rent sits behind a stately, expensive home, and the owners have been away for the last week. There's a boarder who rents a suite inside the main house. I thought he was still around, although it's hard to tell with him. The guy's kind of a ghost, and I don't normally run into him much.

Once my speech processor is in place, I notice some kind of intermittent scraping noise outside. A tingling sensation crawls up my scalp. They have a dog, and she's not barking. But then I haven't heard her at all this week, come to think of it. *Maybe they took her with them?*

I peek out the window, poised to call 9-1-1 if someone is burglarizing the house, and I spot my landlord—at least I think it's my landlord—dragging a large duffel bag across the lawn. It seems heavy, and he's straining to move it. He whips his head around towards me, and I quickly duck down and out of sight.

Did he see me?

My heart starts to race.

I hear a voice, barely above a whisper. "Hurry up," it says.

A woman's voice?

I'm terrified of the dark, so I keep the bathroom light on when I sleep. I'm hoping it's not bright enough for him to see inside my place. I lift the curtain just a hair and look out again. His back is to me, so hopefully he didn't notice me.

What the hell is he doing?

I thought they were away until tomorrow. Did they come home early and I didn't hear them? But this is strange. And this living arrangement made me uneasy from the start. Maybe I need to look for another place, although the thought of that puts my stomach in knots. It's a nice unit at a decent price, and the rental market is extremely tight here. Perhaps he has a good explanation for what he's doing, although I can't imagine what it could be.

I double-check the dead bolt on the door, turn off the bathroom light, and get back into bed. I'm not taking my speech processor off though, so I probably won't be able to get back to sleep; I'm used to total silence. I grab my phone, hold it under my comforter, and start thumbing through apartment listings as I wait for the sun to rise.

TWO

Allie

One month earlier

I rush into Starbucks to grab a pick-me-up before I embark on my next round of apartment viewings. It's packed in here, and I need to use the bathroom. *Badly.* I've never been to this Starbucks before. Rancho Shopping Center, according to my app.

"I've got a to-go order," I say to the barista. "Is there a restroom in here?"

"Over there," she says, pointing towards the other side of the café. "Past the pickup area."

I'm also hungry and hot. But I'm on a tight schedule, so although I'd like to chill for a while, I need to keep going. I locate the restroom and, thankfully, there's no line. When I come out, I rush up to the counter to look for my drink order. I pick up a few cups that could be mine and examine them, but my latte's not ready yet. I let out a long sigh and glance at my watch.

A frazzled worker glares at me but quickly softens her look. I offer her an apologetic smile, not wanting to stress her out any further. I'm surprised she heard me over the whir of the blenders and the milling of the coffee grinder. They're very backed up and seem hopelessly understaffed. I worked my way through college at jobs like that, so I know exactly how she feels. And if I can't get my idea off the ground before my funding dries up, I might be right there behind that counter with her.

But I can't be late for my next appointment, so if my order doesn't come up soon, I'll need to leave without it. I've just finished a two-week boot camp along with the other women in my cohort, a requirement of the organization that gave me the funding for my start-up venture. I've also been looking at apartments on this visit, and I'm starting to think I might have to give up and go back to Milwaukee, at least for now, which is not an ideal option.

The man standing to my right says something, but I don't catch it. I can't hear anything out of my right ear, and the background noise is making it harder. And I remind myself that this is exactly why I'm here, trying to bring my concept to market.

I turn to face him so I can read his lips. "I'm sorry. I didn't hear you."

"New in town?" he asks.

"Yes. Is it that obvious?"

"You went to the wrong side of the store for your pickup," he says, "and you're holding a rental car key."

His wandering eyes look out from a kind, almost jovial face. I glance down at the key in my hand, wondering if I should be more discreet. I don't need to advertise the fact that I'm a single woman traveling alone.

"You're very observant," I say.

"Not always," he replies.

I hope he's not hitting on me. He's nearly twice my age if I had to guess. There are a lot of rich guys around here who can probably get women half their age to go out with them. He's dressed down in jeans and a t-shirt, sporting a Patek Philippe on his wrist—and not an entry-level one. Money's a compensating factor for some women, but not for me. Not for that big of an age gap. Then I notice a wedding ring and relax a little. Perhaps he's just being friendly.

"Looking for a place to live?" he asks.

"Um, yes."

"I'm in real estate," he says.

"Oh." I nod.

That explains it.

Now I'm going to get the sales pitch. I should tell him to move on and not waste his time. I'm not planning to buy. But I realize he's just doing his job. Maybe I can learn something from him. Networking in person isn't my strong suit, and I need to get better at it.

"Mike Tabernaky," he says.

"Allie Dawson," I reply.

"Is it just yourself, or do you have a family?"

"Just me." Saying that out loud makes me feel vulnerable all of a sudden.

"Well, it just so happens we have a guest house behind our home that's become available. It's nearby, in Cupertino.

Just over the border from Los Altos. Perfect for a single person."

Generally, I'm a trusting person, but this seems a bit too good to be true. My mind flashes to the shower scene in *Psycho*.

"That's great, thanks. But I think I may have found something."

He nods as he chews on his lower lip.

"Allie? Your order's ready," the barista calls out.

"Well, that's me," I say. "I need to run. Nice to meet you, Mike." I offer him a fluttery wave and flash my best Midwestern-girl smile. If I end up living in this neighborhood, I'll probably see him again, so I don't want to seem rude or unappreciative. Plus, he might know some venture capitalists he can introduce me to.

"Here. Take my card. In case it doesn't work out." He reaches out to me with his business card perched between his thumb and forefinger. I pluck the card from his fingers without touching them.

"Thanks," I say.

"You're welcome, Allie Dawson. Hope to see you around."

I head outside and mentally prepare myself for another round of apartment viewings, trying to lower my expectations. The market's supposedly softening for renters, but it doesn't feel that way to me. And without a steady stream of income, I've been having a hard time qualifying for a place to rent. I gave up my stable job as a luxury branding specialist to pursue this opportunity. At the moment, I'm hoping that wasn't the biggest mistake of my life.

It's a competitive market, and I'm sure there are a ton of prospective renters who seem more desirable, with longer track records in the area. That's why I'm a little overdressed for the occasion, in my red cap-sleeved Tory Burch dress paired with strappy black sandals. I want to make a good impression and try to appear a bit more mature than my twenty-nine years.

When I open the door to my rental, a white Kia Soul, the heat inside the car hits me and nearly knocks me off my feet. It's late August, so hopefully it will cool down soon. They say it doesn't get this hot here too often—just my luck. I see heat waves radiating off the black vinyl interior. I run around to the other side and open the door to air it out a little. I don't want to show up sweaty and disheveled. Then I shut the passenger door, head back over to the driver's side, and hop in.

The seat is warm but, thankfully, not burning hot. I sit down, strap myself in, and realize that I still have the business card in my hand. I tuck it into my wallet, start the car, crank the a/c, and pull up the address on my app. Then I take one last look in the rearview mirror, apply some lipstick, and fluff my hair. I make a mental note to find a hairdresser. My dirty blonde roots are showing, and I'm badly in need of a trim. Still, I'm presentable enough.

The dark circles under my eyes are gone because the loud people renting the front half of my Airbnb left yesterday morning, and I finally got a good night's sleep. I'm not used to sleeping with my speech processor on, so any noise at all bothers me. I felt vulnerable sleeping without it in an unfamiliar place though, so it seemed safer to sacrifice deep sleep. Last night was better, and the extra hit of caffeine is starting to kick in.

I can do this.

———

Today's apartment search was even worse than the previous ones, probably because it's Saturday and everyone's available. I had four appointments, and each rental had a steady stream of prospective tenants, including the unit that was totally unacceptable to me with no air conditioning, smelly, dog-pee-soaked carpets, and communal laundry.

Even the cramped one-bedroom suite I'm sitting in right now is better than that one, but I can't afford this Airbnb for much longer, even if I could stand sharing part of a house with a revolving door of random travelers. I'm burning too much cash and energy on this trip, and although I filled out applications at the other three apartments, I'm not holding my breath.

Now I'm taking some time to regroup. I decide I'll reach out to the organization that helped me with my pre-seed funding and see if they can give me some suggestions. I reach into my wallet to grab the executive director's business card. But I come across the card I got from Mike Tabernaky, the real estate agent I met at Starbucks, with the guest house. I pull that out instead. He's a luxury property specialist and the principal broker at the firm. Maybe he *does* have a pipeline of wealthy venture capitalists he can introduce me to. At the very least, I should try to connect with him on social media.

But why would he be giving his card out to people at Starbucks when the rental market is this hot? Perhaps he doesn't want to deal with a parade of random strangers at his home? Or maybe he wants a single person, but he can't say that in the advertising because of antidiscrimination laws. I do a search and find his website. It's a small firm with two other agents and a few upscale listings on the site.

I tell myself that if I'm going to be a successful entrepreneur, I need to take some risks. If an opportunity like this dropped in my lap, maybe it's fate. Part of the success story I'll tell one day about how I was ready to give up when I found a place to live from a random guy I met at Starbucks who introduced me to so-and-so…and then it all fell into place.

Am I this desperate?

Yes, but I'm also not stupid. I'll make an appointment to see the unit, and I'll have my brother on the phone with me when I go see it, just in case.

It'll be fine.

I pull out my phone, take a deep breath, and punch in Mike's number. I'm a little surprised when it goes to voicemail and a little relieved. It would be more concerning if he was sitting around waiting for my call. Perhaps it's rented already and I missed my shot. The thought of that makes me want it more.

I open up my email and start drafting a message to Mina Rao, Executive Director at Start-Her, the accelerator that's sponsoring me, hoping that something comes through before I have to hang it up and head back east rather than burn through the money they gave me before I even get started.

THREE

Laura

It's Monday morning and I'm in my home office when Mina calls. The ringtone wakes my sleeping three-month-old, and Kai starts wailing. I could kick myself for not remembering to silence my phone. I pick up the call, put it on speaker, and reach for him.

"This can wait, Laura," Mina says to me as Kai continues his fussing.

It annoys me that my subordinate is second-guessing my decision to pick up the call, and I fight the urge to snap at her. She means well, but Mina's not the only person in my life insinuating that I should take more time off. It's wearing on my frazzled nerves. It's not the baby or my career that's making me stressed. It's the horrible image that haunts my dreams. The one I can't tell anyone about. But that's not Mina's fault, so I take a deep breath and let it go.

"No. He'll settle down. Hang on a minute."

"Take your time."

I lift my shirt, place him on my breast, and grab a pen.

"Okay. What's up?" I ask.

Mina runs through a slew of information in record time. She's my executive director. We met at a now-defunct start-up that folded a little over a year ago. I've since founded an accelerator for female entrepreneurs, and my first class of ten awardees has received an initial round of funding. The timing is less than ideal with a newborn, but I'm not letting motherhood stop me. There are some promising ideas on the table, ones that could really make a difference in the world.

One woman developed a prototype of a blood-testing machine that could be a game changer in health care, if she can bring it to market. Another is working on a clip-on screen that would allow eyeglass wearers to read captions of conversations in real time. Now is not the time to step back.

"What happened to Allie Dawson? Did she find a place yet?" I ask.

Allie Dawson is working on the caption device, and her project excites me because it serves an unmet need in the market, it won't get bogged down in a ton of regulatory red tape, and it's not overly capital-intensive to produce.

"Not yet, but she has a lead on a unit in Cupertino. She's got an appointment this afternoon, and she's a little wary of going by herself, so I offered to go with her," Mina says.

"Why?"

"It's a guest house. Of some real estate broker guy who approached her at Starbucks."

Mina gives me the rundown. It sounds fine to me, but I can see how a single woman might be a little uncomfortable renting a place from a stranger who befriended her at a coffee shop, although that's what real estate professionals tend to do. It's nice that Mina offered to go with her.

"Give me his name and I'll check him out," I say.

We go over the rest of the items on my list and sign off. I'm more tired than usual this morning and not only because of Kai. I had the nightmare again. It took hours for me to fall back to sleep, only to be woken again an hour later by my baby's cries.

I can't go on like this. I search my inbox for the therapist I contacted a few weeks back, to finally schedule an intake appointment. But a call comes in from a venture capitalist I've been courting, and then Kai needs to be changed, so it goes on the back burner once again.

———

My husband, Peter, enters my home office, and I glance at the clock. It's after six already. The hours flew by, and I still haven't reached out to the therapist.

"How was your day?" He places his hands on my shoulders and kisses the top of my head. Then he scoops up Kai and cradles him in his arms.

"Fine. And yours?"

"Always a ten."

My husband's been on cloud nine since I told him about our unplanned pregnancy. I must admit, I'd been looking forward to an empty nest after over a decade of raising my stepchildren. It took me a while to get used to the idea of starting all over. But I'm enjoying motherhood far more than I'd anticipated.

It doesn't hurt that we came into some substantial money around the same time we found out about the baby, from stock gains at Peter's biotech company, which brought a cancer drug to market. There are no financial pressures bearing down on us anymore. Not like there were before. But I'm not about to back down on my career, partly because I love what I'm doing, but also because slowing down might give me too much time to think about the craziness of last year.

Four attempts on my life.

The threat is gone, but not the anxiety. I sometimes wonder if Peter's as jubilant as he seems. How can he be, after everything that's happened? But his happiness seems genuine, and I'm even a little envious of his ability to move on and forget about it.

"I have some more work to finish up. Can you take him for a bit?"

"Just try and stop me."

"Thanks."

He starts walking out the door, and I go back to my inbox to search for the therapist's email. Then he interrupts me again.

"Laura?"

"Yes?"

"Why don't you try and move the nanny to full-time?"

Ugh. We've talked this to death, and I'm so sick of repeating myself.

"I can manage for now. I don't want someone here all the time, hovering over me. I told you."

"You like her?"

18

"I do."

"Then just get her here full-time. You can lock yourself in your office, and she can sit and wait around until you need her. It's better than losing a good nanny. What if someone else offers her full-time?"

"Peter. *Enough!*" I throw up my hands. "I need to focus right now. If you want to help me, then please, give me some space. This isn't helping." He thinks I'm on edge because the baby and my career are too much for me. But that's not the reason.

His eyes widen, and then he lowers them in defeat. It's obvious my words stung. His expression is somber as he turns from me and walks out the door.

"Close the door, please," I say, in a softer tone. Then I rest my heavy head in my hands and take a deep breath. I remind myself that he means well, even if he is annoying me.

I know I'm being short with him, and that's another thing to put on my list for the therapist. How to get over the resentment I feel towards my husband. I pull up the therapist's email, click on her scheduler, and secure an appointment for next week. Next, I locate the web page of Mike Tabernaky, luxury real estate broker. At first glance, he seems legitimate. But it does give me pause that someone like him is renting out his guest house. The market's pretty hot right now, and he has some high-end listings on his page. It seems a little desperate.

I check his broker credentials on the state website, and he's in good standing. No formal complaints. No red flags. There's nothing in the criminal or civil databases either, aside from a few speeding tickets. Maybe he has kids in college, or perhaps he's just the kind of guy who likes to maximize his property value. We live in an expensive area, and people do rent their guest houses. I tell myself it's fine and mentally cross it off my list.

There's more to do, as always, but none of it is urgent. It's dinnertime, so I close my laptop and head out to join my family, vowing to be more congenial to Peter. But I'm not telling him about the therapist. He doesn't know what's bothering me, and it needs to stay that way for now.

FOUR

Allie

It took Mike Tabernaky two days to call me back, and by the time he did, I was kicking myself for being too cautious. I was convinced I'd lost out on the opportunity. I was so desperate that I called the agent with the dog-pee carpet unit, and even that dump was already taken. But it's Monday afternoon and here I am, pulling up to his place to look at the guest house which, amazingly, is still available.

I feel my heart race with anticipation and excitement. It seems like a wonderful neighborhood. The house sits on a cul-de-sac, a quiet tree-lined street with larger, mostly Mediterranean-style homes that aren't overly ostentatious—nice, upper-middle-class-looking houses, priced like small estates. It floors me that these homes go for so much money. I could probably buy a whole block of houses like this back home for the price of one of these.

Mina Rao pulls up behind me in her entry-level Tesla, and I wonder if I need to upgrade the aging Honda I left in Wisconsin in order to be taken seriously here. It's the last thing I want to spend money on right now, so I sure hope not.

Mina and I only met for a short time at my Airbnb before our drive over, but she seemed nice. We're around the same age, and she's not at all what I expected. I pictured a short-haired, clipboard-sporting woman jacked up on caffeine, but she's the opposite: with her long, flowing dark hair and matching soulful eyes, she gives off a yoga teacher vibe.

Before we even exit our cars, I see Mike step out the front door onto the stoop along with a tall, thin woman around his age with light brown shoulder-length hair. I'm assuming she's his wife. Her arms are folded, and her body language isn't too welcoming.

"Hey there, Allie Dawson," he says with a friendly smile. That's the second time he's used my full name, and I wonder if he does that with everyone.

"Hello, Mike. This is Mina Rao. She's my...associate."

"Nice to meet you, Mina." He shakes Mina's hand, and it's not lost on me that he didn't use *her* last name. His wife looks over at him as if she's expecting him to introduce her, but he doesn't.

"I'm Susan Tabernaky," she says to me with a half-hearted smile.

"Allie Dawson. Nice to meet you, Susan."

Much to my surprise, Mike invites us into the main home. I assumed he would bring us around the side yard to the back of the house, but he's treating me more like a friend dropping over for a visit than a prospective renter of his guest house. A large tan dog lets out a hesitant bark and rushes over to sniff us. I like the fact that they have a dog. They're good protection.

"Dolly!" he commands. "Get back."

The dog obeys.

"She's very friendly. Don't worry," Susan offers.

"No problem. I love dogs," I say.

But then I realize she's not talking to me. She's talking to Mina, who's taken a step or two away from the dog and is still looking suspiciously in the animal's direction.

We step into a spacious, unremarkable living area that leads to an open-concept kitchen on the opposite side. It seems a bit new money to me with a ridiculously massive television set, an overstuffed sectional, and a matching leather recliner that looks like it has a massage feature. French doors and a nice-sized picture window look out to the backyard, and I spot the small guest house behind the pool, a little to the right. It's lovely and inviting, but I get a weird feeling about this. I don't like the thought of them sitting in their house, looking out at me.

He offers us a drink, but Mina declines for both of us, explaining that she needs to get going. We exit through the French doors to the backyard and head over to the cottage. Along the way, he asks me how long I'll be staying and what I'm doing in Silicon Valley. I reveal that I'm one of Mina's grant recipients. They gave me pre-seed funding to try and bring my product to market. It's a screen that clips on to eyeglasses and converts speech to captions in real time. I explain that even with my cochlear implant, I miss chunks of conversations. My product would eliminate the need to hear a conversation. The words would simply appear in a person's visual field.

"I love it! What a great idea. We love helping young entrepreneurs. I may even have a few investors I can introduce you to. We've got a young man living in our guest suite who's working on a new type of battery to store energy. You'll fit in perfectly here."

He's talking as if I've already gotten the unit, and I haven't even filled out an application yet. But he knows I've got the backing of the foundation, so he probably figures I've got money. Still, it seems a bit presumptuous.

The unit is as charming as I imagined it would be. It's cozy and clean. A galley kitchen sports shiny, new stainless steel appliances. There's a small bedroom, a sitting area that fronts the picture window facing the side of the house, and an outdoor sitting area to the back of the cottage. It's furnished with the basics, including a queen-size bed that takes up most of the space in the bedroom, a small sofa, a bistro table and chairs, and a TV. There's even a small stack washer-dryer tucked away in a closet, so I won't have to use theirs.

"Do you want me to fill out an application?" I ask.

"I already looked you up, and you seem to check out, although I'd like to do a formal background check before we seal the deal.

"Of course," I say.

"But since, I'm assuming, you don't have steady income, I'd like to ask for three months paid. Up front." He offers me a firm nod of his head.

I feel my eyes widen, but the monthly rent he floats is fair, especially since it includes utilities. Still, it seems a little unorthodox.

"Like an Airbnb," he offers. "Without all those pesky fees. Gives us both a chance to see if it's a good fit."

"Um, yeah, I suppose I could do that."

I glance at Mina and she shrugs, as if it sounds fine to her. I mean, what's the big deal? I even asked some of the bigger apartment complexes to do this for me, let me pay in advance, and they said no. So why is it giving me pause that he's suggesting it now?

"If that works, I'll draw up a contract."

"I think it's—"

"Geez. Allie. So sorry! I'm getting way ahead of myself. Do you even like it? I should have asked that first. It's fine if you want to take some time and think about it. But not too much time. I've got two other showings lined up tomorrow, but I'd prefer to wrap it up today. If you decide to take it, I'll cancel them."

"I think it's perfect," I say.

And it's true. The unit *is* perfect. And it's only three months. So what if he's a little overly friendly and he doesn't like to pay Airbnb fees? I can keep to myself. There's a window that looks out to the side yard, so I won't feel so claustrophobic. I plan to have the front curtains drawn most of the time.

"I'll take it," I say.

"That's terrific, Allie. Just terrific," he replies.

His head bobs up and down as he speaks, and I find his enthusiasm a tad over the top. I hope he's not the type to stop over and bother me all the time. But it's only three months. And it's a great unit at a decent price.

What's the worst that could happen?

FIVE

Laura

My computer is open, and I'm waiting for the therapist to start our first session. I'm not sure exactly what I'm hoping to accomplish or how to even start. After a few minutes, I see a fifty-something woman with short dark hair and kind eyes looking back at me.

"Good morning, Laura," she says. "I'm Dr. Taylor."

We engage in the requisite introductory remarks, and then she gets right to it.

"So, what's troubling you?"

That's a great question, and I don't know how to reply, or rather, which trouble to start with. A few responses flash through my mind.

My husband's daughter tried to kill me last year, the one he didn't know about.

There's a chance my stepson is a murderer.

I don't know if I trust my husband anymore.

My infant son is part of this family.

I settle on something a bit less sensational for my opening remark.

"I went through some trauma last year. And I'm having nightmares. I'm not sleeping well."

"I see. Do you want to tell me about the trauma? Is it something you feel comfortable talking about? Or would you rather focus on the dream first?"

"I can tell you about it."

When I hear myself recounting the events, it sounds fantastical, like something out of a soap opera, and I almost feel like I'm talking about someone else. I explain that my husband had an affair during his first marriage. Although he didn't know it until recently, the woman had a daughter—his biological daughter. She snapped and came after me in a delusional attempt to reunite her family, when she found out the truth about who her father was.

"Came after you?"

"She tried to kill me."

"Is she still a threat to you?"

"No. She…um. She's no longer a threat. She took her own life."

"My goodness, Laura. That's a lot to process."

"And just a month afterwards, I discovered I was pregnant. I have a three-month-old son."

"Congratulations." Dr. Taylor offers me a warm smile.

"Thanks." I nod. "But I'm not sleeping well. And I have a career to focus on. And a son to care for."

"How are things between you and your husband?"

"They're…fine."

She challenges me. "Fine?"

I shrug.

"I know it's only our first session, Laura, but our time together will be more productive if you share with me what you're feeling."

"I'm not feeling much of anything for him. Besides annoyed, sometimes."

We delve into this some more, and I explain that although Peter didn't know about the surprise daughter for much of our relationship, he did find out about her a few days before I did. And there were some other things he'd kept from me, including the fact that he'd had an affair during his first marriage.

"Why do you think he kept these things from you?"

I think about this for a while before I reply because I realize that it's an important question. "Because he was embarrassed. And he didn't want to damage our relationship."

"Do you believe that he loves you?"

"Yes. I know he loves me."

"And you want the marriage to work?"

This is a difficult question for me. Of course, my answer is yes, in terms of how I feel about Peter. He's the father of my child, and we love each other. Even after all the strain on our marriage, we still enjoy each other's company. The physical chemistry has never faded.

But I am concerned about this family in general. They don't have a great track record. His first wife was unstable. My stepdaughter, Lydia, had troubles as a teenager, although she's doing better now. And his surprise daughter with his ex-lover turned out to be a homicidal maniac. And then there are the concerns about my stepson, the ones I haven't shared with anyone. I worry about my infant son and hope it's not genetic. I sometimes feel I'd be better off leaving, taking Kai away from these people.

But then, am I that much better? Keeping secrets from my husband?

I decide to play my cards close to the vest for now.

"I think so."

"Well, that's a place to start. We can try to get you to a more definite place on that."

"I'd like to talk about sleep."

She asks me about the dream, and I need to lie because it's about my stepson. I want to keep that to myself for now. I tell her some of it though. A shadowy figure is trying to smother someone in their bed. The therapist assumes it's me who's about to be smothered, but it's not. She interprets this as a manifestation of the unprocessed trauma from the attempt on my life. Then she explains to me about PTSD and that I might be suffering from it.

We work through the final attempt on my life, and the fact that Ella had a gun pointed at me. She asks me how that felt.

Terrifying.

She takes me back to that moment in my kitchen when I turned around to face Ella and saw the gun, the young woman's hands shaking as she vacillated between fantasy and reality. I make myself breathe through it with Dr. Taylor's assistance. It seems to help a little. She instructs me to do the breathing exercises when I feel the panic well up or if I wake from the dream, unable to sleep. But then our time is up, and we need to sign off.

It's a weird feeling, being in therapy. You're sharing your deepest fears, about to divulge something you haven't told anyone on the planet, and then you realize it's just a business arrangement. This person is a stranger, and I remind myself that I can't give up too much about myself or my family to this woman.

SIX

Allie

It's been nearly two weeks since I secured my rental, and I'm finally moving in. I pull up to the house and park my decade-old blue Honda CR-V in front of it. My vehicle's not as big of an eyesore as I'd imagined it would be. It's well-kept, and I'm not going to squander the funds I have on a car just to impress people. Perhaps I can even turn that into a selling point, the fact that I run a lean ship and that I'm careful with other people's money. I need to focus on taking my concept to the next stage and use all the funds I've gotten to move me in that direction, not waste them on something I don't need.

I step out of my car and spot a lanky, thirty-something guy in jeans and a t-shirt walk past my car and head towards the stone walkway that leads around the left side of the house. His hair is sandy brown and in need of a cut, or maybe that's just his look. I assume he's the other renter Mike spoke about, the one working on battery storage technology. I wonder if it's a coincidence that he has two

31

aspiring entrepreneurs renting from him or if he prefers renting to people like us.

But then, this is Silicon Valley, the Hollywood of high-tech hopefuls, so there are probably scores of us descending on this place from all over the world every day, hoping to launch the next big thing. It makes sense that people like us would end up in rentals like this.

I can't tell if anyone's home. I don't see any signs of Mike or Susan, but their cars could be in the garage. They gave me the key when I rented the unit, so it's fine if they're not here. I gather up as much as I can take in one run and head around the back to my unit. I hear their dog bark, but I still don't see anyone.

When I'm almost to the guest house, I turn back and see Susan standing in front of the French doors with her arms crossed, staring in my direction. She doesn't wave hello, and I can't very well either because my arms are full. Instead, I smile and raise my eyebrows, and she lifts her hand and offers me a half-hearted smile. I wonder if this renter situation is more her husband's idea than hers. I get the feeling she's not too thrilled about it.

As soon as I get inside, my phone vibrates with a text. It's Mina Rao, welcoming me to Silicon Valley and reminding me of the upcoming weekend retreat that starts tomorrow. I shoot off a text to say I'll be there. I've given up everything for this, including my lukewarm relationship with a guy I've been dating on and off since college that probably needed to end anyway. We mulled over the idea of a long-distance relationship, but on this last trip back we landed on a clean break.

It's exhilarating and terrifying at the same time, knowing how much I have riding on this and how little I have to fall back on if I fail. My only option would be my mother's modest little tract home in Waukesha, a middle-class suburb of Milwaukee, but I don't want to think about that now.

This project is important to me on a personal level. I have to make it work. I was one of the first kids to get a cochlear implant back in the nineties when they were still quite controversial. I wasn't born deaf. Rather, I lost my hearing when I was two because of meningitis, and I didn't get my cochlear implant until I was four. The fact that I'd heard before I had the surgery helped since I had already developed speech and auditory skills.

The sound from the implant is totally different though, not at all like the hearing I was born with. I had to relearn everything, and although the device works well, it's not perfect. I need to lip-read to fully understand people, and background noise makes it harder. This caption screen could be life-changing. There are already a few solutions on the market and a few more in development, so I need to move fast.

My product would easily compete with what's currently available: VR glasses paired with an app, tethered to a cell phone. The virtual reality glasses are clunky and heavy with a dark lens, making them impractical for everyday use. With a starting price of nearly five hundred dollars, they're not exactly affordable either. Waveguide, a more promising technology, is on the near horizon. Those lenses will be clear, lighter weight, and even more expensive, with a price tag of over two thousand dollars. I'm racing to beat them to market.

My idea is to produce a clip-on screen that can attach to a user's regular eyeglasses, versatile and affordable. A device that can pair with a wide variety of frames. Fashionable and stylish ones, so people can have a choice about what they wear. That way, wearers can blend in and not stand out. The device can also translate over seventy languages, so I've generated some excitement about it. And I hope to offer it at a reasonable price point.

I have a lot to learn though about the technical aspects of the project. My brother, Kevin, my partner, is the engineer. I'm the designer. I have a substantial following on social media—I'm a micro-influencer—and I've already generated some buzz about them. Branding is my specialty, and I'm pretty sure that's why I was selected to join this cohort, even though I don't yet have a product on the market like most of the others in my group. I don't want to let my followers down. Now that I'm out there with my idea, the pressure is on.

I'm about to head out to get another load from my car when I hear a knock at my door.

"Yes?" I call out.

"Hey, Allie. It's Mike."

I open the door and Mike's standing there, all smiles and sunshine. We say our hellos. He asks if everything is okay, and I assure him that it is.

"Need any help?"

I don't really want to make small talk right now, but I need to start pushing myself out of my comfort zone. I'm here to make connections, and I can probably learn something from him about how to network. Verbal communication has always been difficult and uncomfortable for me, so I've shied away from it in the past, but I need to build my confidence. This seems like a safe place to start.

"Um, sure. If it's not too much trouble."

"Not at all."

We head back out to my car, and I don't have to worry about making small talk, because he's a chatterbox, filling the space with the events of his day as he bounces along beside me. We make three trips before we've gotten all my belongings from the car.

I missed some chunks of what he said while we were walking, but I got the gist of it. That happens if I'm not facing the person or if they talk too fast or turn away from me. Most people don't know that. And I don't like asking people to repeat themselves. I'm afraid I'll come off flaky or inattentive or stupid if I do that.

Mostly, he was talking about the high-end real estate market and the fact that it can take a long time to make a sale. I wonder if that means he's having a financial dry spell, which could explain the renting of the guest house.

He's standing at the doorway of my guest house now, and I'm attempting to get inside and start unpacking. I'm eager to get inside and organize my life before the weekend retreat. I don't want to appear rude though, so I continue to chat with him for a while.

"I'm having some people for dinner tonight if you'd like to join us," he says. "You can meet my other renter, and I also have an investor friend who'll be joining us."

Although I'm exhausted from the long drive, I can't pass this up. Plus, I'm hungry, and I haven't gone grocery shopping yet, so it's surely convenient. On the other hand, I'm a private person, and I worry a bit about setting a chummy precedent with my landlords. But this is exactly why I'm here in Silicon Valley, not back in Milwaukee. I need to reach for opportunity, not bat it away.

"That would be...perfect. Thanks, Mike," I reply.

"Come over around six thirty," he says, and he goes on his way.

I close the door and take in my temporary new residence. I've got three months to try to make something happen, so I might as well start tonight. I've got close to two hours before dinner, so I get to work unpacking and making this guest house my home.

———

Susan walks me into the dining area, through an arched doorway, and into an alcove tucked off to the side of the living room. It seems odd to me that this room is so secluded, considering that most of the house is open concept. It feels like a private dining area in a fancy restaurant, designed for intimacy. I arrived about fifteen minutes later than Mike's six thirty directive, partly because I ran out to get a bottle of wine, but also because I figured there would be drinks and chitchat before we got started on dinner.

I figured wrong.

Mike is seated at the head of the table at the far end of the room, and the table is longer than it needs to be for the size of our party. The place settings are all at his end of the table but set a bit of a distance from him, giving the impression that he's holding court.

There's an older Asian man at Mike's side, facing me. Next to him is the sandy-haired guy I saw earlier, who I assume is the other renter. Two empty place settings sit across from the two guests, which I figure are for Susan and me.

Mike stands as I enter. Then he introduces me. "This is Allie Dawson," he says. "Allie, this is Barnat Kovaks, the young man who rents our guest suite. And this is my good friend Charlie Yang."

I offer my apologies for being late, greet Charlie and Barnat, and sit down.

"Nice to meet you, Allie," Charlie says. Barnat gives me a head nod.

"No need to apologize, Allie. You just arrived from Wisconsin today. How long did you drive today? Ten hours? We're just glad you made it."

"I...yes. I'm exhausted. And hungry. I appreciate the meal."

A mouthwatering smell wafts in from the kitchen. Garlic with a hint of charred meat. There's some antipasto on the table: mozzarella cheese, salami, olives, and crusty Italian bread with an herbed olive oil mixture to drizzle onto our bread plates. I see that people have already started on it, so I dig in. Susan comes in and places two bowls of salad in front of our place settings and then heads back out.

We engage in some small talk about my drive, the route I took, and where I'm from. I tell them I've been living in Milwaukee, in a trendy neighborhood called Bay View, near the shores of Lake Michigan.

"Are you from Wisconsin? Originally?" Mike asks.

By this time, Susan has come back in from the kitchen with the remaining salads. She's seated next to me and we're all nibbling on our first course.

"Yes, from a suburb farther inland called Waukesha."

"And your family is there?"

"My mother's still in Waukesha, and I have an older brother in Chicago."

"And your dad?"

"He's...passed."

"Oh. Sorry, Allie. I shouldn't be prying," Mike says. "Me and my big mouth."

"No, it's fine," I reply.

I want to change the subject and get this conversation to turn away from me. I look across the table to the renter guy.

"Barnat. Where are you from?" I ask.

"Hungary," he says with a thick accent. "But I was living in Germany for years before I came here."

"How long have you been here in Silicon Valley?"

"Six months," Barnat replies.

I notice that there's no cross talk. I ask, he answers—and then there's silence. I don't press it any further. But I'm happy to know he's lasted six months here. Then Charlie and Mike start to discuss some project they're working on, and the rest of us listen politely as they move on to finance and investments.

As Susan starts to clear the salad plates, I offer to help, but she insists I stay put. Mike jumps up to help her and leaves the three of us alone.

"So, Allie. Mike told me about the grant you received for your start-up. Very exciting. Sounds like your project has real potential to do some good in the world," Charlie says.

"Hopefully. I'm only in the beginning stages. Pre-seed."

It seems to me like I'm miles away from getting anywhere on this project. Only a fraction of early-stage start-ups make it to series A funding, never mind series B, C, or the elusive exit: being acquired or going public. I'm not even at the seed round yet, and I probably shouldn't think about how slim my chances are, but I can't help it.

Truthfully, if all I do is call attention to this unmet need and get other companies working harder on this technology, that alone would be a victory. But it sure would be great to make it financially too. I explain that I'm one of ten women selected in the inaugural cohort of a new foundation with a mission of helping women gain access to the male-dominated world of venture capital.

"I'm in pre-seed. We get initial funding, training, and access as part of our award."

"Yes," he said. "Laura Sato Foster's foundation. I've read about it. I'm a micro VC."

My eyes widen. That's exactly the kind of investor I need, a venture capitalist who funds smaller projects. A VC who might be interested in a new founder like me.

I explain more about my idea and my goal of fostering communication for people like me who find it difficult to converse. I share more about my cochlear implant and the impact of my hearing loss on my ability to communicate verbally.

Barnat's expression softens when I mention how difficult it is for me to engage in conversations. Then I point out the other applications for my product, such as language translation.

"It is hard for me too." Barnat nods. "Not understanding. Your product is a good idea."

"Isn't there something like that on the market now?" Charlie asks. "VR glasses that can pair with an app?"

"Yes. But you need to be connected to your cell with a wire. And they're clunky. And uncomfortable. And dark."

"And your solution is…" Charlie smiles.

"Not in existence yet." I smile back. "But it will be. Soon."

"You sound quite determined," he says.

"It's very personal for me."

"That's what we all look for in a founder, Allie. A personal stake. I have a feeling you'll do well."

I want to pinch myself. A VC just gave me a compliment.

I'm about to ask for his card when Mike and Susan return with our meals: chicken in a white wine sauce with roasted potatoes and asparagus. We start on our main course, and it's delicious.

"Susan's an excellent cook, isn't she?" Mike says. "I've often said she should open a restaurant."

I think about asking her what she does for a living, but then I don't want to insult her. What if she does nothing, and I make her feel bad about it?

"I'm doing fine in life insurance," she says. "Mike's always looking for a new angle. One of us needs to keep our feet on the ground."

"Restless, she calls me. But she loves it." There's a sly smile on Mike's face. They catch each other's eyes for a long moment like it's some kind of inside joke.

"Sure, honey. Restless." Susan narrows her eyes on her husband. They remain fixed on him a moment longer before she returns to her meal.

Mike changes the subject and asks Barnat about his battery idea. He has just as hard a time as I did getting anything out of him. I'm fading and in need of sleep, so I start to tune it all out and enjoy the meal.

Thankfully, we wrap up our evening rather quickly after the main course. Everyone declines coffee and dessert, citing early morning commitments. We say our goodbyes. As I'm about to leave, Charlie Yang offers me his business card. He tells me to keep in touch about my progress. I feel a giddy grin spread across my face and worry about appearing too eager, but I can't hold it in.

I walk out the French doors at the back of the house and head over to my new home, feeling great about my first official day in Silicon Valley. Great, but exhausted. Once inside, I wash my face, brush my teeth, and fall into bed. As I'm drifting off to sleep, I think about what Susan said to Mike and the way they looked at each other.

Restless. What did she mean by that?

SEVEN

Laura

Peter's holding Kai in his arms as he comes into the kitchen to grab another coffee. I reach for my son to get in a snuggle and one last feeding before I leave for a long stretch.

"What do you guys have planned for the day?" I ask.

"Oh, you know. Knock back a few beers. Watch a game. That sort of thing."

I smile and kiss my husband on the lips. He runs his hand through my hair and smiles. We had a nice evening, capped off by a tender if subdued lovemaking session, which is about all I can handle this soon after Kai's birth.

Today is the start of the first weekend retreat for my inaugural cohort, and I remind myself to thank Peter for being so supportive. This is as much a learning experience for me as it is for my funding recipients, and it's totally exhilarating. I've never worked in venture capital before, and I haven't launched a business of my own, although

I've worked for start-ups. It was a bold move, founding this accelerator.

I hope not too bold.

When we came into money last year, I wanted to do something to make a difference in the world. To help women gain access to venture capital and become successful entrepreneurs. Peter's been nothing but encouraging. I'm trying to focus more on the positives of our relationship rather than the negatives, and the therapy seems to be helping.

"I got that speaker lined up. The one you referred to me."

"The micro VC?"

"Yes. Thanks." I smile at him. "For everything."

He shrugs, brushing it off, as is his way. He's always been supportive of my goals and generous with money. "We're a team, Laura. No need to thank me."

It was Peter's stock gains that funded my accelerator, even if, legally, the money was half mine. But he's given me carte blanche with it. After a decade of putting my career on the back burner to care for my family, I know I deserve it and so does Peter. But still, I want him to know that I appreciate it.

"Glad it worked out. Oh, and the kids are coming over for dinner," he says.

"Sorry I'll miss them," I say.

"Well, they might still be here when you get home. Lydia wants to run some of the wedding details past you. If you're up for it, that is."

My stomach lurches. My stepdaughter's wedding is in nine months. It's in Hawai'i, where I lived until middle school, so I've been helping with the planning. It's been a lot of fun, and it's not what's making me nervous. It's the thought of seeing Carson, my stepson. I've been avoiding him.

"Sure. I'll try to make it back in time."

Peter excuses himself while I start to feed Kai. As I gaze down at his precious little face, I tell myself I must find out the truth about Carson. I need to know for sure if he really did what I think he might have done.

Before it drives me crazy.

———

"And really, it's not the slide deck or the elevator pitch or the slick logos that make or break our funding decisions for first-time entrepreneurs. It's the core idea and the dedication and drive of the founder. Is there space in the market for your product? And are you going to dedicate your life to making this happen? That's what'll take you to seed, series A, and beyond."

There's a round of applause as Ted Williams, VC extraordinaire, finishes his presentation. We're in a conference room at the local hotel in East Palo Alto off the 101 that I booked for our weekend retreat. I thought long and hard about whether having a male VC present to a group of women would send the wrong message, but that's the reality of the venture capital world and exactly what I'm hoping to change.

His talk was perfect, exactly what I needed, so I'm glad I went with him. He delivered the right mix of reality and hope. I vetted my recipients on those two factors: the marketability of the core idea, and the drive of the founder.

Of all of them, Allie Dawson probably has the most skin in the game. She's got a personal stake in making her product a reality, but she's also the least experienced in terms of business start-ups and not as far along as the others. I used a rating scale for my selection process, and she just made the cut. My other grantees all have a minimum viable product—MVP—and some are even in the market already, looking to scale up. Allie's still working on her prototype. But Allie's a micro-influencer with a strong track record in branding, so that's something in her favor.

Plus, I feel a connection to her. Allie reminds me of myself at that age, although we look nothing alike. I'm a petite brunette of Japanese and European ancestry, and Allie's a tall, buxom blonde. When I was Allie's age, I had already married a widower and dropped out of the workforce to help raise his two kids. Perhaps I'm living vicariously through the younger woman, seeing where my life could have gone, or maybe I'm genuinely excited about the social utility of her product. For whatever reason, I'm rooting for Allie to succeed, even more so than the others.

We've just finished lunch and are moving into the workshop phase of the session. I'm planning to meet with all my awardees individually, and I'm starting with Allie, not because I'm more invested in her, but because I'm going alphabetically.

"How's the new place working out? Are you settled in?" I ask.

"Yes, and it's working out fine. My landlord is friendly. Landlords, I should say. It's a husband and wife. But he takes more of a lead."

I nod. "That's—"

"Oh, and last night, they had me over for dinner. And I met an investor named Charlie Yang. He's a micro VC. And he's interested in my project!" Allie's eyes widen, and I don't have the heart to tell her it probably means nothing. They always say that.

She hands me his card. I take a moment to examine it and then give it back to her. "Well, that's certainly…convenient," I remark.

"Yeah. He said to keep him updated on my progress."

"Good. You should do that. Now, about your progress." I smile warmly as I raise my brows. I have ten awardees to get through.

"Right. So, the prototype should be ready in about two weeks. The screen will snap on to most frame types. Right now, we think it will work when connected to a phone, but not wirelessly. Kevin's working on it. But I'm planning to bring on someone who's more of a computer engineer to help with the wireless feature."

Kevin's her brother and a materials engineer. And she's right. She needs a collaborator who has the software expertise that both she and her brother lack. I'm pleased that she realized that on her own.

"It'll work with the other existing apps? It works with XRAI Glass?"

"It should, but we won't know until we get it in hand and try it out. Right now, it's only theoretical. But the screen will need to be connected by a cord to the wearer's phone. For now."

"I know it's better than the dark VR glasses, but the word on the street is that Vueit's waveguide product is a few months away, and it'll work wirelessly. How will you be able to compete?" I ask.

"My screen, combined with a regular eyeglass lens, is even thinner than their lens, and it works with most frames. Most of the waveguide glasses are for VR in general, not specifically for captioning. They're expected to handle way more than just text to speech and translation, so they need to be heavier and thicker. That's what makes mine different. We're focusing on one feature, so the battery and memory requirements are much less.

"Plus, theirs will cost over two thousand dollars. We're thinking we can bring ours in at around three hundred, or even less. We'll have the ability to do language translation, so I'm confident that the market will be robust enough even without the other VR features."

She makes good points. I'm impressed. "If you can get yours to work wirelessly, you'll be the clear winner. But that might take time."

"I may have to do it in stages. I feel like if it's a choice between their thicker glasses with no cord and my clip-on solution with a cord, I'll be able to capture market share. I can make the cords in different colors so they can blend in with the wearer's clothing, or accent it. I've already generated a lot of excitement about my product."

She shows me her posts, and I can see that her followers are extremely supportive. She has over twenty thousand of them with over a thousand likes on the two posts she showed me. There are hundreds of comments, most of them from potential users of the product.

> *Great for you, Allie.*
> *I can't wait to try it.*
> *That's wonderful news.*
> *You're such an inspiration.*
> *We're rooting for you!*

Her level of engagement is phenomenal. I was a VP of monetization before I founded my accelerator, and our team was never able to generate that kind of interaction with our users. She's got a built-in customer base. All she needs is the product.

"And I'm working on the wireless part, so don't worry," she adds.

Allie goes on to tell me that she's found a computer engineer, a graduate student named Ethan who is already working on wireless technology. He's confident he can get the device to operate without having to be tethered to a cell phone.

I feel my eyes widen. "A grad student?" I ask. I don't like the idea of gambling on a novice.

"Um, yes. Why? Is that a problem?"

She appears a little wounded by my comment, so I soften my expression. "Not necessarily. As long as he can deliver."

She discloses to me what she's planning to offer him, and it's more than reasonable. I wonder if he'll even go for it. But I don't want to discourage her, so I keep that to myself. I'm struggling to find the right balance between directing my grant recipients and letting them own their decisions. Part of being an entrepreneur is learning from failure.

"Sounds like you're off to a great start, Allie," I say.

Then I move on to the next woman in the cohort, and the afternoon flies by. My head is filled with new energy, new ideas, and the possibility of a bright future for all of us.

———

As I pull up to our modest Los Altos home, I see Lydia's Tesla and what I assume is Carson's brand-new BMW SUV parked on the street in front of our house. Carson's been saying he was going to buy a new car, although he didn't need one. It looks like he went through with it. I let out a sigh, hit the garage button, and park my Audi A6 next to Peter's aging Nissan SUV. I stay seated and take a moment to switch gears from CEO and founder to wife and mother. It's not a seamless process, but it's getting easier.

I think about my stepchildren, born into old money on their mother's side and how it's shaped them in so many ways. Even with Peter's stock gains, his children still have a substantially higher net worth than the two of us. Peter and I didn't grow up like that, and I've given a lot of thought about how to raise Kai in a way that won't leave him feeling entitled. There are no easy answers, though. It's natural to want to give your children everything you have at your disposal.

After a moment, I head in. We bought this house a little over a year ago, before the stock gains. Initially, I loved it, in no small part because it was a welcome change from where we'd lived for over a decade. A welcome change from the large, secluded family home in Los Altos Hills Peter had shared with his first wife and his children. Lydia bought that house from us last year. We purchased this smaller, tasteful home close to the Los Altos town center.

But Ella pulled a gun on me in the kitchen of this house, and I can't help but wonder whether that memory is holding me back, keeping me stuck in the trauma. Thankfully, nobody was killed here. With my pregnancy and all the changes in our lives, we haven't even discussed the idea of selling and moving. But perhaps we should.

"Hi, Laura." Lydia runs over to greet me, while Peter and Carson stay seated on the sofa.

"Where's Christopher?" I expected her fiancé to be here.

"On a business trip," she replies.

It's hard for me to believe how much things have improved between the two of us over the years. She was a teenager when I joined the family a few years after her mother's death. Lydia felt threatened by the new woman in the house, and she made it very difficult for me. I've never admitted to Peter how many times I thought about leaving.

Our relationship has steadily improved, and the experience with Ella brought us even closer. Not to mention the fact that Lydia arrived at the house that day just in time to save my life. We embrace, and then Lydia starts to fill me in on the wedding plans. Kai's asleep, and although I feel a little guilty that I can't cuddle him and kiss him goodnight, I'm exhausted. And grateful for the downtime.

Carson is sitting next to Peter, and they look more alike to me every day. He's looking more mature these days with his dark hair cut a bit shorter like his dad's. He's filled out his thin frame, growing into his new phase of life.

"Hi, Carson," I say. He stands up to hug me. "How's the new job?"

"Going well," he replies.

He's just started his first job after graduating from college, deferring his law school admission for a year. He decided that he needed a break from school and that working in corporate America would give him an edge in his law program.

I take a seat in one of the chairs across from them, and Lydia takes the other one.

"We were just talking about the wedding logistics," Peter says. "We're thinking of doing a private cruise for the families a few days before the wedding. Is that doable?"

"Of course. I'll look into it," I say.

Although I grew up in the islands until my middle school years, it's primarily a destination wedding with most of the guests flying in. We haven't landed on a venue yet, or even an island, but we need to do that soon. It's been enjoyable for me, planning Lydia's wedding. I'd wanted to get married there myself, but Peter's mother was too sick to travel at the time, part of the deal when marrying an older man.

The age difference between us doesn't seem so big now; I've just turned forty, and he's a handsome and fit fifty-one.

51

But when I met him, I was twenty-seven. Carefree and single. And it had seemed almost insurmountable. I think about how far we've come as a family, and I'm glad that I finally feel like I'm a part of it.

I sit back and take in our family dynamic with Lydia babbling away about the wedding and Carson chiming in about his new job when he can get a word in. It feels nice to be a family again. But it's getting late, and I'm grateful when the conversation winds down and we say our goodbyes.

As I'm getting ready for bed, the video pops into my head again. The one my private investigator sent me. The video that shows a young man who looks a lot like Carson, heading out the side door of a long-term care home the day Jeanine Randall was pronounced dead.

EIGHT

Laura

It's been nearly a week since I saw Carson, and although the panicky feeling has finally subsided, I know I need to do something about that video. He's my stepson and Kai's half brother. I can't continue to live like this, avoiding him or practically having a nervous breakdown after I see him.

But what's my next move?

I'm not telling my therapist, and I'm not sharing this with Peter. If I tell anyone, I'd be putting them in a bind. If Carson harmed Jeanine Randall, they'd have an obligation to report it to the police, so I can't burden anyone with this. Plus, what does it say about me, that I've kept my mouth shut this whole time?

My only viable option is to go to the private investigator my husband initially hired to find out who was trying to kill me. Shep Shackler's his name. I secretly hired him afterwards, to keep tabs on Jeanine Randall, Peter's former lover. The woman who destroyed their family. The woman whose daughter tried to kill me. Shackler found the video and sent it to me. He's so far kept quiet about it, so I'm reluctant to rock the boat.

I'm in my home office, and the nanny is at our house today, out in the living room with Kai. I finally caved and hired her full-time, as Peter suggested. And although I do miss having the house to myself, the convenience of having her here all the time is worth the sacrifice.

Haley is her name. She's in her early twenties. Kind and reserved. Respectful and unobtrusive. When Kai's asleep, I often send her to the store, and then I have the best of both worlds. I've been more productive with her here, and I'm glad I made this decision.

I pull up the video from Shep Shackler and view it for what feels like the millionth time. Jeanine was in a long-term care home, following a bad car accident. From what we could piece together from Ella's ramblings, she and her mother had a big fight after Ella figured out she'd been lied to all her life. Ella fled the house on that very stormy night. Jeanine went looking for her and had a terrible car accident that left her in a "minimally conscious" state. That seems to be what made Ella snap and come looking for Peter, hoping to get me out of the way and reunite her family.

Peter assured me I had nothing to worry about after Ella's death, that Jeanine was harmless and incapacitated. But I wasn't so sure. She didn't take it well when Peter wanted to break it off and save his marriage. She confronted Peter's wife, Cynthia, in a desperate attempt to win him back. A confrontation that likely caused Cynthia to take her own life, although Peter kept that from everyone to hide his affair.

What if Jeanine recovered and found out what happened to her daughter? From my research on her condition, a recovery wasn't probable, but it was possible. As long as Jeanine was alive, I'd never feel completely safe. So, I hired Shackler to keep tabs on her condition, and a few weeks after breathing a sigh of relief when she passed on, I received this video. It was taken the day she was pronounced dead.

The video is grainy, so enlarging it doesn't really help. It shows a young man with dark hair, about Carson's height and weight, walking out of a side door of the care home. He's wearing scrubs and a mask. He takes off the mask, scratches his nose, turns briefly towards the camera, and puts the mask back on. Then he looks away and walks out of view. I freeze it where he's looking at the camera and try to zoom in, but that only makes it blurrier.

If it wasn't potentially incriminating, I could give it to some tech expert to try to sharpen the image, but I don't dare involve anyone else. And I'm sure the police have the tools to do that, so I want to keep it from them. Because in my opinion, Jeanine Randall got what was coming to her after everything she did to this family. And that's something I can't admit to anyone.

What kind of person am I if I'm willing to turn a blind eye to this?

My interest in finding out if my stepson did it isn't to bring him to justice. It's to find out if he really could do something like this. Although I'm willing to keep quiet about it, I could never do something like that myself. And there must be something wrong with someone who could. Is this a trait my son will have? Is Carson capable of snapping and doing something like that again? That's what keeps me up at night.

I'm staring at the screen, searching for answers, when a knock at my office door startles me. My wrist jerks, sending coffee splashing all over my desk, and I quickly slam my laptop shut.

"Yes? Come in." My voice is louder than it needs to be.

"Kai's asleep. Do you need me to run to the store?" Haley's curly brown bangs hang down over her eyes, bouncing off her glasses. She's constantly flipping them back, and I wonder why she doesn't trim them. She's dressed in baggy jeans and a t-shirt, her usual outfit, a timid smile on her face.

"Sure. But can you text me next time rather than knocking? Like we discussed? I could be on a call."

"Right. Sorry about that." She glances down towards the carpet, averting my eyes.

I hope I haven't hurt her feelings. She's a sweet girl, and I appreciate her help. I smile, trying to soften the intense look on my face, which has nothing to do with her.

"No problem. You have the grocery list, right?"

"Yes. Should I leave the door open? So you can hear Kai?"

"Please." I have the baby monitor, but I still feel better with the door open.

She turns and starts to walk away.

"Haley?" I call out.

She turns back to me.

"Yes?"

"Keep up the good work. You're doing a great job."

A smile lights up her face. "Thanks, Laura," she says.

I head out of my office to check on Kai and get some paper towels to mop up the spilled coffee. I decide I'll leave it alone for now regarding the video. Maybe I'll check in with Shackler at some point, but I'm not ready to go there just yet.

———

I'm at a table for two at Le Bistro, a cute sandwich and salad shop in Menlo Park, waiting for my best friend, Sophie, who's even later than usual. But at least she texted me that she was running twenty minutes late. She should be here any minute.

Since Haley's employed full-time now, I decided to treat myself and get out of the house for a girls' lunch. It's Friday, and I've been stuck in my office all week. I needed a change of scenery. I'm enjoying it so far, even sitting here by myself waiting for Sophie, savoring the downtime and simply being out and about.

Sophie arrives with a vengeance, making a grand entrance, as is her way. I see her blonde curls bobbing towards me as she maneuvers through the crowd and plops down across from me.

"You're not going to believe what happened to me!" Her eyes widen and her hands shoot up. I can always count on her to distract me from whatever it is that's bothering me.

Before she starts on her story, we order, both opting for salads, and I dig into the fresh French bread the waiter has placed on our table, still warm from the oven. As the creamy butter melts into the crevices and drips onto my fingers, I think about the fact that I need to get back to my normal workout routine.

I've lost the baby weight, but my fitness level has gone down, my lifelong goal of competing in the Kona Ironman World Championship slipping away with each day I fail to make time to train. I didn't realize how hard it would be to juggle a newborn and my career.

"So. What happened? What won't I believe?" I ask.

She goes on to tell me that as she was leaving her office to come see me, she bumped into some guy whose name I'm supposed to know from our grad school days, someone she briefly dated, who last week ran into another acquaintance of ours I also can't remember, and it all added up to some business for her. Then she shares a bit of gossip about his messy divorce. That's why she's in PR and I'm not. She remembers everything about everyone she's ever met, and I'm an out-of-sight, out-of-mind kind of person.

Our salads arrive, and she turns the conversation to me.

"So, how're things with you? How's my little godson?"

Peter and I aren't religious, but Sophie insisted on being deemed "godmother," whatever that means, even though we didn't have any kind of ceremony. Peter doesn't have many guy friends, so her husband, Jim, is Kai's godfather.

"He's fantastic. Getting bigger every day. And he's smiling now."

"Wait until he starts belly laughing. It's the best sound in the world."

Sophie has two kids, a daughter in middle school and a son in elementary. I'm a late bloomer as far as babies, although when we were in our twenties, I was the one who broke up our swinging-single gal-pal duo to become a stepmom.

"I was starting to think you were avoiding me, I've tried so many times to get you to come out," she says.

"Why would I be avoiding you?" I reply.

But she's right. I have been avoiding her. *Because she knows me too well.* She knows when I'm worried or upset, but I'm hoping I can pass it off as new mother jitters. She knows about the nightmares, sort of. Like my therapist, she probably assumes it's PTSD.

"How's the therapist?"

"She's fine." Sophie's the one who recommended her to me.

"Fine?" She raises her brows at me and gives me a look.

"She's as good as anyone. I'm sleeping better, but I don't know if it's her or the fact that Kai's sleeping for longer stretches now."

"How're things with Peter?"

"Good. Better."

A month or so ago, I confided in her that I'd been feeling resentful towards him, but it's gotten better. I don't want to dwell on that now, so I change the subject to my work, a topic we stick with through most of our lunch.

As we're winding down, I'm dying to tell her what's really bothering me. There's a part of me that hopes she picks up on my anxiety and uses her powers of interrogation to wrestle it out of me, despite my best efforts to keep it under wraps. I've never had to keep a secret like this before, and it's so damn alienating.

But she doesn't pry. Perhaps I'm getting better at the art of deception. And although it lifted my spirits to get out for a bit, as we say our goodbyes, I feel lonelier than I have in my entire life.

NINE

Allie

It's Saturday, a week since I officially moved in, and I must say that my first week in Silicon Valley was quite productive. I met with Ethan, the software engineer I told Laura about. I was able to secure him for a three-month contract. He thinks he can get the screen to work wirelessly rather than being tethered to a cell phone. That would be an important milestone. I hired him on a contract basis at a decent hourly rate. I won't have to pay benefits, which saves me money and makes it less complicated to terminate the arrangement since he's not an employee.

The prototype will be ready in about two weeks, my brother assures me. Hopefully in time for our next retreat. I've got a lead on two factories that can produce the clip-on screens, and I'm doing research on the latest trends, trying to figure out which eyeglass styles will work with it. The frame needs to be a certain size and shape, so not all eyeglass frames will work with it. But I can offer way more choice than my competitors. I've been chronicling my progress for my followers, helping them feel like they're part of the process.

My little cottage is working out just fine so far. After dinner with the Tabernakys last week, I haven't interacted with them too much, and I haven't seen Barnat at all. It feels lonely with an entire weekend ahead of me with nothing planned. That's something I hadn't even considered when I moved. Last weekend I was busy with the retreat, so it's just starting to hit me now that I'm all alone. In Milwaukee, I had a nice circle of friends. A lukewarm relationship. An office full of people.

I'm planning to join a health club to have more social interaction, and I've got an appointment at a swanky one close by later this afternoon. It's a bit of a splurge, but it's the perfect place to network or chill when I need a break, and I like to keep fit. Well, if I'm being honest, I like to *be* fit. The getting fit, not so much. But I make myself work out, and it helps if it's at a facility with the extra luxuries like a sauna and steam that serve as my reward, which this place has.

I put on my speech processor and tune in to the sound of water splashing outside. I glance out my front window and see Barnat swimming laps. It's a pleasant late summer morning, not too hot yet, so I decide I'll make myself presentable, head out with my coffee, sit by the pool, and try to strike up a conversation. I'm here to network after all.

Hopefully, he won't take it as an invasion of his privacy. He seems reserved, and I remember how hard it was getting a word out of him at dinner. But I'm dying to compare notes with him about his progress and his experiences in Silicon Valley in general. Not to mention how this living arrangement is working out for him.

I open my door and head over in shorts and a tank top. I don't plan to go swimming, but I'd like to get some sun. He's taking a break, or maybe he's finished. He's standing in the pool fiddling with the paddles on his arms, which are surprisingly muscular. He's not a big guy. He's got the upper body of a swimmer though. Broad shoulders that taper to a smaller waist. Lean but fit.

"Hi, Barnat," I say.

His head whips around towards me. "Oh." His eyes widen. "Hi…"

"Allie," I say.

"Yes. Allie."

"I hope I'm not disturbing you."

He pauses for a moment. "No. I'm finishing with my swim."

Perhaps it takes him some time to translate what he wants to say into English. I place my coffee mug on a side table and make myself comfortable on a lounge chair. He lifts himself out of the pool in one fluid motion, wraps a towel around his waist, and strolls over towards me.

"Do you swim often?" I ask. *Stupid question.* It's obvious that he does, but I can't very well unsay it.

"Yes. I swim for a long time. In school."

"Like in competitions?"

"Yes. But not anymore."

"I'm going over to join the Bay Club this afternoon. I don't really know anyone here, so I figure it's a good way to meet people."

He nods.

"Have you met many people here?" I ask.

"No," he replies.

I gather he's not too interested in meeting people, so I'm not going to read too much into that reply.

"How's your battery project going?"

"It's going fine."

He shakes his head, and water droplets fly off his floppy hair. A few land on my arm and chest and I flinch, but he makes no apologies. Then he takes a seat on the lounge chair next to me. He flips his hair off his face. I'm leaning back in my lounger, but he balances on the edge of his like he's not planning to stay long. It seems like this conversation is a chore for him, and I wonder why he came over to me. If he didn't want to socialize, he could have just walked away and gone inside. I feel like there's something he wants to tell me, but he's not saying anything, so I start to fill the silence.

"I'm making some progress on my caption screen and the—"

"Allie." He holds up his hand. "It's not a good idea to talk about your project so much."

"Oh, I…I'm sorry, I didn't mean to bore you."

"No." He shakes his head. "That's not what I mean."

"I don't understand."

He looks me in the eye. "This is Silicon Valley. It's competitive here. Be careful who you trust. There's…sabotage. People who want to steal ideas."

My eyes widen. That hadn't even occurred to me, but I guess it makes sense. But then how can I generate interest in my ideas if I can't tell anyone about them?

"Thanks, Barnat. Good advice."

I'm about to ask him how he likes living here. What he thinks about Mike and Susan. But he stands up, sending a clear message that this conversation is over.

"Have a good day, Allie," he says. Then he turns from me and heads to the house.

"You too," I reply.

He doesn't look back.

His warning seems a bit cynical to me, but then it's possible that his battery technology is more valuable than my project. I can't imagine corporate spies lurking in the background trying to hijack my caption screen, but I guess you never know. It wasn't discussed in any of our sessions last weekend. In fact, a significant chunk of the time was devoted to our elevator pitch and slide deck, two of the tools we use to try to get funders interested in our ideas— which also involves telling them about it. I'll run his advice past Mina and see what she thinks.

Then I look up and see Susan in the kitchen window. I decide it's probably time to head inside and give them some privacy. Even though Mike said we're welcome to use the pool anytime, I don't want to overdo it. They probably don't appreciate me staring into their living quarters any more than I want them peering into mine. I can't have it both ways.

I sit up, grab my coffee mug, and head back to my unit.

———

I feel like a new person after a vigorous workout at my new club, followed by a steam and whirlpool. Now I'm about to meet Mina for an early dinner. It was so thoughtful of her to reach out and offer, and I hope I'm not being too much of a pain. I confided in her that I was feeling lonely, but I don't want to appear weak or whiney.

I felt like we connected though, and that we might even become friends; I could really use one. She had me meet her at the Los Altos Grill, a trendy spot in downtown Los Altos, where I'm planning to spend more time now that I see how cute the town is. Laura Foster lives in Los Altos. Although Mina lives farther north, she didn't mind meeting me closer to where I live, which is one town south of here.

Silicon Valley is suburban. A collection of small towns, each with its own unique vibe. Most have a quaint downtown with shops, restaurants, and other establishments. Los Altos is my favorite so far. Businesses large and small are peppered throughout the region. If not for the occasional glimpse of a famous one, it would be hard to know that you were in the valley. People dress down here, too. It's not like New York or Chicago. And so far, I've found people to be quite friendly.

The restaurant is warm and inviting with dark wood paneling and dim lighting that must feel cozy when the weather gets colder. There's a large, rectangular, festive-looking bar area where the light reflects magically off the glassware, and lots of people are eating their dinner around it. It seems like a great place to meet people. Maybe that's why she picked this spot. It's the kind of place you could come in alone, eat at the bar, and not feel lonely.

I stop and snap a quick photo, which I'll post later. I'm not addicted to social media or anything, but I need to engage my followers. They're critical to the success of my venture, and they're invested in my journey. That sounds like I'm being manipulative, but I'm not. I enjoy the interaction with them, especially now that I've moved and started all over.

The hostess seats us in a booth that's bigger than it needs to be for two people, but quite comfortable. When the waiter arrives, I order a gin and tonic, and Mina selects a California pinot noir. Then she suggests a chopped salad to start, and I tell her that sounds perfect.

"How long have you known Laura Foster?" I ask.

"About five years. We worked together. She was my boss before she started the accelerator. At another company."

"What kind of company?"

"An app developer. For college applications."

"What happened to the company?"

"It went under when the new AI apps hit the market."

The waiter arrives with our drinks and some bread for the table, and we both stop to slice off a piece. I'm starving after my workout.

"Speaking of which, the guy who rents a suite where I live? Remember Mike Tabernaky mentioned him?"

"Um, yes, I think I remember him saying something about another renter."

"He's developing some kind of new battery to store energy."

Mina nods and takes a sip of her wine. "What's he like?"

"He's from Hungary. Maybe mid-thirties. Very quiet. But he warned me this morning against talking too much about my project, and it struck me as an odd thing to say."

"Warned you?"

"He said I shouldn't talk too much about my idea. That there's sabotage. People waiting to steal people's ideas."

"I guess that can happen around here. But there are caption glasses on the market already. You're just improving the product. I don't see what they would be stealing. You don't have to advertise the actual technology to people if you can get them to work wirelessly. But you need to tell people about your product. How else will you find funders?"

"That's exactly what I thought."

"Maybe he's into you and that's just an excuse to talk to you?"

I mull this over. He's cute, but kind of aloof for a guy who's interested in me. Perhaps that's a strategy he uses, or it could be the European way. But then I remember how he cut off our conversation, and the fact that it took him a while to remember my name.

"I doubt it," I conclude.

"I don't. You're stunning."

I roll my eyes. "Anyway. Do you think my idea is original enough to file for a patent?"

I realize how much I need to learn, and the challenges ahead suddenly seem almost insurmountable.

"I'm not sure. Maybe. My wife's an attorney. I can run it past her and see what she thinks."

"Thanks," I say. "That would be great."

We order our meals. Rotisserie chicken for me and cedar plank salmon for Mina. I turn the conversation back to Laura Foster. She's a closed book. Hard to read. Totally different from Mina, who seems much more open.

"So, what made Laura want to start the accelerator?"

"She's motivated by the mission, really. Of empowering women."

"How did she make her money?"

The minute I say it, I wish I could take it back. I probably sound like a gossip. The gin is loosening my lips, and I need to be more careful.

But Mina doesn't bat an eye. "Mostly it was her husband. He was working on a drug for ovarian cancer, and they got FDA approval last year. The stock shot up. One of those rare but legendary Silicon Valley success stories."

Laura Foster's bio doesn't include starting any companies of her own, which I found a bit strange when I applied to her program. But then, I suppose if she worked at startups, she probably has the background to give us what we need. Still, I'd feel better about being under her guidance if she'd taken a concept to exit. Of course, I'm not going to say anything like that to Mina. I can't afford to look a gift horse in the mouth.

She turns the conversation back to me and my background as our meals arrive. I take a bite of my chicken. The savory smells have been making my mouth water. Mina asks about my family, and I explain that it's small.

"Well, you know about my brother," I say. "He's my only sibling. My mother's retired. She worked in customer service for a major printing company, and she took early retirement. My dad died when I was in middle school."

"Sorry to hear that."

"It was a long time ago."

"I'm sure your mom misses having you around."

I could tell her that my mom and I don't talk much. We love each other, but our relationship has always been a little strained, not like the one between her and my brother. But I don't know Mina very well, so I keep that to myself.

"She understands why I need to do this. And Kevin's married with a three-year-old son. My mother's into being Grandma."

After we've finished eating, the waiter clears our plates, but we still have drinks to finish.

"Let's sit up at the bar and finish our drinks," Mina says as she reaches for the tab. I offer to pitch in, but she insists on covering it.

"Only this once," I say. "Next one's on me."

She doesn't acknowledge my offer as she stands and saunters to the bar.

When we reach it and take our seats, her head turns towards the front door. A smile lights up her face. I turn around. A striking man in his early thirties with dark hair and haunting eyes like hers waves to us. He strolls over, makes his way through the crowd of people waiting for tables, and gives her a hug.

It takes me a moment to process what's happening. Mina turns to me, and it's soon clear from the mischievous smile on her face that this isn't a coincidence.

"Allie. This is Ricky Rao. My cousin."

TEN

Laura

I'm sitting in the lobby of Shackler Investigative Services, waiting for my appointment with Shep Shackler, which should start in about ten minutes. I'm early, and he's normally right on time. He's fixed up the lobby since the last time I was here, no doubt with some of the hefty fees we paid him last year. But he delivered for us, so I'm not complaining.

Plus, I'm a lot more comfortable now. He's replaced the aging, cracked vinyl furniture with two cushiony but firm black leather chairs and a modern side table, and there's a water feature that blocks out the background noise. It's quite relaxing.

My reason for being here, as far as he knows, has nothing to do with the video, but I plan to find a way to segue into it. After my lunch with Sophie and my feeling so isolated, I decided I had to tell someone. But I need to tread carefully and not go after the video issue head-on until I feel him out a little.

Luckily, I found another reason to contact him. A few days after my lunch with Sophie, Mina told me that Allie Dawson was concerned about people stealing her captioning technology. This was due to a warning from some Eastern European boarder who rents a suite from her landlord. Mina thought his comments about corporate espionage were strange, so she mentioned the conversation to me.

At first, I brushed it off, but then I remembered Allie telling me that her landlord introduced her to a VC the first night she was in her new place. Even at the time, it struck me as overkill, and I wondered why he would do that for a tenant. But she mentioned that he's a friendly guy. And some people thrive on being useful to others. Or maybe his VC friend has a genuine interest in new entrepreneurs. Or perhaps her landlord has some kind of financial arrangement with the guy, a finder's fee for bringing him new leads.

Although I'm mostly using this as an excuse to meet with Shackler, I must admit it's a little unsettling when I put it all together, especially combined with the fact that he befriended her at a Starbucks.

Soon, Shackler comes out, and I stand up to greet him. He ushers me into the office, and we engage in the requisite pleasantries—but not for long. He cuts to the chase, and that's something I like about him.

"So, what can I do for you?"

I explain the situation with Allie and her landlord while he jots down a few notes.

"Hmm," he says, pressing his lips together as he processes the information.

"Right." I know exactly what he means. It's not really adding up to anything concrete on the surface, but it is a little odd.

"I mean, I could run some background on the guy if that would make you feel better."

"It would, yes. Would you do that?"

"Sure. You're really going above and beyond for one of your...recipients."

"She's young. And a bit naive. She's not from around here."

"We're not exactly in the hood, Laura. Where's she from?"

"Milwaukee." I suddenly feel very transparent, like he knows I'm here to talk about the video and this is just an excuse.

There's an awkward silence. I look away, down to the floor. I can see him in my peripheral vision, sitting back, twirling his pen between his thumb and forefinger.

"So, is there anything else?" he asks.

I take a deep breath. And I decide to go for it.

"The video you sent me?"

"Ah, yes." He nods. "The video."

"What did you do with it?"

"I destroyed it. After you told me it couldn't have been your stepson."

"Good," I reply.

"Why? Has something changed?" he asks.

"No. Not at all. I just wanted to make sure that the issue was officially—"

"Laura. Case closed. I've got no interest in making problems for you or your family or looking into it any further."

I nod.

He pauses, twirling his pen again.

"Unless, of course, you want me to," he says.

Nothing has changed. I'm not lying to him. Carson said he was in Mendocino with his girlfriend that weekend. When he volunteered that information, I took him at his word and tried to make myself move past it. I never confronted him about the video.

Carson's not big on social media, unlike his sister, so I wasn't too concerned that he didn't post any photos of his trip. But wouldn't this girlfriend of his have an online presence? And wouldn't she have posted photos and tagged him in them? And then there's the fact that we never actually met her. The relationship was serious enough for a weekend getaway, but not serious enough to meet the family. And they conveniently broke up a few weeks after their trip.

But I don't share any of this with Shackler just yet.

"Hypothetically speaking," I ask, "what would happen if someone asked you to look into something like this, and you found out...something?"

"Hypothetically, I would be obligated to report a crime, but only if I knew for sure that one had been committed. In practice, PIs have discretion. And it's nearly impossible to know for certain that a crime happened without gathering evidence."

"I see."

I think about the fact that Shackler checked up on Peter and Jeanine Randall when he thought Peter might have been responsible for his late wife's death and was possibly trying to kill me too. And I wonder if he really would keep quiet. As if reading my mind, he continues.

"Now in the case of my investigating your husband, that was different. I wasn't going to let someone be murdered just to protect my client. It's a little different if we suspect a crime is going to happen."

"Got it."

"So. Is there anything more I can do for you? Anything else you want to…share with me, perhaps?"

"There's nothing more to tell you about that day. But I've been having a hard time moving on. I'd feel a lot better if I knew for sure where he was that weekend. I never asked Carson about the video, and when he told us about his weekend getaway to Mendocino with his girlfriend, I dropped it. But I have no proof that he went on that trip. Or that he didn't go to Jeanine's care home in Nevada. And I've been having nightmares. My relationship with my stepson is strained. I'd feel a lot better if I could know for sure it isn't him in the video."

"That's understandable. I can check into it. See what I can dig up."

"This stays between us?"

"Always," he says. Then he narrows his eyes on me. "Unless I find out you're planning to kill somebody."

I expect him to smile, but he doesn't.

I swallow. "Got it."

"I'll be in touch," he replies.

As I exit the office, I feel like a giant weight has been lifted off me.

ELEVEN
Allie

It was clear from the minute Ricky Rao was introduced to me that my dinner with Mina last weekend was all a setup. I suppose it makes sense. Mina can't give everyone in the cohort the kind of individual attention she's been giving me, so I'm not surprised she had an ulterior motive.

She didn't come out and say it was a setup that evening. Rather, she introduced him as a fellow entrepreneur, a bit ahead of me in terms of the process, who'd just secured series A funding for his project. We didn't stay at the bar very long, about an hour, but he asked for my number. He called a few days later and invited me to dinner. It's Saturday morning, and we're going out tonight.

He's funny and handsome, and it's nice to have something to look forward to this weekend, although I do wonder what will happen if it doesn't work out. Will Mina hold it against me, if I decide he's not for me?

Mike and Susan are away this week, so I've been spending more time doing my work, sitting out by the pool. The evenings are lovely this time of year. The heat wave broke as we moved into September. A cool breeze usually comes in around sunset. I like to sit out there alone, without my speech processor, and take it all in. My other senses are heightened when I can't hear. The colors appear more vibrant, and the wind rushing across my bare arms tickles me ever so slightly.

I haven't seen Barnat at the pool at all this week, and I wonder if he's actively avoiding me. I ran into him once, when I was returning to the house with my groceries and he was pulling up to the curb. He said hello, but aside from that, he didn't seem at all interested in engaging with me. I wonder if I've offended him somehow, or if that's just his way. I suppose it doesn't matter. He means nothing to me or my life in terms of the big picture.

So why am I even thinking about him?

———

Ricky just dropped me off in front of the house. It's early, only half past eight, and it's not quite dark yet. He offered to walk me to my door, but I told him it wasn't necessary. I notice that Barnat's car isn't here. He seems like such a hermit. If he's got a more exciting social life than I do, I'm really in trouble.

I'm not sure what Mina was thinking, trying to set me up with her lovesick cousin. He's a nice guy, but he's still hung up on his last girlfriend, who dumped him about a month ago. He spent most of the night talking about her. He's obviously not over the relationship. He mentioned that Mina couldn't stand her, nor could the rest of his family, who haven't been shy about expressing their relief that it's over. I commiserated about my recent breakup just so he wouldn't feel bad, although I'm not very upset about it.

I'm sure Mina meant well, but as a date, this was pretty much a disaster. We had a good time once we got past the idea of dating each other. He gave me some advice about how to secure funding. He and Mina grew up in Silicon Valley, and this start-up stuff seems to come naturally to him. He even took an elective in entrepreneurialism back in high school, something that wasn't an option at mine or at most other high schools back then, I imagine.

I told him about the sabotage warning from Barnat, and he thought it sounded like a strange thing to say. But he also mentioned that finding a new method of battery storage is a hot research area. Not only companies, but nations are competing to find an alternative to lithium-ion batteries. It made me wonder how good Barnat's idea is and how impressive a background he has. Maybe he's someone well-known back in Europe.

Once inside my place, I start to get ready for bed. I'm wondering how I might fill my days with more social interaction. I have a slew of meetings next week, but none of them will take up an entire day. I'm used to having a tight schedule, and I feel a little untethered with so much unstructured time at my disposal. There's always something to do for my project, of course, but until I start making some headway, it's a lonely life. I don't want to sit around this guest house day and night. It's depressing.

I notice a text message from my mom and make a mental note to check in with her tomorrow. I should make more of an effort. She has her flaws and we've had our problems, but she loves me. And I know she's worried about me, all alone out here. She's always been overprotective in her efforts to shelter me from pain and disappointment. It borders on being insulting though, like she thinks I can't do anything without her assistance.

"You're doing what?" she said when I told her I was quitting my job to take advantage of this opportunity. "What are you going to do for health insurance? What if it doesn't work out?" Then she went on to point out the dismal statistics on start-ups. The staggering rents in Silicon Valley. The dangers of living alone...*for someone like me.*

So, of course, I haven't told her anything about how hard it was to find this place. If she knew I moved into the guest house of some guy who chatted me up at Starbucks, she'd probably have an anxiety attack and start drinking again. But as the homesickness washes over me, I get an urge to connect with her. It's too late to call her back now, but I'll check in with her tomorrow.

In the meantime, I decide to make myself a schedule. We have online coursework to complete for our program, and I can map out a plan to take morning classes at the gym and then do the coursework for an hour or two afterwards. They have an inviting coffee and snack bar at the club, where people sit and work. All my meetings are after lunch next week, so that should work to keep me less lonely, at least until I make more progress.

I plop into bed with a printout of some of the research Kevin has synthesized for me on how to get the device to work wirelessly with our prototype, so I can share it with the grad student next week. I'm fighting to stay awake though. Soon, I feel my eyes flutter as the papers slip from my hands and I sink into the pillow.

TWELVE

Allie

Present day

I wake to the sun's rays beaming into my eyes. I feel disoriented and confused. There's a sinking feeling in my stomach like I'm waking up from a nightmare I can't quite remember. Something's hovering on the edge of my consciousness. I reach for my phone on the nightstand, but it's not there. Then I remember I had it in my hand in the middle of the night.

But why?

I pat around the bed and locate it next to me under the covers. And then it hits me.

What on earth was my landlord dragging across the lawn last night?

I had my speech processor on when I got back into bed, and now I don't hear anything. I feel my head and it's not there. I see it on the floor, pick it up, and make sure it's not damaged. It must have fallen off, which is probably why

I slept so late. At least it's daylight, and I made it through the night.

I replay the events in my mind's eye. First, I woke up suddenly, after feeling some kind of...vibration? I remember thinking it could have been an earthquake. Then I looked outside and saw Mike dragging a duffel bag across the lawn.

Were those two events related? Did I dream that vibration? And what the hell was in that bag? Because I certainly didn't dream that. More importantly, did he see me when I peeked out the window? And whose voice was that I heard? I think back. *Hurry up,* someone said. Susan maybe? It was faint, and I'm not even sure it was a woman.

I really don't know how to play this. If something strange is going on, it's safer for Mike to think I know nothing about it. And I'm not about to ask him what he was dragging across the lawn in the middle of the night. I need to find a way to talk to Barnat and see if he heard or saw anything. I wish I had his cell number.

I get up and pop a K-cup in my Keurig so I can get some caffeine in my system. I know Mike and Susan were supposed to come home today, not last night. Why were they back early?

As I drink my coffee, I search for Barnat on every social media platform I can think of, but he's nowhere to be found. But then, I'm not even sure I have the right spelling of his name. And it wouldn't surprise me if he has little to no social media presence.

After a few minutes of searching, I give up and go make some toast. Then I see a text from Mina. I distract myself as we volley back and forth.

> *Mina: How was it?*
> *Me: Well...*
> *Mina: Don't tell me. He's still hung up on his ex.*
> *Me: Yup.*
> *Mina: OMG I'm so sorry! He's hopeless.*
> *Me: Don't be! It's fine.*
> *Mina: You sure?*
> *Me: Yes! No worries. All good.*
> *Mina: :)*

She's a nice person, and I'm sure she meant well. Plus, I might need to call her later and get her to rescue me from this bizarre living situation. I'm happy that she kind of owes me one. I don't need to tell her that I wasn't all that interested in her cousin anyway.

I take another sip of my coffee. The caffeine is perking me up, but it's also making me more nervous. And as I fixate on the image of my landlord dragging a duffel bag across the lawn, my vision starts to blur. I grab the counter to steady myself as my heart races.

Not this again.

The lights pulsate, and my thoughts begin to race. I struggle to breathe. I can't think straight anymore. Soon my heart is pounding like a bass drum. I grab my chest as the panic grips me in its vise, squeezing me tighter and tighter.

Am I having a heart attack?

I see flashes in my mind's eye now, memories I've tried so hard to bury. A dark figure coming towards me. The visceral, primal fear that engulfed me.

It's getting worse. I pace around the apartment, accomplishing nothing. With my hands trembling, I struggle to punch in the code to my phone. On the second try, I open it. I press the numbers 9-1-1, but I resist the urge to hit the call button. Instead, I force myself to sit down.

I can see. I can smell. I can feel.
I can see. I can smell. I can feel.
I can see. I can smell. I can feel.

As I repeat this mantra, I move my hands from my eyes to my nose to my forearms, stopping to pinch myself. When my pulse starts to slow down a bit, I breathe.

In for five, out for ten.
In for five, out for ten.

I visualize the dark figure turning from me and running out of my room. I force myself to remember the sudden rush of relief I felt. Rushing to the kitchen, I run my hands under cold water. The pounding has subsided, but my heart is still beating faster than normal. The worst is over though. I can tell. It's not a heart attack, and I suppose I should be happy about that. But I'm not. I'm crushed.

I haven't had a panic attack in years. I thought that was all behind me. I haven't thought about that night in a long time, the night that started it all. A night I don't want to dwell on now. Last night must have triggered the memory. This brings me back to my present dilemma and what to do about last night.

Did he see me? Should I say anything? Should I move out?

Leaving this place would be a terrible financial burden for me. I paid three months' rent in advance, and I've hardly made a dent in my time here. And what excuse would I give? If I leave, he might think I suspect something. I wish I knew for sure if he saw me or not. I'm probably safer playing dumb unless I can team up with Barnat and figure out what's going on.

I dump out the rest of my coffee, finish my toast, and get dressed in my workout clothes. I don't really feel like working out, but I need to do something to get my mind in a better place. Plus, I'd like to run into Barnat and find out if he saw or heard anything. I remember the text from my mother and decide it's not the right time for a call. I send off a reply instead, telling her we'll FaceTime tomorrow.

Grabbing my gym bag, I head out my front door and scan the yard. I don't see anyone, but my eyes land on the shed in the far corner of the yard. A shiver runs up my spine as I wonder what might be stuffed in there.

I walk around the side of the house to my car, hoping to see some signs of life. As I come around the corner, I spot Mike sitting on the stoop with his head in his hands. He lifts a hand and peeks out at me. His eyes are red and glassy.

"Mike?" I say.

He takes a deep breath. "Hi, Allie."

"Um, how was your trip? Did something...happen?"

"It's Dolly," he says.

The dog.

"Did she..."

"She got sick on our camping trip. I think she ate something in the woods. Maybe some kind of poison for the mountain lions or something. We tried to get back in time, but we didn't make it. She died on the way home."

"Oh, Mike. I'm so sorry."

I feel like a perfect idiot for thinking such dark, crazy thoughts. He was dragging Dolly somewhere. To the shed, maybe. Not wanting to keep her remains in the house. I'm not going to mention to him that I saw him since there's nothing to gain by admitting I was spying on him. I'm pretty sure I ducked down in time. And if he has nothing to hide, he shouldn't care anyway.

"It'll be okay. We just need some time. Susan's beside herself."

"I'm sure. Is there anything I can do?"

"No. But thank you."

There's an awkward silence, so I say goodbye, head to my car, and start it up. As I'm driving, I reflect more on what happened last night. Dolly dying explains the dragging. But I still wonder about that thud I felt.

Was it a small earthquake? Or did I dream that part?

———

I stop at the front door with a bouquet of flowers for my landlords that I picked up on my way home from the gym. It's the least I can do. They've been so helpful to me, and I feel horrible for being so suspicious of him. Mike comes to the door and thanks me, but I still haven't seen Susan.

When I step into the backyard, I see Barnat in the pool, and it feels like things are getting back to normal again, if normal means a completely new life filled with relative strangers I somehow suddenly find comforting. And I don't care if he's antisocial or I'm bothering him, I'm going to head over and talk to him but not before I go inside and get some water.

After I drop off my things inside my place and fill my water bottle, I head back out, still in my black yoga shorts and hot pink jog bra. He stops to take a breather from his laps, still standing in the pool. Then he turns to me.

"Hi, Allie."

"Hi, Barnat."

At least he remembered my name this time.

He's taking a break, but I don't think he's done yet. He grabs the paddles from the side of the pool and puts them on. I wait patiently, catching up on my social media channels as I watch him swim. I have a handful of clients who pay me to promote their products, and it brings in some nice side money. After about twenty minutes, he finally stops and gets out of the pool. He turns to me and waves goodbye.

"Barnat?" I call out. "Can I talk to you?"

He nods and heads my way, but when he reaches me, he doesn't sit. Rather, he stands over me, the water dripping off his slick backed hair and glistening on his taut, tanned torso.

"Yes?"

"Did you hear their dog died?"

"Yes. He told me this morning."

"Did you...hear anything last night? Or feel any kind of a thud?"

"Thud?"

"Like a boom. And then some shaking." I push my hands down to simulate something falling and shake my arms to illustrate a vibration.

He smiles. "Allie, you are a curious person, no?"

"What?"

"I keep to myself. I don't concern myself with these things. You should try this."

"I thought it might have been an earthquake."

"No, I didn't feel anything. You'll get used to it," he says.

"Okay."

Does that mean it was an earthquake, and he doesn't notice them anymore? Or that it was something else and I should mind my own business? Why is he always so cryptic? He starts to walk away, but then he turns back to me.

"So how was your date?"

I feel my eyes widen. He wasn't there when I came home. Maybe he saw Ricky pick me up? It seems totally out of character for him to mention it. I find this intriguing. I thought I had him pegged, but it seems like I don't.

"Not great." I shrug.

He nods, but his face registers no reaction.

Then I smirk. "Now who's being curious?"

As he turns and walks away, I see the faint hint of a smile on his face.

THIRTEEN

Laura

It's been a little over a week since I met with Shackler, and I feel better now that I'm taking some action. Airing my fears, even to a guy I'm paying, seems to have worked to alleviate some of my stress.

I've been trying to figure out what I'll do if he comes back with some kind of evidence that Carson was at the care home when Jeanine died. Would I confront him? Would I keep it to myself? One thing I won't do is turn him in to the authorities, and I'm convinced that Shep Shackler won't either. He hasn't gotten back to me yet, but I know from experience that these things take time.

Everything's going fine with the foundation so far, and we're gearing up for another round of individual meetings next week. Progress check-ins with each of the recipients. There's so much I need to learn, but it's exciting, and I'm making more progress now that I'm sleeping better and I can focus. I haven't had the nightmare since I met with Shackler, and I've put a pause on the therapy for now.

Peter's home, although I haven't seen him yet. I heard him when he came in, and I'm sure Haley's gone, so it's time to join my family.

I head into the living room. Peter's watching the news, and Kai's lying on a blanket on the floor, playing with a rattle. I rarely feel the age difference between my husband and me these days, but this is one time I do. I'd never sit and watch the evening news, but it's sort of a ritual for him if he gets home in time.

"Hey, you," he says. "Join me." He pats the spot next to him. I see he's got an open Beck's sitting on the side table, but I can't tell how full it is.

"Let me get something to drink. You hungry? I'll have dinner in about thirty minutes."

"Maybe some cheese and crackers."

"Want another beer?" I ask.

"No. I'm fine," he says.

I walk into the kitchen to get a glass of sparkling water and our snacks, and I'm thankful that Haley put some chicken and potatoes in the oven for dinner. All I need to do is make us a salad. Peter would gladly help, but he's not that great at it. I tell him I like doing it myself, although that's not true. But I don't want to hurt his feelings.

With our cheese and crackers in hand, I head back into the living room and sit down next to my husband, just in time to see a "breaking news" banner flash across the screen. It's the local broadcast, so it stops me in my tracks. It must be something important. Someone famous died? Or a murder? Then my stomach sinks. I hope it's not a mass shooting. Perhaps watching the local news isn't the worst idea in the world.

The anchor cuts to an upscale home somewhere in the hills. Portola Valley maybe? Or Woodside? The reporter on the scene is talking to someone to his right until he notices he's on the air. He fiddles with his earpiece, and then he starts.

> *We're here live on the scene in Portola Valley, at the home of local venture capitalist Charlie Yang, who was officially declared a missing person late Monday afternoon. Mrs. Willa Yang, his wife, reports that he never came home on Saturday after leaving midmorning to play a round of golf. She tried to report him missing on Sunday but was required to wait twenty-four hours to officially launch an investigation.*

He introduces Willa Yang, the wife of the missing man. We see a tear-streaked but stoic woman who looks to be in her fifties take the stand, trying to compose herself. She reiterates what the reporter said and appeals to the viewers to contact the police with any information.

The police captain is up next, but he doesn't tell us anything more, just that the first few days in a case like this are critical and that nothing is insignificant. Then they cut back to the studio, and the anchor tells us they'll bring us updates as the story develops.

"Wow," Peter says. "He disappeared. Maybe he's got dementia or something."

"She's not that old, Peter."

"Maybe she went for an older man. Like you." He gives me a tickle.

I shift to the side, almost spilling my water.

"You're certainly jumpy," he says.

"I don't think they'd involve the police or make this kind of appeal if they thought it was dementia," I reply.

"I mean, what else could it be? Someone kidnapped him? Murdered him? That seems unlikely around here."

"Yeah," I say. But I'm only half listening because something clicks in my mind, and my stomach lurches.

"Peter!" I grab his arm.

His eyes widen. "What?"

"Charlie Yang."

"Yeah. And?"

"I think I heard his name from one of my grant recipients at the retreat. I think she met him recently. She mentioned to me that she'd been introduced to him by her landlord. The name sounded familiar when the reporter said it, but at first, I figured it was just one of those names I'd heard around town."

I'm pretty sure it's the name of the VC Allie Dawson met at her landlord's house, although I could be wrong. I try to pull up my memory of the business card. I'm almost certain that was the name on the one she handed me that day.

"So?" My husband's looking at me curiously. "What's the big deal if she did?"

I'm hesitant to tell him the whole story for fear that he might even suggest that we go to Shep Shackler about this. Peter knows him, because he hired Shackler last year to find out who was trying to kill me. But I don't want

Peter to know that I retained him to keep tabs on Jeanine Randall. I tell him that Allie's landlord befriended her at a Starbucks and that she felt a little weird about him at first. And then I explain about Allie being invited to dinner by her landlord the first night she was in her new place and being introduced to a VC.

"Well, that's a strange coincidence," he says.

"Yes, it certainly is."

Then he picks up the remote and turns off the television, not seeming to grasp the implication, mostly because I'm not telling him in a way that would make him suspicious.

"I'm starved," he says. "Let's eat."

"Sure," I reply, although suddenly, I don't have much of an appetite. As I start into the kitchen, I hear my phone ping. It's a text from Shep Shackler.

> *I have some information for you.*
> *Call me in the morning.*

PART
TWO

FOURTEEN

I'm not sorry about what I did. Still, I don't want anyone else to get hurt. That wasn't part of the plan. But I will accomplish what I set out to do, and I won't let anyone stand in my way. Charlie knew the stakes going into it, and his suddenly growing a conscience was something I couldn't tolerate. He got what was coming to him, although I'm still troubled by the fact that it had to come to that.

But Allie Dawson's innocent in all of this. And I'll do what I can to spare her. Still, she saw what she saw, so I'll need to keep tabs on her. Collateral damage is an unfortunate consequence of my profession, and if I feel she's a threat to me or my objectives, I'll do what needs to be done.

FIFTEEN

Allie

Charlie Yang is missing.
I'm trying to process what Laura Foster just told me. She texted me a few minutes ago, confirming our check-in meeting for tomorrow. I rarely hear from her directly, so I was surprised to see her text. I figured Mina would confirm the meeting, even though it's at Laura's home office.

But then she asked me for the name of the venture capitalist I met at dinner with my landlord a while back, so it seems she had an ulterior motive for contacting me directly. When she asked me about him, I assumed it was because she wanted to include him on some kind of VC list for the foundation. I felt, for a moment, very pleased with myself for being useful already. Now I'm floored.

He's missing?

I send off a text asking her to FaceTime me. Talking on the phone is hard for me, but thankfully, the captions on FaceTime work well now, and it'll go faster that way.

She calls, and soon I see her on my phone, looking a little stressed.

"What happened?" I ask.

She explains that Charlie Yang went missing over the weekend, but she only found out last night, via the local evening news. The name sounded familiar so she thought to mention it to me.

"I figured you might want to know since he's friendly with your landlord."

My landlord who was dragging a duffel bag across his lawn in the middle of the night.

"That's...terrible. Do they have any idea what happened?"

"Not yet."

"Is this...unusual? In this area?" I ask.

"Yes. Very," Laura says.

She goes on to tell me how this is generally an extremely safe area, and although they've had the occasional high-profile murder case over the last few decades, she doesn't remember many missing person cases. She mentions there are some rumors about Charlie having issues with depression in the past and that he might have been having financial problems.

A suicide, maybe?

I hear a knock at my door and ask Laura to hold on.

"Yes?"

"It's Mike," my landlord calls out from the other side of the door.

I open it, and he's standing in front of me with flyers in his hands. Flyers with Charlie Yang's image on them. He appears as deflated as he did on the stoop the other day, and I wonder where his exuberant personality went.

"I don't know if you heard, but my friend Charlie Yang is missing."

I nod. "Yes, I just heard about it."

"We're putting flyers up. Can you help? Take them to your gym, or wherever else you go? I emailed you an image to put on your social media if you wouldn't mind." He runs his hand through his hair, seeming quite out of sorts about this. I guess they're pretty close.

"Yes, of course." I take the flyers from his hand.

"I wanted to let you know that Willa, his wife, will be staying with us for a week or so. In the event someone's... done something to him, she feels safer here. For now. We're keeping that out of the media, so please don't disclose that to anyone. For her safety, as well as ours."

My phone is cupped in my hand; I don't think he can see I'm on a call. There's nothing to gain by telling him, and I'm sure Laura can keep this quiet.

"Of course. Let me know if there's anything else you need."

"Thanks," he says.

I shut the door and go back to my call.

"Did you hear that?" I ask Laura.

"Most of it. The wife is staying there with them, and he wants you to hand out flyers."

"Yes."

"Tag me on your social media when you put up the info, and I'll repost it," she says. Then Laura tells me she needs to go, and we sign off.

The fact that his wife will be staying here makes me feel better about Mike, but it also raises other issues. What if someone was targeting Charlie and they find out that his wife's here?

I've been nervous about this place from the start, and I don't need all the additional stress. But I have a full schedule for the rest of this week, and I can't afford to lose all the money I've paid out for rent. I decide I'll run it past Laura Foster at my meeting tomorrow and see what she thinks. Perhaps I'm overreacting. But this is a lot to absorb, and the last thing I need right now. I need to focus on my work, and this is a distraction I can't afford.

———

It's late afternoon, and I'm back from a busy day. I had a virtual meeting with my brother and my software engineer. Kevin's very close to having a functional prototype that tethers to a phone, but we're far from making it work wirelessly. Overall, things are moving along, but not as fast as I'd like. I also need to start cultivating a list of seed-funding possibilities to take me to the next stage. And with Charlie Yang missing, my one lead, I've got nothing. Funding has been tight lately, I've heard. Just my luck that it would dry up now.

I hear a knock at my door, and I assume it's Mike again. "Allie? It's Barnat."

I open the door, and Barnat's standing there in jeans and a t-shirt, his hair a bit damp but not dripping wet. His eyes meet mine, and then he looks away. His lips are pressed together, and I can't tell if he's nervous or if he's struggling to convert what he's thinking into English.

"Hi," I say, but he doesn't reply. "Do you want to come in?"

"Sure." He enters and scans my apartment.

"Can I...get you anything?"

"Some water if it's not too much trouble."

"Sure. Please, have a seat."

I motion to the compact sofa, thinking about the fact that we'll soon be sitting close together. It makes me a little wary. Although I find him intriguing, I'm not sure how I feel about his being here or why I'm so nervous. I was the one trying to strike up a friendship, but something feels off about this.

Rather than sitting, he starts nosing around my place. I turn and head to the kitchen to get his water and fill a bowl with tortilla chips. I'm tucked behind the wall that divides the kitchen from the living area, so I can't see exactly what he's doing. I saw him stop and look at the photos on my bookshelf as I was walking in.

I head in with the water and chips, and he's still standing, looking out the side window towards the shed.

He turns to me. "Do you mind if I ask you something?"

"Um, sure. Go ahead," I say.

"How much do you pay for this place?"

My eyes widen. That wasn't what I was expecting. I tell him my monthly rent, and he nods. Then we sit next to each other on the sofa as I place the water and chips on the coffee table. I lean back against the sofa arm and turn towards him.

"Why do you ask?"

"I was wondering if I'm paying too much. I wanted to see this place. Compare it to mine." He stretches his arm across the back of the sofa.

"I see. And are you? Paying too much?"

"No. I think it's a fair price. But I'm surprised Mike didn't tell me when this was vacant." He lets out a sigh. "I would have taken it. But he rented it to you."

"Oh. Well. Sorry about that."

And now I'm wondering if that's why he was cold to me when I first moved in. Perhaps he resents the fact that I'm in this place and he's stuck in the main house with the Tabernakys.

"It's not your fault," he says. "But now, Willa Yang is staying there too." He rolls his eyes. "I would like to have more privacy. And I only have the hot plate and a small minifridge. You have a full kitchen. And your own laundry, yes?"

I nod. "A small stack washer-dryer. Are you looking for another place?"

He shakes his head. "No. I can't. I paid for a year in advance."

"Wow. A year. That's a lot."

"I'm new to the United States. I didn't know any better." He shrugs.

"I paid three months in advance, and I'm not new to the United States. It's hard to find a place here."

"Well, if you decide to leave, could you tell me first?"

"Um, sure. But I'll probably stay for the three months at least."

Although I was thinking about leaving, the thought of him nipping at my heels has me feeling a little defensive and more protective of what I have.

"I understand."

"How do you like it here in the States?" I ask.

"I plan to go back home when I finish what I came to do."

He didn't really answer my question. This seems to be a habit of his. Then he asks about my family, and how I like it here compared to Milwaukee. I tell him it's hard because I've left my friends and I don't have many new ones.

He understands, he says, because he's got a language barrier to contend with, on top of being new in town. I explain that I have a difficult time communicating also, even in my native language, because of my hearing loss.

"It's okay right now, talking with one person, but with a group, it gets more difficult."

"Even in your own language?" he asks. "That's...hard."

"It's life." I shrug. "I'm used to it."

Then he asks me about sign language, a question I often get. I explain that when I was a child, the idea was to get me to use my hearing, and not rely on sign language, so I didn't start learning it until later. The thinking has since changed on that, but as a result, I didn't learn it as a child. I studied ASL as a second language in high school and college, but I'm not a native speaker. And I don't know ASL well enough to feel comfortable in the Deaf community, meaning people who identify as culturally Deaf and use ASL as their main mode of communication.

Yet I don't blend effortlessly into the hearing community either.

"You can hear with this?" He pats his ear. "What's it called?"

"Cochlear implant," I say.

"How does it work?"

"It hooks over my ear and attaches to my head with a magnet, which connects to the one inside my head. Then the sound is converted into electrical impulses, and it stimulates my hearing nerve."

"Does it work?"

"Yes, sort of. But not so well in noise. And it gets uncomfortable sometimes, having it on my ear. And I still need to lip-read, especially in noise, which is tiring. Getting the caption screen off the ground would help a lot."

"Yes, I can understand that. Do you sleep with it on?" he asks.

"I, um…not normally, no."

"Is that scary for you, not being able to hear?"

"Not really. I'm used to silence. I don't like darkness though. I need to be able to see."

"You sleep with a light on?" he asks.

Odd question.

I nod.

"How's your battery project going?" I ask.

"I'm making some progress."

"What company did you work for in Germany? And where in Germany did you live?"

"It was a small company. Outside Hamburg. I'm sure you've never heard of it."

Hamburg. At least that gives me something to go on.

"So, what do you think about Charlie Yang's disappearance?"

His jaw tenses a bit. "I don't think anything about it. It doesn't concern me." He glances down at his watch. "And I'm afraid I need to get going. I have a meeting in an hour. I need to prepare for it."

I wonder if I've struck a nerve or if he really did lose track of time. He stands up and I follow his lead. Then I walk him to the door.

"So, if you decide to leave, you will let me know first?" he says.

"Sure."

He stares down at his feet for a moment and then looks back up at me. "Do you like to hike, Allie?"

"Not really. I'm more of a gym girl. Why?"

"I thought you might want to go with me."

I must say, I'm tempted. He's cute—in a mysterious-European-guy kind of way. But I'm not about to go off with him into some deserted wooded area. He's too cagey, and I don't fully trust him.

"I like to walk," I offer. "I'm just not that into roughing it. In the wilderness," I add.

"Do you know the Dish?" he asks.

I do. He's referring to the Stanford Dish. It's a popular walking and running loop, hilly and winding—and normally very crowded—that houses a giant radio antenna. I've been wanting to go, and I tell him this.

"How about next weekend?" he asks.

We agree on a date and time, and I see him out the door.

Susan Tabernaky is spying on us out her kitchen window as he exits. She's not even trying to hide the fact that she's looking in our direction, and I wonder why she would even care that Barnat's been over at my place.

When we're out at the Dish on Saturday, I'm planning to pump him for all he knows about these people and what they're up to, as well as what's going on with Charlie Yang and his disappearance. I'm sure he's got plenty of thoughts about it, even if he's not sharing them with me. There's more to Barnat Kovaks than meets the eye, and I'm determined to find out what it is.

SIXTEEN

Laura

Shep Shackler gets right to the point at our Monday morning meeting. He informs me that he hasn't been able to find any evidence that Carson was in Mendocino at an Airbnb with his girlfriend the weekend Jeanine Randall died. On the other hand, he hasn't found any indication that he was in Nevada at the care home, either, aside from the video I've already seen. The recording from the camera feed inside the hospital, he says, has long since been erased. The only way to say for sure where Carson went that weekend would be to check the GPS from his car.

But Carson sold his car.

I tell him this.

"That's interesting," he says. He looks off to the side, tapping his pen on his notepad. "When?"

"About a month ago," I reply.

He jots something down on the pad.

"So now what?"

"I have an idea. But there's some risk attached to it," he says.

He explains that he could do some old-fashioned legwork at the hospital. Ask around and see if anyone saw anything. See if there are any rumors floating around about suspicious circumstances regarding Jeanine's death. But there was no formal investigation, he reminds me. So right now, there's no reason for anyone to look into it any further. And if he starts poking around, he could stir up something that might be better kept under wraps.

"You can't find out some other way?" I ask.

"Like?"

"Hacking into her medical records?"

"Illegal. And risky. Bad combination."

"Right."

"There is one other option," Shackler offers.

"What's that?"

"Show your stepson the video and ask him if he was there."

"I'm not ready to do that."

"Then I think the only move is to find out more about the cause of death. If there's nothing of concern, that would ease your mind, wouldn't it?"

It would, but I need to give his idea a little more thought. Because he's right. If he starts asking questions, he might dredge up something or put ideas into people's heads. The power of suggestion is strong.

"Yes. But I need a day to think about it."

"Take your time," he says. "And about the landlord you had me check out—"

"Oh, I almost forgot. You heard on the news about the missing VC? Charlie Yang?"

"Yes, of course."

"Turns out he's the guy Allie Dawson met at his house her first night in the new place. Remember? I told you about him. He was interested in Allie's project."

His eyes pop open. I don't think I've ever seen Shackler look so surprised, and we've told him a lot of shocking things.

"That's certainly... curious," he says.

"What do you make of it?" I ask.

"What do you mean?"

"The whole thing seems strange to me. The landlord befriending her at Starbucks. The mysterious Hungarian guy warning Allie. And now a missing VC."

"The news report said he's suffered from depression. Maybe he killed himself."

"Maybe," I say, mulling it over. I catch myself fiddling with a strand of hair and let it go. "But what about the corporate espionage? Do you think there's anything to the warning?"

"What's your grantee working on again?" Shackler asks.

"A device that can caption speech in real time."

He nods. "And the Hungarian guy?"

"Some kind of battery technology."

"Hmm." His lips are pressed together, and he's tapping his pen again. "What kind of battery technology?"

I shrug. "No idea."

"There could be something to his warning. There's a ton of espionage. Some of it state sponsored. And battery storage is a hot technology."

I nod.

He continues. "China's big on transportation technology. Cars. Airplanes. You heard about the GM case?"

"Yes, I did."

He's referring to the case that resulted in the prosecution of two spies. One was a career veteran at GM, the other a reluctant participant who was coerced into taking part.

"They stole steam engine technology. For airline turbines," Shackler reminds me. "They got caught, but most people don't. Have you heard of the Delta protocol?"

"No, I haven't," I reply.

"The federal government's trying to get firms to crack down and be more proactive about preventing espionage. Especially here in Silicon Valley. They've issued a set of red flags for employers to look for regarding their employees."

"Like?"

"Disgruntled employees. Renegades. People with problems. Secrets. Gambling debts. Drug addiction. And people with family members in autocratic countries. Or people who make easy targets for blackmail or bribery."

"Like the honeypot scandal?" I ask.

I'm referring to the allegations that foreign hookers have been targeting Silicon Valley VCs at certain high-end bars and restaurants around town, trying to get them into bed, get dirt on them, and blackmail them. Or coax secrets out of them during pillow talk, like something out of a Cold War spy movie.

"Those allegations have been floating around for a while now. I'm not sure there's much to them. And even if there were, what could they really get from VCs? The valuable targets are the cogs in the wheel. Engineers. Data scientists. Chemists. They have the cutting-edge technology. The valuable information."

"Right."

"And it's not only governments doing this, although the focus is mostly on China and Russia. That could be a plus for some small-time competitor who just wants to get a leg up on the competition. The hyperfocus on foreign countries deflects everyone's attention. Corporate espionage doesn't need to be part of some larger plot for global domination. Sometimes it's just greed. Or personal ambition."

"Allie's caption device can also do language translation," I say. "There are others on the market that can also do that. Apps that pair with virtual reality glasses. But hers will be more discreet. It's obvious if someone's wearing a pair of VR glasses."

"That might be of value. If, for example, a person could listen in on conversations and translate them without the speakers knowing," Shackler says.

"So you think she has something to worry about?"

"It's always a good idea to be careful and protect your ideas. I was starting to tell you about the landlord," he reminds me.

"Yes. You were. And?"

"No red flags that I could find. I haven't investigated his finances or his background. I wasn't sure how far you wanted me to go."

"I guess we can cool it for now."

"Whatever you say, Laura."

"Oh. Charlie Yang's wife is staying with her landlords now, in the main house."

"Allie told you this?"

"Yes. She told me yesterday when we were confirming our meeting for today. Which starts soon, so I need to get going."

I stand, and Shackler follows. He walks me to the office door and rests his hand on the doorknob.

"I'd say, based on my limited information, I don't think she's in any immediate danger. But the living situation is odd, I'll give you that. It might be better for her to get out of there sooner rather than later. Then you can get this off your plate. Seems you have enough on your mind without adding this to it."

He makes a good point.

"I'll give it some thought."

"And let me know what you decide on the other... situation."

"Will do."

As I'm walking to the car, something hits me. Lydia's living in that big, empty house alone up in Los Altos Hills. She and Christopher are, much to my surprise, waiting until marriage to live together, although they are at each other's places all the time. She claims that moving in before marriage leads to more problems. It's easier to bail on someone when you find out all their annoying habits, she believes, if you're only living together. If you're married, she feels, you're more likely to stick through the inevitable period of adjustment. I'm not sure I fully agree, but it's her decision.

At any rate, she has extra space. The home is built on a slope, and the ground floor is like an in-law suite with a separate entrance. The kids used it as a hangout room, and it became Peter's man cave when they left home. It would be perfect for Allie.

I'll run it past Lydia, and if she agrees, I'll propose it to Allie today. Shackler's right. Something's strange about her landlord, and I don't need my family or my foundation dragged into the middle of it. I'll extract Allie from the living situation, wash my hands of it, and move on.

SEVENTEEN

Allie

The Foster home is not at all like I pictured it. The living room is tastefully furnished, bright and inviting with a pearl-colored fabric sofa and two occasional chairs that I can tell are expensive. The decor in general appears high-end, but the home itself is modest and smaller than the Tabernaky residence. It's not what I expected from someone funding start-up ventures.

After a short walk down a hallway off the living room, the three of us get settled in her home office. Before I have a chance to start in on the details of my progress, Laura Foster brings up my living situation. She points out that it might be a distraction from my project. I can't tell if she's genuinely concerned about my safety or if she's worried about me potentially wasting the money she gave me. It's likely a little of both.

"I have a possible solution," she says.

She turns to Mina, and I can tell by the look on Mina's face this is news to her too. We arrived at about the same time and walked in together, so perhaps they haven't had a chance to discuss her idea.

Laura pauses as if second-guessing herself. Maybe she's going to try to pawn me off on Mina? Or she's going to offer to have me stay here? That would be awkward, if generous, so I hope not.

"Lydia, my stepdaughter, has a house in Los Altos Hills, about fifteen minutes from here," Laura says. "It has an in-law unit with a separate entrance on the first floor. She's agreed to let you use it for the next few months. At no charge. Then you can move out of where you are now and really focus on your work."

I see Mina nod, and I feel myself relax. My living situation has been causing more stress than I realized, and the thought of getting out of it is appealing.

"That's very generous of you. And of your stepdaughter. But are you sure about this?"

"It's fine with Lydia. It's a large home, and she lives alone. She's engaged, but she and Christopher don't live together. He's there some of the time, and some of the time she stays over at his place. He'll move in after the wedding. But that's not for another nine months. As long as it's only for a few months, it'll be fine. That should be enough time for you to accomplish what you need to in Silicon Valley."

"It sounds perfect, Laura. Thank you so much," I say.

"And you two are about the same age. After we finish up here, Mina can take you over to see it." Laura turns to Mina. "That is if you have time. Sorry to spring this on you, but I was just getting off the phone with Lydia when you two arrived."

"It's fine," Mina says.

We move on to my project. I tell them about my progress with the prototype and about my upcoming meeting with Ethan, the graduate student engineer I've put on retainer.

Laura's a little concerned that he might not have the experience to pull it off, but I assure her that I've done my homework on this—which I have—and that he's exactly the kind of person we need on the project. Someone with a fresh way of looking at the problem. She's not an engineer, so I'm surprised she's pushing back so much.

But then neither am I.

What if I'm wrong about him?

"Allie?" Mina says, seeming to sense my trepidation.

"Yes?"

"Ricky would be more than happy to sit in on the next meeting if you need an objective opinion about the guy."

That's not a bad idea. Ricky's background is in electrical engineering, and we got along well, even if there was no real spark. And the fact that we won't be dating makes it a lot less complicated to involve him in my business.

"Sure. That would be great," I reply.

I explain that with Charlie Yang missing, my one lead on a seed funder has dried up. I feel a bit callous for voicing that concern. The guy is missing, and I'm thinking about myself and the impact on my career. But neither of them bats an eye.

"Focus on the product, Allie," Laura says. "If the product's good enough, the funders will come to you."

It's wise advice, so I'll take it to heart.

Mina's Tesla winds up Moody Road into the rolling hills. We're in Los Altos Hills now, a separate town from Los Altos with a smaller population. The lots are much larger than the ones close to town. Some of the homes are visible from the road, but many are set back, concealing their grandeur, letting nature take the spotlight.

We're only twenty minutes or so from the headquarters of many of the companies that drive our economy, yet we're in a wooded wonderland with stunning vistas and natural beauty that rivals some of the most scenic places in the world. No wonder this is one of the most expensive areas of the country.

She maneuvers her car around a group of cyclists riding single file on the narrow road. My stomach does a flip-flop. I get carsick sometimes, but only when someone else is driving. I see some hikers on the other side of the road and think that this could be a peaceful place to live and work.

It's a stark kind of beauty. Not lush, but serene. The rolling hills are mostly golden and dry, but there are patches of green here and there. Splashes of red, yellow, and lavender dot the landscaped homes, framed by a bright blue sky. I think about the harsh, long winters in Wisconsin and that I'd never have to endure one here. Thank goodness, because these roads would be treacherous covered in snow and ice.

We drive for another ten minutes or so and then she turns down a gravel road. Trees form a tunnel, sheltering us from the relentless morning sun. It's not an overly long road, but I bet it feels like that late at night. I see no streetlights and it's isolated from the other homes. A chill runs up my spine when I picture it pitch-black in the dead of night and imagine what it would feel like to drive it alone.

Laura said Lydia would be away some of the time, and for a moment, I consider that I might be better off at my current place. What if someone tries to break into the house when I'm sleeping alone without my cochlear implant? What if there's a fire, and I can't hear the alarm? I have a portable visual fire alarm that's fine for the small cottage I'm in now, but it's not adequate for a home this size. Perhaps they have sprinklers. As we drive up to the home, I'm relieved to see there's a gate with a security keypad. Mina punches in the number, and we drive in and park.

It's a large, rustic-looking home surrounded by towering trees that block the sun. I'm not sure what kind they are. I was expecting something imposing and intimidating, but the house appears comfortable and inviting, if a bit secluded. We get out of the car and make our way to the house. Mina turns to me.

"So what do you think, Allie?"

"It's..." I look the place up and down, struggling to find the best way to express my concerns without seeming ungrateful.

"Isolated?" she says.

"A bit."

She smiles and rubs my arm. "It might take some getting used to. But this is an extremely safe neighborhood. I promise."

She's right, but I have concerns that don't occur to most hearing people. Still, I'm probably better off here than in

Mike's guest house, especially considering the recent turn of events with his missing venture capitalist friend.

"I'm sure it will be fine," I say. "And I appreciate the offer. Very much." I don't want them to get the wrong idea. Mina and Laura have gone above and beyond to help me.

"Of course. Don't worry about it. Now, the guest quarters are on the first level, through that entrance on the side." Mina points to our left. "Let's go have a look."

"What's that smell?" I ask. It's pungent and overpowering.

"Eucalyptus." She motions to the trees.

We go inside. The unit is a little bigger than my current one, although not as updated. It has a kitchenette, a full bath, a living area, and a small bedroom. It will work out fine, and it's only for a few months. If I get my seed-round funding, I can move to a different place or even go back to Milwaukee and work from there. All I need is a little more time to focus. Laura's right. I can't afford any distractions, and my current living situation certainly is one.

"It's perfect," I tell Mina.

"Wonderful!" she replies. "Let's make it happen."

———

As we drive back down Moody Road, I wonder how Lydia Foster can possibly afford a place like this. I probably shouldn't pry, but then it's Mina, not Laura. I feel like she won't really care.

"So, is Lydia some kind of Silicon Valley phenom? That seems like a pretty expensive house for someone around our age."

"Family money," she replies.

"Oh. I see." That makes more sense. Sort of.

But then why do the Fosters have a modest home compared to this one?

"It's from their mother's side," she says, as if she senses that it's not quite adding up for me. "They inherited much of her wealth when she died. And then a ton more when her grandmother passed last year."

"Oh wow. When did she...um, when did they lose their mom?"

"Years ago. When the kids were small. I think Lydia was seven? And Carson was four? Laura met their father about five years later."

"That's so sad. Was she sick?" I hadn't realized that Laura Foster married a widower. That must have been hard, to come into a family after a tragedy and try to pick up the pieces.

"No. She fell off a cliff when she was out hiking. At Windy Hill Preserve, over in Portola Valley."

Peter Foster's first wife fell off a cliff?

"Wow," I say.

"Yeah," she replies. "It was ruled an accident, but there wasn't much of an investigation." She shrugs. "I'll leave it at that."

I've felt an undercurrent of tension radiating off Laura from the first time we met. That's one of the consequences of not being able to hear very well all the time. Growing up, I had to rely a great deal on body language and facial expressions before I learned to use my hearing. As a result, I'm sensitive to people's emotions. It's a valuable skill. I can tell when someone's anxious or upset.

One thing's for sure. There's more to this family than meets the eye, and I'm going to dig around and see what I can find. Something's eating at Laura Foster, and I'd like to figure out what it is. I've put all my eggs in the woman's basket. If there's any chance she's distracted by her own problems, how do I know she's steering me in the right direction on my venture and not off a proverbial cliff?

"Sounds like the family has been through a lot."

"You can say that again. Especially with what happened last year."

"Why? What happened last year?"

Mina sighs. "I, um, I thought you knew about it."

"Knew about what?"

My eyes nearly pop out of my head as she goes on to tell me how Laura was almost murdered last year. By her husband's daughter who nobody knew about, conceived during an affair twenty years before, when Peter was married to his first wife. No wonder I'm getting a weird vibe from her. The poor woman.

"And then having a newborn on top of it all," I say.

"I know. She's amazing. She didn't have to start this accelerator now. She could have just sat back with their new money and focused on her family. But she really wants to make an impact and help women become successful entrepreneurs."

Now it's all starting to make sense, why Laura seems so guarded. I knew there was something more going on. On the surface, she has it all. But she's tense and often seems preoccupied. There's a sadness about her, and now

I know why. She's probably traumatized and exhausted. I feel grateful that she's so committed. She believes in me, and I can't let her down. I've got to make this work. For all of us.

———

I'm back home. It's late Monday afternoon, and I need to decide how to break the news to Mike that I'm moving out this weekend. He shouldn't be too upset since he'll get to keep all the rent money. And if he and Susan saw me looking at him through the window that night, I expect he'll be relieved to be rid of me.

It's a beautiful evening. The late summer heat wave broke, and there's a hint of fall in the cool breeze that comes in around this time of night. I decide I'll go sit out at the pool. Maybe Mike will come out, and I can break it to him then. I don't like the idea of knocking on their door. Susan makes me uncomfortable, and I don't want to deal with her. I change into shorts and a t-shirt and head out with my book.

After about twenty minutes of reading in my lounge chair, much to my dismay, Susan comes out into the yard with a woman I assume is Willa Yang. She looks a little younger than her husband. Late fifties maybe? But then you never know. Maybe she's had work done.

Now I regret coming out here. I hope they don't come over and talk to me. What do you say to a person with a missing husband?

Susan waves at me as they head towards the grill, which is under a covered area to the side of the pool. She turns it on, I suppose in preparation for some kind of barbeque. Then they turn and start walking in my direction. Susan probably wants to introduce me to Willa Yang.

I get up from my lounge chair to greet them. For once, Susan looks approachable and friendly. I should get this over with and tell her now, while she has a smile on her face. I'm planning to stay for the rest of the week and move to Lydia's place on Saturday.

"Allie, I wanted to introduce you to Willa Yang. She'll be staying with us for a while."

"Mrs. Yang," I say. "I'm so sorry to hear about your husband. Has there been any news?"

"Thank you. No, nothing yet. And please call me Willa."

She's a petite woman with a stunning silver-gray bob that becomes her. Her look is elegant and refined. She's wearing stylish white shorts with a navy polo shirt, accented with simple pearl earrings and a matching necklace. Her kind eyes are at odds with her stoic affect, and I sense that she's the type to keep her emotions in check.

"He was very kind to me. Please let me know if there's anything I can do," I say.

"Charlie was excited about your product, Allie."

"Really?" I'm totally shocked that he even mentioned me to his wife.

"Yes. Your story moved him. Deeply."

"Well, thank you for telling me that, Willa."

"Of course. We tire of hearing pitches about silly apps that do nothing for the greater good. So much greed and excess in the world these days. We started this fund to support projects that can genuinely make a difference in the world. And your caption device has the potential to do that."

I remind myself that this woman is in pain. I try not to feel sorry for myself because I've missed out on what could have been a wonderful funding opportunity.

"I certainly hope so. That reminds me. Susan? I have some news."

"Oh?"

And then I decide to lie.

"I've decided to move back to Wisconsin," I tell her.

"Really?"

"Yes. I can do my work from there. I'm very homesick."

"That's...unfortunate."

What does she mean by that?

I offer her a halfhearted shrug.

"When will you be leaving?" Susan asks, as her eyes bore a hole in my skull.

"This weekend."

"Oh, wow. That's quite sudden." She pauses. "You know that we can't—"

I hold up my hand. "I know I can't get my money back, Susan. It's fine. I understand."

Willa is looking off to the side, seemingly uncomfortable with how Susan is reacting. I'm relieved I'm not the only one who finds her off-putting. Susan glances in her direction and then turns back to me.

"Well, let me talk to Mike and see if we can figure something out. I'm sorry it's not working out for you."

"It's not the living arrangement. Really. You've both been nothing but supportive," I reply, trying not to choke on my words.

She smiles and thanks me. For a moment, she looks almost like a normal person. We engage in some further forced pleasantries, and then the two of them go on their way.

Of course, now I need to figure out what I'll say if they catch me in the lie. But what do I care? I'll never see these people again. *Hopefully.*

I grab my water bottle and book and head back to my guest house, thinking about how wonderful it will be to get the hell out of here.

"Allie?"

I turn around. It's Willa. Susan has gone into the house, but she's still outside. I start to walk over, and we meet in the middle of the yard.

"Yes?"

She holds out her hand. "Take my card," she says. "Charlie was very enthusiastic about your project. I'd be happy to take a look at it when you have something to show. I'm sorry you're leaving so soon though. It would be much easier to fund you if you were staying here. But perhaps we can try to work with you long distance."

I look down at the card. Willa Yang is the CFO of the company. *I still have a shot.* But now I've backed myself into a corner with my lie. I would love to stay in touch and court this relationship, but I just said I was leaving.

"Thank you, Willa."

"My pleasure," she replies. "I'm not making any promises. It's a competitive process. But keep in touch, and I'll see what I can do."

"I understand. And I will," I say. "Thank you."

As I head back to my cottage, I think about how I might be able to backpedal from my fake decision to leave town. At least I have a funding lead, and that's something. Overall, I consider it a win. But I'll have to get better at thinking on my feet.

I must admit that the thought of not having Barnat around anymore makes me a little sad. I feel like he has my back around here, which is weird, given the fact that he's so curt with me most of the time. We still have that walk at the Dish planned for Saturday, so perhaps we will keep in touch.

Barnat! Damn it!

My hands fly to my head. I told him I'd let him know if I was moving out. I should march right over there now and do it, but I don't want to face him. I send him a text instead, letting him know of my decision, and then I place my phone on my nightstand, face down.

With that taken care of, I make myself a salad, curl up with my book on the loveseat, and call it a day.

EIGHTEEN
Allie

It's Wednesday afternoon, two days since I told Susan I'd be moving out, and three days before I plan to leave. Oddly, I haven't run into anyone all week. Not Mike, and not even Barnat. He replied to my text, thanking me for letting him know about the upcoming vacancy, but he didn't say anything about our Saturday Dish walk.

I wonder if Susan and Mike told him that I'd be leaving for Milwaukee that day. Probably. Perhaps I should tell him the truth, but not while I'm still living here. I should have thought it through before I blurted it out to Susan. Now I may have to let the friendship go, and maybe that's okay. He's attractive and intriguing, but a little cagey. The practical course of action is to wash my hands of him completely, cut my ties with this living situation, and rid myself of this whole bizarre chapter of my life.

I have another iron in the fire anyway. Ricky Rao went with me today to meet with Ethan, to discuss my goal of making the device wireless. And I have to say, I was impressed. Ricky gave off a commanding presence at the meeting, which is something I didn't pick up on when we were alone together. Maybe that's how he is around other guys, or perhaps it was because he was in his element. He wasn't a jerk or anything, just confident and reassuring. And his vetting Ethan will go a long way towards making Laura Foster more comfortable with my decision to hire the guy.

During the meeting, I started to think that I should give Ricky another chance, and I was wondering if he felt the same way. When we walked back to our cars, after I'd thanked him for his help, he turned to me.

"Allie?"

"Yes?"

"I'm sorry I wasted our first evening together complaining about my ex."

"It's okay, Ricky, I—"

He held up his hand. "No." He shook his head. "It's not okay. It was rude."

"You can't help the way you feel."

"The way I *felt*." He smiled. "That's in the past. I'm looking to the future now."

"Interesting. And what do you see? In your future?" I felt a little flutter in my stomach, but I wasn't going to let on about it. I was trying to play it cool because truthfully, it *was* a bit rude of him to obsess about his ex on our first date.

He paused and looked down at his feet, seeming a little nervous. I found it endearing. Then he looked up at me.

"Another dinner date?" He cocked his head to the side, his big, brown, soulful eyes wide with anticipation. "With you?"

"And when do you see this happening?"

"I see this happening on Saturday night. At seven o'clock."

"That's a very precise premonition."

"I'm an engineer. I'm into precision."

I smiled at him. "Precision is good." I was planning to say yes, but I let him stew a bit, just for fun.

"So what do you say, Allie?" A tentative smile sat patiently on his face.

"I say yes, Ricky. I'll have dinner with you at precisely seven p.m. this Saturday."

His half smile grew to a full one. A confident one that reached the eyes. Inviting and sexy.

I left feeling excited about my Silicon Valley reboot, ready to move out and move on, forget all about the Tabernakys, mysterious Barnat, and the missing VC, and focus on the business of making my dream a reality.

———

I'm about to get ready for bed when I hear a knock at my door. It's about a quarter to nine in the evening, and I feel my stomach lurch. It's an odd time to have a visitor, and I wonder if something's happened.

"Yes?" I call out.

"Allie? It's Barnat."

I hope he's not upset with me if he somehow found out that I told Susan before I told him. I open the door.

"Hi. What's up?"

He doesn't seem angry, but he looks a bit somber. Is he perhaps sad that I'm leaving?

"There's been some news about Charlie Yang," he says.

I invite him in. He goes on to tell me that they found Charlie in a hotel in East Palo Alto, off the 101. He died from a gunshot wound that appears to be self-inflicted, although that's still under investigation.

My stomach sinks. Sure, I've had my share of challenges and heartaches over the years. Losing my hearing, for one. And then my father. But Peter Foster's wife falling off a cliff? His secret daughter trying to kill Laura? And now Charlie Yang, taking his own life? What is with this place? Part of me wishes I *were* going back to Wisconsin.

"That's terrible," I say.

He nods. "So, you're leaving on Saturday?" he asks.

"Yes," I reply.

He looks down at the floor and then up at me. "It seems very...sudden. You leaving town." He locks eyes with me. "Are you sure it's the right move?"

"No, I'm not sure."

"Well then. Maybe you'll change your mind."

Then I get an idea, a way to set the groundwork for a possible change of plans later.

"I need to go home, for now. My mother's got some health issues, and I need to help her out. I can always come back later if things improve."

"I'm sorry to hear about your mother. Is it serious?"

"I...um. I don't really want to talk about it right now if that's okay."

"Sure," he says.

"I guess I need to cancel our Dish walk." I shrug.

"I was looking forward to it," he says.

"Me too."

"Are you going to move into my unit?"

"I'll talk to Mike about it today."

There's an awkward silence as we struggle with how to wrap this up.

"Okay then. I should probably get going," Barnat says. Then much to my surprise, he reaches over and hugs me.

"Keep in touch, Allie," he says. "And take care of yourself."

"I will," I reply.

After he's out the door, I plop down on the sofa, take off my speech processor, and stare off into space, trying to process the events of the last few days. I'd be lying if I said I didn't feel a spark for Barnat. He's such an enigma.

Then I remind myself that foreign romances can be tricky. With the mysterious accent and the language barrier, it's easy to get carried away and lose touch with reality. To see things that aren't there. Ricky Rao? He's reality, and that's what I need right now.

Then something catches my eye on the bookcase. It's dark, the same color as the case, but it's protruding out from under one of the shelves, although it's tucked back a bit. I walk over and feel underneath. It seems to be stuck on with something, so I get a knife from the kitchen to loosen it.

I try to pry it off, but the knife springs back and slams my knuckle against the shelf. Hard. I pull out my hand and shake it. It's a butter knife, so it didn't cut me, but I'll probably have a bruise. Then it dawns on me that if I remove it, whoever placed it there might know I found it.

Instead of removing it, I reach in and snap a photo of it with my phone. It looks like some kind of bugging device. And I think about the fact that Barnat was standing there, that day he came over to ask about my apartment.

Did Barnat bug my apartment? Or was it Mike and Susan?

My heart is beating so hard, I wonder if they can hear it. I think about leaving right now. Packing up my car and going to a hotel until Saturday. But that would only call attention to the fact that I'm onto them. As much as I want to get out of here, I think sticking with the plan is my best option. Two more days and I can leave this place behind.

But who are these people?

And what do they want from me?

I need to tell someone, and I run through my choices. It's kind of late to bother Mina or Laura, and even later for my brother, in Chicago. Then I land on the perfect person, fire off a text, double-check the bolt on my door, and grab my computer.

I've cued up a slew of tech videos on electrical engineering to watch. I'm sure I won't get much sleep tonight, so I sit on the sofa and start on them now. I glance over to my front door, pull a blanket tight around my body, and settle in for a long, dark night.

NINETEEN

Allie

I finally fell asleep on the sofa around one in the morning and got about four hours of sleep. I'm more tired than usual, but I can function. I texted Ricky last night. Told him I needed to talk to him in person about a pressing work issue. He offered to come over to my place right away, but I told him I'd meet him at Peet's in downtown Los Altos first thing in the morning.

Now I'm sipping my second latte, waiting for him to arrive. I've been here for an hour. It's a great place to work or meet, spacious enough to find a secluded table away from people, and busy enough so that background chatter will drown out our conversation.

Hopefully. I'm not as trusting as I was a month ago.

I'm looking at the image of the device they planted. I tried to match the photo to a bunch of different bugging devices I found online, but I couldn't find anything that looked exactly like it. I look up from my phone and see Ricky coming through the door. He rushes right over to me.

"Are you okay?" he asks, placing a warm hand on my shoulder.

"Yes, I'm fine."

He motions to the counter. "Do I have time to grab a coffee?"

"Of course."

"Can I get you anything?" he asks. He places his laptop on our table across from me.

"No, I'm good."

He heads over to order. I'm so freaked out that for a short moment, I start to question his renewed interest in me, as if he might have an ulterior motive. But I push that crazy thought from my mind. I need to trust someone, and why would Mina's cousin be scheming against her grant recipient? It's hard not to get completely paranoid though with everything that's happened.

Soon, he sits down across from me at our small table off to one side of the café.

"So," he asks, "what's up?"

I take a deep breath. "I think someone bugged my apartment."

His eyes pop open. "Holy shit, Allie!"

"You can say that again." Then I pull up the photo. "Take a look at this. It was stuck under one of the shelves in the bookcase." I go on to describe the encounter with Barnat when he showed up at my apartment that day, when he made an excuse to come in and look around.

"So you think he stuck it under there? When he was in your place?"

"I can't say for sure. It could have been my landlords. It could have been there the whole time."

"Maybe this is some kind of scam they run. Find aspiring entrepreneurs. Offer them housing. And then steal their ideas."

"Right. But then, Barnat's an aspiring entrepreneur too."

"Or that's what he wants you to think. He could be part of the scam."

That thought makes my stomach sink.

"But you said my technology's not that valuable. Not like his battery storage venture."

"Well, hold up. You said there are applications for language translation, right?"

"Yes. The app it pairs with, XRAI Glass, can translate about seventy different languages in real time."

Ricky nods. "The translation option could be valuable. And your device would be a lot less obvious than a pair of VR glasses."

"True. So, you think it's possible they want to steal it? But why would they introduce me to Charlie then?"

"Who knows? Maybe to throw you off? Or maybe Mike's got some kind of deal with the Yangs. A finder's fee? And they're not trying to steal it? I'm just glad you're getting out of there. Any way you slice it, it's odd. I'm sure Laura will let you move in earlier, given the circumstances. You should get out now. *Today.*" He nods.

I tell Ricky I've thought about it. And I feel that sticking with the plan is the best option. It's only two more nights, and I don't want to make it obvious that I'm onto them.

He shrugs. "Sure. But I don't like the idea of you staying there alone."

"I don't have much choice."

He pauses, biting his lower lip. "I would offer to stay there with you, but I don't want you to get the wrong idea."

"I, ah…I don't think—"

"On the couch, of course," he adds.

I sigh.

"Bad idea. Sorry," he says.

"No, it's not that." I explain that I lied and said I was moving back to Wisconsin because I'm lonely and homesick. Having a guy sleep over might cause them to question my explanation.

"How about we video chat on our computers? Overnight?" Ricky offers.

That seems like a good idea, and I tell him so. With that settled, we move on to the business of figuring out what to do next.

"Let me call Mina and tell her what's going on," he says.

"Not here." I glance around the room and then turn back to Ricky. "You never know who might be listening."

"Right. I'll do it from my car. You sound like a real Silicon Valley pro now."

"Hardly." I let out a chuckle.

He examines the photo and tells me he's sure it's a bugging device and not a low-level one like you can get online. It looks to him to be rather sophisticated and possibly one that's not available in the United States.

Which points once again to Barnat. I feel so betrayed.

Could Barnat be in on this with the Tabernakys? Is that why he befriended me?

That thought sickens me, along with the fact that I felt an attraction to him. Perhaps it was all an act, his mysterious-stranger vibe interspersed with mild flirtation. Thank goodness I called off our Dish walk.

"Have you said anything in that room that would compromise your project? Or have you said anything to any of them directly?" Ricky asks.

I think about it for a few moments, trying to recall my conversation with Barnat and what I said at dinner that first night. I don't talk on the phone much at all. And I don't think I gave much up to him that day.

"I spoke to my brother, Kevin, over FaceTime. About the prototype. In my conversations with them, I didn't say anything more than I've said in any other meeting I've been in."

"That's good. But let me check your computer. They could have tried to clone it."

Crap! I hadn't thought of that. My hand goes to my forehead. "What if they've taken all my work?" I feel as if I might start to cry, and I'm trying to hold it back.

Ricky takes my hand in his. "I tell you what we're going to do. We're going to file for a provisional patent today. Even if you don't get it, at least you'll be taking some action to protect yourself. And nobody can steal your idea while the application's being processed."

"But I don't have proof of concept."

"That's why you file for a *provisional* patent. You'll have to pay fees twice. Once when you file the provisional one and again when the design is finalized. But you'll be protected in the meantime."

"How much does it cost?"

"Not much. Provided I do all the grunt work, and you won't have to pay out of pocket for that." He smiles.

"You'd do that for me?"

"Sure. For you. And for Mina and Laura. They have skin in the game too."

"Of course. And Ricky?"

"Yes?" he asks.

"Thanks."

"My pleasure. I'm not letting those fuckers screw things up for you and my cousin. Let's get to work."

We dive in and start on the application, and soon I'm feeling better about everything. I'm taking back control of my life and moving myself in the right direction. Then I glance around Peets, wondering who might be lurking in the shadows, waiting to steal my work.

Sorry suckers. I'm not going to let that happen.

TWENTY

Laura

My stomach's been in knots for the last two days. Shackler called on Wednesday and said he had some information for me. I'm headed into his office now to hear what he has to say. On top of that, I just found out that Allie's apartment was bugged. *Bugged!* I'm starting to have some moments of doubt, feeling like I'm in over my head with this accelerator. There's a lot I don't know about venture capital and start-ups, not to mention corporate espionage.

Is this something I should have discussed with my grant recipients?

I feel my pulse speed up as I enter the building to face what he's uncovered, and I wonder if I should have left well enough alone.

"Have a seat," he says.

I sit with my eyes glued to him as I settle into the chair. "What is it? What have you found out?"

"I've done the legwork, and I'm pleased to say there's no evidence of any kind of shenanigans surrounding Jeanine Randall's death."

My relief is tempered by an undercurrent of annoyance. *You couldn't have just told me that on the phone?* But then I notice that his jaw is tense and his lips are pressed together. I sense there's more to it.

"Is that...all?" I ask.

"No." He swallows. "There's more."

"Go on," I say. A prickly sensation creeps up my spine.

"There was chatter that day at the care home. About a young man who fits Carson's description, leaving her room earlier that day. A few hours before she died."

"Chatter?"

"From a nurse on the floor. She saw a young man coming out of Jeanine's room. He was dressed as an orderly, but she didn't recognize him. When she called out to him, he sped up and kept walking. She was about to follow him when she got a call from a patient, so she let him go."

"It was the day Jeanine died?"

"Yes."

I take a deep breath. "I see."

"But it was much earlier in the day. Jeanine was alive when he left," Shackler reports.

I feel my shoulders relax. If she was alive when he left, chances are he didn't do anything to her. But my gut had been telling me there was something going on with Carson. Something seemed off with him. The story about his trip to Mendocino. The mystery girlfriend we never met. And it seems I was right. Perhaps he just went to confront Jeanine. To get some kind of closure.

"I can't say for sure that it was Carson, of course. I'm not sure if this helps. But at least you can be sure she wasn't..." He pauses for a moment, his lips pressed together. "That she died of natural causes."

"It helps a lot. Thanks, Shep."

I let the information sink in while Shackler fiddles with his pen.

"Is there anything else?" he asks.

With my personal matter taken care of, I pivot to the matter of protecting my business interests. I tell Shackler about the bugging device Allie Dawson found in her guest house.

"That's unfortunate but not unheard of, I'm sorry to say." He's tapping his pen, deep in thought with a faraway look in his eye.

"It seems that—"

"Unless?" He turns to me. "Sorry. What were you saying?"

"I was saying that it seems her landlords might be running some kind of scam. But what were you going to say?"

"Her technology can be used for language translation too. Isn't that what you said?"

"Yes."

"That could have value."

He goes on about the possible applications. Companies doing international business. Eliminating language barriers between employees or supply chains. Or for covert operatives of foreign nations.

"Like...spies?" I ask.

He shrugs. "Stranger things have happened."

That seems far-fetched to me. I tell him so, and he agrees. In all likelihood, he tells me, they're small-time scammers who try to sell the information to competitors.

Then we discuss the options. Allie could go to the authorities. File charges. California is a two-party state, and it's illegal to record someone without their consent, not to mention a violation of the landlord-tenant laws.

"She doesn't want to press charges," I say. "If these people are criminals, they could be dangerous."

"I get that," he says.

"Plus, it will distract her from her project to involve herself in something like that."

"When is she moving out?" he asks.

"Tomorrow."

His brow furrows. "Seems a shame to let them get away with it."

Then I inform him that she applied for a provisional patent. Her technology is protected for now. I tell him I'm not looking to take it any further.

"Good thinking on her part. Sounds like you've got the bases covered as far as your business is concerned."

"I don't like the idea of them getting away with it, either. But it's Allie's decision. And I've been through enough over the last year. If there's any chance these people could be dangerous, I don't want to get involved. I'm sorry if that's shortsighted, but it's not my problem. Not after tomorrow."

"I could do some digging around. Get it on the radar of law enforcement on the down-low. I don't need to mention her name. Or yours."

Shackler's a former police detective, and he doesn't like to let things go. I'm starting to regret telling him about it.

"Keep us out of it. Please. I've been through enough."

"I'll keep you out of it, Laura. But let me keep an eye out, just in case. Do a little investigating. If they're at all dangerous, it's prudent to have a heads-up about it."

"I can't put any money towards it."

"Pro bono, Laura. A public service."

"Sure," I say.

I'd feel better if he just dropped it, but I know he won't. And it's a fair point. Keeping tabs on them isn't the worst idea in the world. With our last order of business settled, I leave the office feeling lighter, but still untethered.

As I'm walking to my car, it suddenly dawns on me what's been missing in my life. Why I've been feeling so out of sorts. I head home with a vengeance, eager to get my life back on track.

———

My hands are shaking as I mount my bike. I've taken some rides since the bike crash, but only around the flats. Never on hills. I try to tell myself that it won't happen again. That it wasn't an accident. I didn't make a mistake. It was an attempt on my life. But somehow, I still have doubts.

I was racing in the Santa Cruz Half Ironman last year, starting on the dangerous downhill part, poised to finish with a personal best for me. A record time that could qualify me for the Kona Ironman World Championship.

And then it all came crashing down.

I remember my confusion when the handlebars gave way under my arms. I was leaning on the aero bars, the upper bars, where I rest my forearms when I'm jamming along. I leaned left to pass a pack of cyclists ahead of me and the bars collapsed, catapulting me to the pavement.

It happened so fast that all I could do was close my eyes and tuck. I woke up in the ER with a broken collarbone and considered myself fortunate. It could have been a lot worse. I haven't done a real bike ride since that day. Partly, it's because I still have moments of doubt about the incident.

I have proof that Ella cut the brake hose on my Audi. I have proof that she drugged my coffee at work. I stared down the barrel of a gun as her shaky hands pointed it at me in my kitchen. But I have no proof that she tampered with my bike, and it's holding me back. It's possible the bolt came loose on its own. Maybe I was so distracted with all that was happening, I didn't check it properly. Or maybe I did something to make it come loose.

But it's time to leave those doubts behind.

I push off and start riding. I'm doing thirty miles today, and it's going to include hills. I realize now that racing isn't simply a hobby for me. It's a part of who I am. It's how I clear my head. It's what allows me to handle all my other responsibilities. And I can't let motherhood or the foundation get in the way. I'm putting my goal of qualifying for Kona front and center.

As I'm finding my groove on this ride, I realize it's the right decision. It's the only decision that will set me free from being mired in anxiety and doubt. I'm about halfway up Moody Road when another realization hits me. I need to confront Carson. For his sake as well as mine. I'm certain he's suffering, holding in whatever happened that day. I need to face my fears.

All of them.

Now.

———

I'm back home, dripping in sweat, feeling like a new person. Well, not exactly a new person. More like the old Laura. The one with the boring life, where soaring downhill is the most exciting part of my day. I greet Haley, give Kai a kiss, and head upstairs to shower.

Truthfully, my life had been relatively uneventful up until last year. I'd always had some doubts about Peter's first wife and her untimely death, and there was some intrigue regarding the circumstances of it. But that was my husband's drama, not mine.

Me? I grew up in Kailua, a suburb of Honolulu, body-surfing and doing my homework. We moved to California when I was in middle school, and I gave up the bodysurfing, replacing it with distance running—and doing my homework. Both my parents are academics, and they had high expectations. Sure, I had my share of adventure in college, but aside from that, my life was happily run-of-the-mill. And that was fine with me.

Then I met Peter about five years after Cynthia's death. I was twenty-seven. Carefree. Getting my career off the ground. Racing in triathlons. Barhopping with Sophie. And a year later I was a stepmom, putting my goals on hold, trying to heal a broken family.

It made no sense when he first told me about his late wife's accident. She was an experienced climber, and she "fell" out on a hike? Last year, Peter confessed to me that the family assumed it was a suicide, but they'd kept that quiet. Officially, the police ruled it an accident. He and Cynthia's mother didn't push it any further, so as not to call attention to her history of mental illness and to protect the children.

After some prodding on my part, Peter also disclosed that his wife was pushed over the edge that day, metaphorically, by his lover, Jeanine Randall. She followed Cynthia to Windy Hill Preserve and said all kinds of ugly things to her, attempting to break the marriage up for good. Peter assumes that's what made her take her own life. And he insists that Jeanine didn't literally push Cynthia off the cliff. The position of the body indicated a fall, not a hard shove. The manner of death was ruled accidental.

But I still wonder. How can they know for sure?

This all came out over dinner last year. It was the four of us: Peter, me, and the kids. I can still see the look on Carson's face that night. He knew then that Jeanine was responsible for the death of his mother. And I can hardly blame him for wanting to confront her. I'm relieved that my stepson's not a murderer. Just a wounded little boy who lost his mother in a tragic, heartbreaking way. I need to help ease his pain.

"Hi, Carson," I say.

I'm surprised he picked up my call. I was planning to leave a voicemail.

"Hey, Laura. What's up?"

"I need your help tomorrow. Are you busy?"

I can't very well disclose that I want to talk to him about Jeanine Randall, so I'll ease into it when I get him alone with me. He informs me that he has plans in the afternoon, but he's free in the morning.

"Perfect." I start to explain that we're moving Allie tomorrow, but it seems Lydia already told him about it. He mumbles something about scumbag corporate spies.

"Can you give us a hand?" I ask.

"Sure," he says. "What time?"

We settle on ten o'clock, which is perfect. Peter has taken up golf, and he'll be out then. The fact that Peter's so unfazed by the events of last year is starting to grate on my nerves. I wonder if there's something wrong with him. Maybe the new golf hobby is a deflection? Finding out you have a daughter and then losing her in the space of a few weeks must take some kind of toll on a person, although he seems fine. But I wonder. Is he?

I suppose I'm a little jealous. I wonder what it's like to be able to let go and not dwell on the past. It must be great. After I talk to Carson, I'll come clean to Peter about all of it. Then maybe I'll find peace of mind. I feel like a hypocrite, complaining about his lack of transparency when I'm keeping this from him.

With that taken care of, I head into my office. I've got nine other grant recipients, and they all need my attention. Allie Dawson's gotten enough of it for today, so I open the folder of a thirty-something single mom who's working on a travel app and get to work.

TWENTY-ONE

Allie

The day is clear and the weather is perfect. A crisp October day, and a welcome change from the heat wave we were having when I first arrived. Ricky came over to help me pack up my car, and we've just finished.

Ricky's being here had the added benefit of preventing any unnecessary interaction with my landlords. Otherwise, one of them might have offered to help me pack up, and I'm trying to avoid them. Although I'm eager to wash my hands of all of them, I don't want to burn my bridges with Willa Yang. It's good to have options, and if she turns out to be my only lead, I'll reach out to her.

Ricky just left, and now I'm cleaning the apartment. Mike will be over in an hour to inspect it. They offered to give me half of my unused rent money. I checked into it, and if they rent this unit out again during the period I've already paid for, it's illegal for them to keep any of my rent money. Mike could be putting his real estate license in jeopardy, which reminds me how shady he is. But for that reason, I don't want to make an issue of it. You never know what a person like that might do. I'll take the partial refund he's offering and move on.

I'm mopping the floor when I hear a knock at the door. It's not time yet for my inspection, so this catches me by surprise. I open the door and see Barnat standing there, his arms folded.

Great.

"Hey," I say, forcing a smile. "What's up?"

"I came to say goodbye."

Rather than invite him in, I step outside and close the front door. I look him up and down, wondering if he was the one who planted the bugging device.

"I'm in the middle of cleaning," I say.

He nods. "So. You're headed back to Milwaukee?" His tone sounds taunting, as if he's daring me to lie to him again.

"Waukesha, actually," I reply. "To my mother's house. I gave up my apartment when I moved."

"Right. How's she feeling?"

"About the same," I say.

"Let me know if anything...changes. I'd still like to show you the Dish."

Yeah, right.

I tilt my head, trying to look cute and gullible. "Sorry about bailing on you, Barnat. But I need to do this. You know, for my mother."

"Of course," he says. "Your mother." A sly smile appears on his face as he eyes me.

"I need to get going," I say.

"Well, good luck, Allie. Take care of yourself," he says.

"You too, Barnat."

Or whoever you are.

———

Mike and Susan both came over to check me out of the unit and say their goodbyes. Much to my surprise, they gave back all my prepaid rent money. They informed me they'd found a new renter who could move in right away. I have no idea if it's Barnat or someone else. Maybe they're not so shady after all.

Susan was quite friendly today, and Mike seemed almost apologetic, as if it were somehow his fault that I'm leaving. I'm hoping that if he did see me peeking out at him that night, he's grateful for my silence. I inspected every inch of the apartment again and didn't find any other suspicious devices, but the one under the shelf was still in place.

It crosses my mind that if Barnat didn't plant it, he could be a victim too, but I don't trust him enough to tell him about it. Chances are I'll never know who put it there or why, and I suppose I'll need to live with that. Laura suggested that I could report it to the police, but I told her I'm not doing that. It's too risky, and I don't need to make enemies out of them.

I exit the guest house for the last time, eager to leave it behind. As I walk to my car prepared to move on, there's a newfound pep in my step. I hop into my Honda, strap myself in, and pull away from the curb.

But as I'm driving down the street, something catches my eye. It glides past me, and my eyes shoot up to the rear-view mirror. I slow the car and let out a gasp.

A large tan dog is trotting towards the house.

PART THREE

TWENTY-TWO

As I watched her get into her car and drive away, I almost allowed myself to breathe a sigh of relief. Almost. But I know better, so I held it in a little longer. And when I saw the dog coming towards us, my stomach sank to the floor.

How the hell did this happen? We were so close. Part of me wishes I hadn't seen Allie's car slow down. What she saw that night I could have lived with. We probably could have let it go. But that changed everything.

None of this was supposed to happen. And none of this is my fault. If everyone had followed the plan, nobody would have gotten hurt. Of course, now it's up to me to fix it. It's clear I'm the only one who has what it takes to tie up all the loose ends and protect us.

I know what I need to do. It will weigh heavily on me. But I'll do it.

TWENTY-THREE
Laura

C arson sits on our living room sofa, sipping a black coffee. I walk over and place a bagel and cream cheese on the coffee table. He continues scrolling on his phone, briefly glancing up to acknowledge my existence.

"Thanks," he says.

His eyes dart back down to the device he cradles in his hand. I look over at Kai napping in his bouncy chair and remind myself to keep him away from screens as long as possible. It's too late for my stepkids. They were raised at precisely the wrong time, when nobody gave it a second thought. I gave up on them a long time ago, but there's still hope for my infant son.

When I sit down across from him, it takes him a few moments to notice me. I rarely initiate any kind of interaction with him and normally let him take the lead. In contrast to his sister, he's reserved, and it seems to make him uncomfortable if I try to force it.

"Is something wrong?" he asks. He hasn't touched his bagel. I have a sudden urge to abort the plan.

I ignore it.

"I wanted to talk to you about something," I reply. "Something important."

"Sure, Laura. What's up?"

My stomach tenses. "It's about Jeanine Randall," I say.

His eyes widen, and then he's silent for a moment. "Jeanine Randall?"

"Yes."

"What about her?" He folds his arms over his chest, gripping his forearms and curling into himself.

"There's something I've never told anyone. And I'd like to tell you, if that's okay."

"Um...okay. Sure." He can't seem to look me in the eye.

I confess that I'd always harbored concerns about the woman. I tell him that I never understood why there hadn't been more of an investigation into his mother's death. And that I've always wondered if there was some kind of altercation between his mother and Jeanine that day.

"I thought Jeanine might have been dangerous. Unhinged. Like her daughter," I say.

He clears his throat but stays silent, looking off to the side. "Carson?"

He looks at me now. "Yes?" he says.

"Did you have concerns about her too?" I tilt my head to the side, awaiting his response.

He uncrosses his arms and places his hands on his thighs, mindlessly rubbing them as he gazes down towards the coffee table.

"Take your time," I say.

He takes a deep breath. "I guess," he says. "Yeah, I had some concerns."

"That's understandable."

I let this sit with him for a bit, and then I continue. "I was worried about something else too."

"What?"

"I was worried she might recover and come after me. After us. So I hired a private investigator to keep tabs on her. He sent me a video a while back. I never told anyone about it. Not even your father."

He swallows. "A video?"

"Yes. A video of a young man leaving her care home. The day she died. A young man... who looks a lot like you."

We're both silent for a few moments. Then Carson starts to tear up. He's trying to choke back the sobs, but he can't hold back the eruption. I've seen him cry as a boy, but only in the whiney way children do when you won't let them have a candy bar before dinner. Never like this, a release of pent-up remorse and guilt, deep and guttural. I move over to the sofa, rub his back, and let him cry it out. After a few minutes, he composes himself.

"I didn't touch her. I swear."

"I believe you, Carson. Do you want to tell me what happened?"

He nods.

"Take your time, honey."

After a few moments, he confesses to me that he went there that day to confront Jeanine. To ask her what really happened up at Windy Hill Preserve.

"She was the only one who knew what really happened. I wanted to know the truth about my mom," he says. "I wanted to know what she saw. And I wanted her to know the pain she caused me. I wanted her to suffer. Like I suffered."

"So what happened?"

"I was angry. Really angry. On the drive. And on the way up to her room. But when I got there and saw her in the bed…" He shrugs.

"It's okay, Carson."

"She looked so helpless. And frail. Her eyes were closed. It seemed ridiculous to even be there. I was about to leave. But then her eyes began to flutter. And then they opened. I started talking. I was calm. Weirdly calm. I told her who I was. And I thought I saw her eyes widen, like she understood what I was saying. I told her it was her fault that my mom was gone. That no matter what happened up there on that cliff, she killed her. I asked her why she did that to our family. And I started to cry." He takes a deep breath.

"Take your time."

"Then I told her about Ella. That her crazy daughter tried to finish what she started. And I told her that it didn't work. And that Ella killed herself. *Now we're even*, I said. And then I left."

"Carson. I'm so sorry you had to carry this around all this time." I reach for him and we embrace. It's been ages since I held him, and it feels good.

After a bit, he releases me and straightens up. "I didn't touch her," he says. "I swear."

"I know. I believe you."

159

"But what I said to her. Could it have…?"

I grab his shoulders and give him a shake. "This isn't on you. You hear me? She got what was coming to her, and none of this is your fault. She died hours later, and she was fine when you left. I doubt she even registered who you were or what you said. Do you understand me? It's *not* your fault."

He nods.

"We're putting this chapter behind us. It's time. Got it?"

"Yeah, Laura. Thanks."

Kai's wail forces us to switch gears. I glance at my watch and realize we're running a little behind schedule. I probably need to change Kai before we leave.

"We need to get going."

He nods.

"Are you okay?"

"Yeah. Thanks, Laura."

I nod. "Now eat your bagel. We're going in ten."

He picks up the bagel and takes a bite.

I'll need to fill Peter in about all of this soon.

I'm not looking forward to it.

TWENTY-FOUR

Allie

My hands are still shaking as I drive up to my new residence. I punch in the code at the security gate. It's a quarter to nine in the morning, and I'm a little early. I hope Lydia won't mind. I drive in and park my Honda in front of the garage door, and only then do I let myself think about what I just saw.

Could the dog have been Dolly?

If so, I got away from there just in time. Thank goodness the Fosters offered me a way out of that living situation. I haven't told anyone about seeing my landlord that night, but I'm thinking about telling someone now. It would be nice to get it off my chest. But then Laura Foster suggested I go to the police about the bugging device.

What if I tell her, and she insists I report it? Or what if she tells them herself?

I decide I'm better off keeping it to myself for now. If Dolly is alive, then Mike lied to me. And I don't even want to think about what that would mean. Whatever's going on at their place is no longer my problem. I'm safer moving on. If I tell the police and they open some kind of investigation, they could force me to testify. Who knows what the Tabernakys might do to me if they think I'm a danger to them. Besides, it could have been a different dog. I didn't see the animal's face, and the dog looked a bit thinner than I remember.

It wasn't Dolly.

I take a deep breath and let it all go.

Lydia's at the door now. I exit my vehicle, determined to leave Mike, his guest house, and the mystery dog behind.

———

Lydia seemed happy to see me. Laura Foster and her stepson arrived about five minutes after I got out of the car, and we got to work moving me in. I'd met Lydia once before, but this was my first time meeting Carson. He's pretty much her opposite, quiet and reserved, and I notice he hardly got a word in. I'm glad she's a talker, though because I don't have to worry about filling the silent spaces.

At first, I found Lydia a bit intimidating, but I've warmed up to her already. It almost feels like she's grateful for some company, living alone at this secluded property. Her fiancé travels a lot, she said. He's in Europe on business for a few weeks, and she's joining him later this month. She exudes confidence, and I wish I could be more like her.

She's attractive in a savvy businesswoman kind of way, almost my height but with a smaller build. Her look would be severe if weren't for her sparkling blue eyes, a striking contrast with her long, silky dark hair. Carson's eyes are deep brown, but otherwise, they look very much alike. She strikes me as the kind of girl who was popular in high school, but not in a mean girl way. More like the kind of girl who could stand up to a bully, but not be one.

I hope I'm right.

We've just finished unloading my car and we're taking a break, sitting in the living room of the main house. It's so different from Laura Foster's home. Almost the opposite. The studded brown leather sofa I'm sitting on is stiff and regal. A heavy, ornate rosewood dining table sits on a dark wood floor. Not much light comes in through the windows because of the tall trees surrounding their property. It's got the feel of a secluded English country home or an upscale hunting lodge.

I imagine it could get a bit depressing here though, and it doesn't surprise me that Laura picked a light, airy home when they moved and decorated it the way she did. It had to be difficult, living all those years in a dead woman's home.

Thinking about all the tragedy this family has gone through, I'm a bit surprised that they kept this home in the family. My mother couldn't wait to sell our house and rid herself of the memories when my father died. Of course, financially we didn't have much choice. I wonder what it would have been like if a stable stepdad had come into my life after my father died, like Laura Foster had for Lydia and Carson. They're luckier than they know.

"Have you set a date for your wedding?" I ask.

"Yes! June fifteenth. We're very excited."

She chatters away about the different islands, the venues she's considering, the logistics of planning a destination wedding, and the endless details that need to be worked out.

"I'm so lucky Laura's helping me. I don't know what I'd do without her."

It seems like they have a great relationship, and I wonder if it was always that way. After a bit, Carson tells us he needs to go. He looks preoccupied, or perhaps he's just sick of hearing about the wedding. We wrap things up, which is fine with me. I'm anxious to start unpacking.

"Thanks so much. To all of you. I'm very grateful."

Lydia squeezes my forearm. "I'm happy to have some company. It's no problem."

Then she offers to cook dinner for me tomorrow night, and I accept. I've got a date with Ricky today but no plans for tomorrow, and it's nice to have something to look forward to.

I'm heading downstairs to unpack when I notice a text on my phone. My stomach sinks, because it's from Mike Tabernaky. I stare down at the screen, trying not to read too much into it.

Safe travels, Allie. Keep in touch.

TWENTY-FIVE

" **D**id you say you want me to blindfold myself?" I ask. We're driving with the a/c on, and I wonder if I heard him correctly.

"Yes. Put it on," Ricky confirms.

"Why?"

"I told you. It's a surprise."

I do like surprises...most of the time.

"What kind of surprise?"

"You'll have to wait and see. Hurry! We're only five minutes away."

It's not really a blindfold. It's his tie. A light blue one made of silk. It feels soft against my face as I secure it in place. Some light comes in through the fabric, so it's not too freaky.

I'm intrigued.

We've been in the car for about forty minutes now. We spotted a Waymo driverless car when we first got on the highway, and Ricky thought it was cute that I snapped a photo. I guess that's normal around here, but my followers

BONNIE TRAYMORE

might like to see one. He's taking the scenic route from the Peninsula to San Francisco for our mystery date. North on 280 from Menlo Park, over to Route 1 near Pacifica, then to Skyline Boulevard, a spectacular drive that runs along the coast. Of course, I can no longer admire the view or share it with anyone. After a few minutes, the car slows down and we pull into a parking space. He shuts off the car.

"Can I take it off now?" I ask.

"Not yet," he says.

This better be good.

He tells me to wait while he comes around to my side of the car. Then he helps me out and hooks his elbow with mine so he can guide me to wherever we're going. *Are people looking at us, wondering if I'm a hostage?* I'm smiling, so probably not.

"Okay," he says. "Almost there."

Soon he stops, and I feel him undoing the knot. The tie slips from my head and into his hand.

"Oh my God!" I say this a few decibels louder than I intended. If people weren't looking at us before, they sure are now.

We're at the San Francisco Zoo. What adult gets this excited about a zoo? A week or so ago, I told Ricky how much I loved my trips to the Lincoln Park Zoo in Chicago with my dad. It was only in passing. I'm amazed that it even registered with him.

"You remembered," I say, my voice barely above a whisper.

He's got a mile-wide grin on his face. "I listen. Most of the time."

166

My eyes widen and my heart warms. "Thank you."

He shrugs. "Well, it's not the biggest one on the planet, but it's—"

I place a finger on his lips. "Shh. Don't spoil it. It's perfect."

———

We meandered through the grounds for about an hour. Visited the elephants. Then the giraffes—my favorite—housed in the African Savanna with the zebras, surrounded by native plants and birds. Now I want to go on a safari. A real one, in Africa somewhere.

One of these days.

This place is amazing. I had no idea. Acres of manicured gardens sit across from the ocean, the foam caps visible from several vantage points. I saw what looked like a wedding rehearsal on the grounds, near one of the restaurants. What a great place to get married.

We're with the lions now. I connect with most animals, and I'm eyeing one of them. He's lying on the edge of a raised platform with his paws stretched out in front of him. His golden eyes look wise, like he's an old soul with something to teach me. They're framed by a fluffy mane in a tawny shade of blonde that's almost the same as my hair.

And almost the same shade as that dog I saw earlier today.

I swallow.

Damn.

I was just starting to put it out of my mind, but now it's front and center again, the questions spinning around in my head. Was it Dolly? Or am I imagining things? Could they have done something to Charlie Yang? It's going to drive me crazy. Maybe I should tell Ricky. But I'm not sure I want to get any further involved. And if I tell him, he might want me to report it to the police.

"Allie!" Ricky jolts me back into reality.

"Yes?"

"Are you even listening to me?"

I realize he's been talking to me for a while. "I'm sorry, Ricky. It's just…" I sigh.

"Is something wrong?"

"No. Not at all. I was busy communing with my lion friend. Sorry."

"Your lion friend?"

"Yeah. He's trying to tell me something. I'm sure of it."

"He's trying to tell you you're lunch. You have heard of the food chain, no?"

"Very funny. Speaking of lunch, let's go get a snack," I say. "Right after I do this." With my phone, I record a clip of my furry friend and post the reel to my Instagram.

I wave goodbye.

He licks his chops.

———

We grab hot dogs and sodas from a kiosk and take a table in the outdoor garden. The birds must be nearby. They're screeching like crazy, as if there's a disturbance in the air. Or maybe they're coming for us, like in that Hitchcock movie. *Wasn't that filmed nearby?*

A chilly gust of wind blasts in from the ocean, and goosebumps sprout up across my skin. I rub my arms and take a bite of my hot dog. I've got to tell someone, and Ricky's my best bet.

"I think something weird is going on over at my old place. But I'm not sure I want to get involved. If I tell you what I know, will you promise to keep it to yourself?"

"Well, that depends. That's a hard promise to make without knowing what it is. Are they planning to blow up the Golden Gate Bridge? Then no, I won't keep it to myself."

"Fair enough. They're not planning to blow up anything, as far as I know. And there's a chance it might be nothing. But I don't think so."

"So, it's somewhere between nothing and blowing up the Golden Gate Bridge?"

I nod, chewing a mouthful of hotdog.

"Okay. And?"

"I'm pretty convinced there's some kind of sabotage going on."

"Don't I already know that? From the bugging device you told me about?" He takes a bite of his hot dog and wipes his mouth with the back of his hand.

"Yes, you do."

"So why are you telling me this again?"

"There's more."

"You think they're trying to steal secrets. And...?"

I pause for a long moment, thinking about how to tell him this complex, involved story. I decide to cut right to the chase.

"I think the Tabernakys might have murdered Charlie Yang." I let out a nervous chuckle.

Ricky's eyes widen, and he nearly chokes on his hot dog. "What the fuck, Allie? Are you making some kind of sick joke?"

"No. Not at all." I shake my head. "It's just that, hearing myself say it out loud, it seems kinda…ridiculous? Maybe my imagination is getting the best of me."

"Okay, well, may I ask why this even crossed your mind?"

I explain to him what I saw my first night in the house. The night Charlie Yang went missing, when Mike was dragging the duffel bag across the lawn. "But when he told me about the dog dying, I figured the dog was in the bag, so I let it go."

"Okay. And?"

"Today as I was pulling away from the curb, I saw a dog that looked like Dolly, trotting towards their house."

"Are you sure it was the same dog?"

"Well…no. I only saw it from behind. And it was a bit thinner than their dog."

"It could have been anybody's dog, Allie. That's a pretty big leap you're making. You didn't see its face?"

"No, I didn't."

He sighs.

"You think I'm overreacting?" I ask.

"Maybe a little?" He's got a hesitant smile on his face.

"I sure hope so."

"Look. They found Charlie Yang days later. In a hotel room. Far from their house. It was ruled a suicide. He died in that hotel room, not at their house. Those are the facts."

"When was it ruled a suicide? I thought they were still investigating."

"Today. I heard it on my drive over to pick you up. There's a celebration of life for him next weekend."

"Hmm. Okay. That does make me feel better."

And I do feel better. It was the right move, getting this out in the open. It's frightening how my dark thoughts can take over, left to fester inside my head.

"A dead dog sounds more plausible. Doesn't it?" Ricky asks.

I shrug. "Sure. But what about the sabotage? Do you think I have any obligation to do something about it? Should I warn Barnat? Maybe he didn't plant the bugging device, and they're trying to steal his work."

"That's not unusual. In fact, it's downright common. Even expected. Don't give it another thought. If Barnat's stupid enough to let them steal his ideas, he's never going to make it here anyway."

"Well, *I* was stupid enough to let them try to steal my idea."

"No, you were smart enough to tell me about it. And then file for a provisional patent."

"I guess you have a point."

I take a sip of my soda and reflect on my conversation with Willa Yang when she told me to keep in touch about the funding.

"So...there's a celebration of life for Charlie Yang next weekend?"

Ricky nods, finishing up a mouthful. "Why?"

I remind him that Willa offered to consider my project for seed funding.

"Right. And?"

"Should I go to the service? Would it be…weird?"

"Interesting idea. Most people would appreciate the support. And it seems like it's open to the public. He was well-known around town, so there'll be a lot of people there. I'm sure you'll blend in."

"But I told them all I was moving away. How do I explain that?"

"Don't you have your weekend retreat coming up? The weekend after next?"

"I do. Good point. I could say I'm in town for that."

He puts his hand on mine. "A new romance could also explain a sudden decision to move back."

I feel a little flutter in my stomach. "You'd go with me?"

Ricky nods. "I'd be delighted. I'm always up for meeting a new VC."

"It's a date, then?"

"It's a date," he says.

"Thanks, Ricky. For everything. It was very sweet of you to do this for me," I say.

We lean into each other and sneak a kiss. Then we get up and toss our wrappers in the trash.

"Now, let's go see the primates," he says. "Maybe I can 'commune' with them." He hunches over like a gorilla and makes a snorting noise as we walk.

I roll my eyes. Then I bat him on the arm. "Hey, did you know that they can learn signs?" I ask.

"I did not know that."

"Yeah. It started with a gorilla named Koko. She was born at this zoo, in fact."

As I continue to educate him about the linguistic controversy about whether gorillas can really understand ASL, I'm once again optimistic about my future—and I know for sure that I want Ricky in it.

TWENTY-SIX

Allie

"Would you like a refill?" Lydia asks.

I probably should say no. I've only had one glass so far, and I'm in that sweet spot where I feel relaxed but not tipsy. I have an important meeting in the morning with Ethan, my software engineer. But it's so nice to feel comfortable and safe, especially after Ricky eased my mind last night about the whole Charlie Yang situation. Plus, as much as I'm enjoying my budding relationship with him, I'm really craving some girl talk. I'm not ready for the evening to end.

"Sure," I reply. "But just a smidge."

Lydia pours some more pinot noir in my glass. I stop her when it's less than half full; she fills hers to the brim.

We got through the basics over dinner. I told her about my background in luxury branding and filled her in on the progress I've made on my caption screen. I learned that she works for a company that launched a new dating app, similar to eHarmony. It matches people based on personality type but also uses DNA to flag any potential genetic issues with a partner.

"That's how I found out I had a half-sister," she says. "We were beta testing it, and I uploaded my genetic data."

I'm not sure I'm supposed to know what happened to their family last year, but she seems to think I do. My inhibitions are dulled by the wine, so I take a chance.

"Is that the half-sister who—"

"Tried to kill my stepmom? Yeah." She rolls her eyes. "She was a real nutcase."

"That must have been terrifying. For Laura. And for all of you."

Lydia explains that she'd arrived with *her* gun—as if we all carry one—just in time. "But then my father came charging in, and it was total chaos. Ella's gun went off. The bullet grazed my dad, and he fell to the floor. Then she ran outside and shot herself. Maybe she thought she'd killed him." She offers me a shrug.

"That's…well, it's just horrible. I'm so sorry, Lydia."

"Oh, don't be." She waves it off. "She's out of our lives now. *Forever.*" She says this with a smug look on her face.

I make a mental note to never get on her bad side.

"Have you and Laura always been close?" I ask.

"Oh, no. I was a perfect little shit to her for years. I don't know how she put up with me. I was…messed up. Angry that my mom was gone. You know?"

"Sure."

"I missed my mother. Terribly. And I took it all out on Laura."

"It's understandable."

"No, it's not. I was horrible to her. Even my dad doesn't know the worst of it. But why am I going on about this to you? What a terrible first impression I'm making!"

"Don't worry about it. I was a perfect little shit to my own mother when I was growing up too. I think we all are, to some degree."

"How's your relationship with her now?"

I sigh. "It's not great. And that's on me."

Seeing how Lydia's matured makes me feel like a spoiled child. I need to try harder with my mom. She's been trying to make amends to me for years, getting nothing in return.

"Do you want to talk about it?"

Normally, I don't. But for some reason with Lydia, I do. I don't know how to start though, so I stare down at the hardwood floor for a moment, avoiding eye contact.

"Go ahead," she says. "This is a safe space."

I swallow and look over at her. "Our problems started when I was about ten. I started to feel self-conscious about my cochlear implant. It was affecting my friendships. It's not like I was teased. More like frozen out. It's hard for me to understand people in groups, and that's how girls interact at that age. Eventually, it got too hard for them to include me, so they stopped asking me.

"And I took it all out on my mother. I resented that she made me wear it. One day, in the middle of a fight, I took it off, threw it on the kitchen floor, and smashed it under my boot. These new, expensive leather ones she'd splurged on the weekend before."

Lydia laughs. "Ha! I was worried you were too wimpy for Silicon Valley. But it seems you've got some fire in you after all."

"Yeah, well the device costs about five thousand dollars. And we weren't well off. Our insurance covered it that one time. We lied and said it was an accident. But she was furious with me. And I didn't want to go to speech therapy anymore. I'd have tantrums in the parking lot of the therapist's office, like a toddler."

"Like you said to me, it's understandable."

"No, it's not. I didn't do that to my dad. Just her. And when he died in a car accident later that year, things got worse. Much worse. My mother started drinking heavily. Kevin, my older brother? He had to grow up fast. I don't know what I would have done without him."

"Is he...does he also have a hearing loss?"

"Nope. Just me." I hold up my hands and shrug.

"Are you close with him?"

I hesitate because I don't know quite how to explain our relationship. We're close, in a co-dependent kind of way. Instead, I redirect the conversation.

"He may have saved my life."

I haven't told this story to anyone in a long time. And suddenly I'm eleven years old, right back there in the bedroom of our ground floor apartment in the middle of the night.

"I woke up for some reason, and I sensed that something was wrong. And when I looked over towards my dresser, I saw a man. A stranger. In my *room.*"

Lydia's hand goes to her chest. "Oh my God," she says. Her blue eyes widen.

"There was a full moon showing through the cracks in the blinds, but it was still hard to see. And without my speech processor on, I couldn't hear anything. I was terrified. I think he was going through my jewelry box. But he must have heard me stir, so he turned around and started towards me. I thought my life was over. I wanted to scream, but I was frozen to the bed. But then he stopped in his tracks, bolted over to my window, shoved it up, and hopped out."

"Holy shit," Lydia says.

"Yeah. It was all over in a minute or so, but it felt like an eternity. I was lucky. Turns out my brother came home at just the right time. It must have spooked him when he heard Kevin come in the front door."

"And where was your mom?"

I let out a sigh. "Passed out drunk. He climbed in through her window, but she didn't hear him. Got her jewelry and some cash, then came for my stuff."

"Jesus, Allie. Did they ever catch him?"

"Nope. He got away with my birthstone necklace, some of my mom's jewelry, and a little cash. I guess it could have been worse."

"And your mom? Does she still drink?"

"No." I shake my head. "She got sober about a year after that happened."

"Well, that's something, I guess."

She's right. It is something. It's been nearly two decades, and I decide I'm going to try harder to mend fences with my mother. I've been punishing her for too long. We're different people, and even without all the baggage, our personalities don't exactly mesh. But family is family, and she and my brother are all I have.

We sit for a bit longer in comfortable silence. I haven't felt this close to another woman my age in a long time. It's nice.

"So. Tell me about Ricky," she says with a warm smile. "Is it getting serious?"

And we move on to lighter topics as I nurse my wine and let myself relax for the first time since I moved to Silicon Valley.

We wrapped up our dinner pretty early, and I spent the last two hours getting organized for my week. Now I'm putting the last of my things away in the bathroom after a pleasant FaceTime call with my mother.

I told her I'd come home for Thanksgiving, and that made her happy. She filled me in on her latest happenings, and I told her I was dating a nice guy named Ricky. It's the most I've shared with her in quite a while. She seemed comforted by the fact that I have a guy looking out for me, and I'm trying not to take offense at that.

I turn around to leave the bathroom and almost jump out of my skin. Lydia's right there, in the doorway.

What the hell?

She looks upset.

Is she mad at me for some reason?

She's talking a mile a minute, but I can't hear what she's saying because I don't have my speech processor on. She's talking too fast for me to lip read.

"Slow down, please," I say, holding up my hand. "I can't understand you."

"My dad had a heart attack," she repeats, slowly enough so I can read her lips.

"Oh my God, Lydia. I'm so sorry."

Her hands go to her head. I get into the bedroom, grab my speech processor, and snap it into place.

"I...I have to go to the hospital," she says.

She's shaking. Probably in shock. She can't drive. She drank much more than I did, and she's beside herself with worry.

"It'll be okay. Let me drive you there," I say.

"He's at Stanford," she says.

"Good. We'll be there in a flash. Don't worry. They know what they're doing. He's going to be fine."

Lydia nods.

I hope I'm right.

Just a few moments ago, I felt better than I have since I got here, and now I'm thrown right back into the middle of another family crisis. I'm starting to think I'm bad luck for people. But that's a crazy thought, and I don't need more of those, so I grab my purse and we head out.

TWENTY-SEVEN

Laura

The waiting room is nearly empty, and somehow that's making this worse. Each time I start to settle in, another booming announcement has me jumping out of my seat. I can hear every detail of another family's frantic ruminations as they wait for news about their teenage son. The mother is hysterical, and I can't say I blame her. Still, I get up and move to the far side of the room.

Sophie comes back from the café with two coffees. She lives a few blocks from here and arrived before me. I couldn't ride in the ambulance with a baby, so I drove myself. She and her husband, Jim, met me here, and he went back to my house with Kai and their kids.

"Any more news?" she asks.

I shake my head. She hands me a coffee and sits down next to me.

They're prepping Peter for surgery. A coronary angioplasty, where they'll open his arteries and place stents in them to increase the blood flow. At first, they thought he might need bypass surgery because the blockage was extensive. But the cardiologist arrived and said this less risky procedure could work for him. There's always a chance it won't completely fix the problem, and then he'll have to have the bypass. But Peter decided it was worth a try, even if it might increase the risk of another heart attack. He'll need to go on statins right away.

"So. What happened?" Sophie asks.

In all the commotion, we haven't talked about how we ended up here. I'd like to tell her the truth, but I can't. Because Peter and I had a conversation that pushed him over the edge, and I need to keep most of it to myself.

For years, I've suspected that Peter was keeping something from me, and I was right. I've been dying to get my secrets off my chest, too. I thought coming clean with each other like we did tonight would fix us, but it appears to have nearly killed my husband, not to mention my marriage. Maybe truth is overrated. Maybe some things are better left unsaid.

"Nothing, really. It was an ordinary evening. We were just...talking."

"About?"

I don't want to outright lie to my best friend, but I can't tell her everything. I shoot for somewhere in the middle. "We were talking about Ella. And Jeanine. And everything that happened last year."

"I see. I thought you guys were past that."

"Working through it," I say.

Sophie nods. "And?"

"And then he got a weird look on his face. He said his chest hurt. He thought it was indigestion and tried to brush it off. But it got worse, quickly. When he said it felt like an elephant was sitting on his chest, I called 9-1-1, although he was still protesting, trying to say it was nothing."

"It's a good thing you did."

"He holds it all in, Sophie. Do you know he's had almost no reaction to what happened last year? Here I was feeling annoyed with his ability to move on and forget. But he hasn't forgotten. He stuffed it down and let it fester."

"Until it all exploded," she said.

"Yes. It all came out tonight. The guilt he felt about Ella's existence. Her attempts on my life. Her suicide. His first wife's death. The impact on his children."

"It's his nature, Laura. Don't blame yourself."

But I do blame myself.

"What if he doesn't make it?"

I suddenly feel very cold, and my body starts to shake. I wrap my arms around myself and rock in my seat.

"He'll make it, Laura. Don't go there."

"What if Kai has to grow up without a father?"

Deep, gut-wrenching waves of grief emanate from my core, and tears flood my vision. Sophie hugs me tightly against her and lets me cry it out. After a bit, she sits up and grabs me by the shoulders.

"That is not going to happen. You hear me? Peter's young and fit, aside from the blockage. This is a very common procedure. You're at one of the best hospitals in the world. He'll be fine."

I nod, and we both grow silent for a while. She grabs her phone and starts texting someone. In my logical mind,

I know she's right. But I can't help but run through the worst-case scenario.

Lydia's wedding with nobody to walk her down the aisle.

Kai's graduation, his father not even a distant memory.

My stepdaughter arrives, snapping me back into reality.

"What's she doing here?" Lydia glances over towards Sophie with daggers in her eyes.

I'm not surprised by her comment. She has a habit of reverting to her younger self when a crisis strikes, and they've never liked each other. Sophie tried numerous times to get me to leave when Lydia was at her worst, and I can't help but suspect that Lydia overheard one of our conversations. I don't see how that would have been possible. We never talked about it at the house or within earshot of her. But it certainly seems like she knows. Or maybe she's envious of our closeness. I hope Sophie keeps that snarky response she's formulating to herself. A war between the two of them is the last thing I need right now.

"Sorry," Lydia says, catching herself. "I didn't mean it that way. I was just...surprised to see you."

I breathe a sigh of relief.

"Jim and I met her here," Sophie explains. "He took Kai and our kids to your parents' house. I was waiting until you got here to leave. I'll be going now." Sophie stands.

"No," Lydia says. "You can stay."

Sophie shakes her head. "No. Jim needs to get our kids back home." Then she turns to me. "I'll stay at your place with Kai, all night if you need me."

"Thanks, Soph," I say.

We hug goodbye.

"Keep me posted," she says and heads out.

With that conflict averted, I turn my attention to Lydia and fill her in about where things are. About ten minutes later, the ER doctor comes out and reports that Peter is stable and doing fine. They'll start the procedure soon. Right now, there's nothing to do but sit and wait.

"You can go if you want," I offer.

"No way. I'm not leaving until I know Dad's okay."

I give her hand a squeeze and we quiet down for a bit.

"How's it working out with Allie?" I ask.

"Fine so far. It's kind of nice, having a friend I can talk to."

I'm surprised she's calling Allie a friend so soon after meeting her. Lydia's never had many close girlfriends, and I always figured that was by choice, but maybe not. She's got a bristly side that some women might find off-putting. She's as loyal and protective as a Doberman if she's on your side, but that's not always apparent until you get to know her. Perhaps Allie's mix of congeniality and deference is a good fit for her. And Allie could sure use someone like Lydia in her corner.

We settle into what's sure to be a long period of sitting and waiting. Lydia pulls out her phone and starts texting someone. I assume it's Christopher, although I have no idea what time it is in Europe or wherever he is. The family with the wailing mother has left, and it's eerily quiet. With nothing to distract me, the conversation replays in my head.

In hindsight, I suppose I didn't really need to tell Peter about Carson's visit with Jeanine at the care home. But I felt compelled to do it. To get it all out there. To clear the air. To share with my husband the fears that had been plaguing me, and my relief when my worst ones weren't realized. I thought it would help bridge the gap between us.

But it didn't.

At first, he was angry. His nostrils flared as he processed what I'd disclosed. "Why didn't you tell me this when you got the video? And why did you go to Shackler behind my back?"

He had a right to demand answers. Peter was the one who initially hired Shackler to find out who was after me. He was Shackler's client first. And the only explanation I could give him was that he had seemed blind to the idea that Jeanine could be dangerous.

Plus, the story never made sense to me. Why did she leave town, pregnant with his child, and not tell him about the baby? Why didn't she stay and fight for him if she was as lovestruck as he'd claimed? His explanation was that they'd worked together, and she'd left to avoid a scandal. But that didn't add up. I knew there was something he wasn't telling me.

Then his anger turned to guilt and shame. He stood up and started pacing around the room. "It's all my fault, Laura!" he confessed.

I thought he was referring to the affair. "Peter. Don't beat yourself up. Cynthia cheated first. She had problems. We've been over this."

"She wanted to work it out," he replied. There was a faraway look in his eyes like he was replaying it in his mind.

"I know. That's why you ended it with Jeanine," I reminded him.

But I wasn't sure he was hearing me. He seemed miles away. I felt perplexed. We'd been over this many times. I didn't understand why he was so upset. What was I missing? Was he more in love with Cynthia than he'd let on?

"No. You don't understand. It's my fault. All of it. I'm just like my father!" He paced around the room some more, running his hands through his hair.

That confused me even more. Peter's father was an abusive drunk. He'd helped his mother get away from him, in fact. But as far as I knew, his father wasn't a cheater.

So what the hell was he trying to tell me?

"What are you talking about?" I asked.

Then he sat on the sofa and rested his head in his hands. He wouldn't look at me when he spoke. And finally, he revealed the missing piece of the puzzle. That one bit of information my intuition kept telling me was out there, waiting for me to find it, so the story would add up.

I already knew that he'd confronted Jeanine after she'd accosted Cynthia at Windy Hill Preserve, but he hadn't shared the details of the altercation with me. Apparently, Jeanine admitted to him that she'd taunted his wife up on that ledge. Showed her their sexting streams. Told Cynthia that Peter was no longer in love with her. That she was a terrible mother and should let him go. Peter got angry, and they started to argue. Then she said something along the lines of *she got what she deserved.*

"I lost it," he confessed. "She was speaking about Cynthia in the past tense. I thought she'd done something to her. I grabbed Jeanine and started to shake her, but she wouldn't tell me what she meant. She just laughed in my face. And then I put my hands around her neck and demanded she tell me what she was talking about. I tightened my grip. And I squeezed..." He put his head in his hands.

My eyes nearly popped out of my head. "What the hell, Peter!" I exclaimed.

He shook his head. "I know. I lost it."

His revelation felt like a gut punch. I didn't have any words to express what I was feeling; it was a mixture of vindication and disgust. I knew all along there was something he wasn't telling me. But in my wildest dreams, I didn't think it would be something like this. Something physical.

He finally looked me in the eye. "I could have killed her, Laura."

"But you didn't, Peter." I tried my best to comfort him, but it took some effort because I was totally shocked. The fact that I'd been right all along suddenly seemed beside the point.

"No, I didn't. I stopped myself. But not before I saw the look in her eyes. She went from love to fear to pure hatred in a matter of seconds. And I don't blame her. I squeezed hard enough to leave some bruises."

"And that's why she left," I said.

It finally made sense, but that was of little comfort to me. I knew then and there that I'd never be able to look at him the same way. I never would have thought he could do something like that.

He let out a sigh. "Yeah. Well, she blackmailed me. She told me Cynthia jumped, and that if I didn't get her the money, she'd frame me for murder. I was hoping she was toying with me and that Cynthia was okay. But I called in a tip to the police from a pay phone anyway. We didn't hear anything for hours, so I hoped she was bluffing. But later that day, when we got the news..."

"*Peter!* Blackmail? Are you kidding me? You should have gone to the police." My voice went up a few decibels as I tried to process what he was saying. "Why didn't you go to them?"

"I don't know! It seemed too risky. They might have believed her. So I just paid her off. And she left town."

That was about as far as we got before he clutched his chest. So, now I have my explanation. It's all out in the open. And I wish I could go back in time and undo it all.

Peter has spent his whole life trying not to be like his father. I try to tell myself that this was a one-time thing. Extenuating circumstances. Jeanine provoked him. He's never been violent with me; never once so much as raised his voice to the kids. He's the father of my child, and we're bonded forever as Kai's parents.

It's not working.

A dark sadness washes over me as I prepare to face the strong possibility that my marriage is over. I know now that he's capable of putting his hands on a woman. And then paying someone off to save himself instead of doing the right thing. I don't know if it's something I can get past. More importantly, I'm not sure it's something I *want* to get past.

And I'm certain Peter knows that.

TWENTY-EIGHT

Allie

There's a chill in the air that's hard to describe. I'm from Wisconsin, so I know cold. It's in the fifties today in Half Moon Bay, and that's a heat wave for October by midwestern standards, but I'm shivering. Chilled to the bone. Perhaps it's the moisture in the air. Or maybe the mood.

Guests in drab colors.

The fog blocking the sun.

I feel like I'm drinking in the sea, with the mist rolling in from the ocean and settling over the high-top cocktail tables that dot the manicured lawn. We arrived a little early. Rows of white folding chairs look out to the ocean, awaiting the guests. Heat lamps sit near the tables, still unlit, promising a respite from the cold. There's an indoor area—a clubhouse—but they're still setting up. I'm assuming that's where we'll go later for refreshments, after the service.

It's not a typical setting for a celebration of life, but it works. There's something timeless about the sea, and

Charlie Yang loved to golf. We're on the grounds of the stately Ritz-Carlton, adjacent to one of the most scenic golf courses in the Bay Area. It sits on a bluff high above the Pacific, a dramatic and bold backdrop. It's a nice place to say goodbye, with the whitecaps rolling in and the endless sea stretching out as far as the eye can see. I wonder if they'll spread his ashes there.

A few other guests are milling around, but no one I recognize. I pull my ebony pashmina tightly around my body. It's covering my simple beige scoop neck dress. All black seemed like a cliché, and not quite right for a celebration of life. I think it works. Ricky's got on a dark gray suit, and he looks so handsome in it. I've never seen him in a suit and tie before.

He puts his arm around me and pulls me in. "You're getting soft, Allie. Midwestern girl like you? Doesn't it get like fifty below zero where you come from?"

"We have coats. And gloves. And indoor venues."

"Fair enough."

People in California seem to be in denial about the cold. They dress as if it's still summer. Nobody here is wearing a jacket, and there's nothing to shelter us from the cold winds. I think about taking a video to post of this beautiful venue, but that might seem insensitive. I'll get some footage later, away from the crowds.

"Want to get a coffee?" He points over to a station near the entrance to the clubhouse that they've just set up. It's midmorning, and the service should start in about twenty minutes.

"Sure," I say.

We make our way over. It's self-service. Coffee. Juice. Muffins.

Ricky pours me a cup. "How do you take it?" he asks.

"Milk. No sugar."

He hands me the cup, and I hold the steaming hot coffee in my hands. I take a cautious sip. Across the lawn, I see Mike and Susan coming our way. My stomach does a little flip-flop, but I try to stay calm.

I elbow Ricky and whisper to him. "That's them. My old landlords."

"I'll alert the FBI," he says.

"Stop! It's not funny."

"It kind of is," he replies.

I roll my eyes and give him a poke in the stomach. I notice he's got rock-hard abs. And it dawns on me that things have been progressing slowly on the physical level. I wonder if he's more hung up on his ex than he's saying or if he's simply trying to be a gentleman.

"Allie Dawson! Whatever are you doing here?" Mike says upon arrival. He's got a goofy grin on his face that's at odds with the occasion. Susan's her usual dour self; she fits right in at a function like this.

"I'm in town for some meetings, so I wanted to pay my respects," I reply.

"And you are?" Mike turns to Ricky.

"Ricky Rao." Ricky offers Mike his hand, and they shake. "Mike Tabernaky."

"I'm Susan," she says. "Mike's wife." She keeps her arms crossed tightly against her front. "Nice to see you again, Allie." Her tone is cordial, but her jaw is tight. I've noticed that her mouth doesn't move much when she talks, almost like a ventriloquist. It's hard for me to understand her sometimes.

"Likewise," I say.

"Rao," Mike says, biting his lower lip. "That sounds familiar. Did I perhaps meet your... sister? Her first name escapes me."

"I think you're talking about Mina Rao. She's my cousin. And she runs the foundation—"

"Right! She came with Allie to look at the apartment."

Mike's tapping his foot on the ground. He's a bundle of energy this morning, even for him. He pours himself a coffee, although it's probably the last thing he needs.

"So, Allie. Are you reconsidering your decision to leave Silicon Valley?" Mike asks.

I decide I may as well get this over with and set the stage for my return. "My mother's doing better. So, yes, I may reconsider."

"Your mother?" he asks.

Damn. I forgot that I used that excuse with Barnat, not Mike, so now I launch into an explanation of my mother's fake "condition." I'm vague and brief. Thankfully, Ricky comes to my rescue.

"I'm working on changing her mind," he says. He puts his arm around me and pulls me close, knocking me off-balance. I spill coffee on my pashmina. Grabbing some napkins, I try to soak up the liquid.

"Ah, young love. That'll do it. But I'm sorry to say Barnat took the guest house and I've got another renter in the suite, so I can't take you back," Mike says.

"I'm happy to take her off your hands." Ricky says this with a sly smile.

"Let's not get carried away," I say. "I haven't made up my mind yet."

Susan smiles at this, a real smile, and I don't get why she finds this amusing. She's so weird. Then Mike looks over towards the cocktail tables.

"That's an associate of mine over there. I need to…" He nods in that direction.

"Sure. No problem," I say, relieved to extract myself from this conversation.

The heat lamps, now ablaze, look warm and inviting. Guests are starting to gather around them, and I would like to join them.

"What's up with him?" Ricky asks. "Is he always that wigged out?"

"He seems especially wiggy today. Maybe it's the guilt. You know, from the cold-blooded murder he committed."

"Such a funny girl," he says.

We sneak a peck on the lips.

Willa Yang and the reverend are at the podium in front of the chairs. She's wearing a navy long-sleeved dress that flatters her small frame. It pairs well with her stunning silver hair. I suppose the service is going to start soon. I missed my chance with the heat lamps though. Too bad.

A few guests are taking their seats, but some are still hovering around the tables. My thoughts drift to Barnat, and I wonder if he'll show up today. He's living in the guest house, Mike said. If he took my apartment, then he probably wasn't the one who planted the device. That means he could be a target of whatever they're up to. I know it's not my problem anymore, but I feel bad not telling him about it.

"Want to go take a seat?" I say to Ricky.

He nods and we head over. I want to position myself where Willa can see me, but I don't want to make it obvious. We sit towards the back, over to the far side of one of the rows, a proper seat for an acquaintance. After a bit, she looks in my direction. She catches my eye and offers me a warm smile. I return it and give her a slight wave of my hand.

Mission accomplished.

———

The service was short but moving. Willa painted a picture of a kind and generous man, full of optimism and goodwill, a person who wanted to make a difference in the world. They have no children, which surprised me. She's dedicating their fortune to advancing the causes he believed in, and I can't help but hope that one of those is mine. Mike didn't speak, but a few other close friends did. I got the impression she doesn't have any family here. She must be very lonely. *I wonder what their story is.*

"I'm going to use the restroom and grab another coffee," I say. "Want one?"

Ricky shakes his head. "I'll grab us a cocktail table," he says.

I dash over to the restroom, trying to beat the rush. My heel sinks into a wet patch in the ground, and my shoe comes off. I glance around, hoping nobody saw me, and step back into my shoe. I'm such a klutz.

Speak of the devil. About fifty yards away, standing near the clubhouse, it's Barnat Kovaks, staring at me with a shit-eating grin. I shrug and smile back, then continue to the restroom. When I exit, he's waiting for me.

"Back in town so soon?" he asks. "Your mother must have made a fast recovery."

"I'm in town for some meetings next week."

"Your second date went better, I take it?"

"Um. Yes. Not that it's any of your business."

"Allie. If you wanted to call off our Dish walk because of him, you should have told me. You didn't need to move out of your apartment."

Is he jealous? Of Ricky?

"I didn't move out because of that. We're…friends. Just like you and me. I told you, my mother—"

"Right. Your mother. I'm messing with you, Allie. Don't worry. I got the guest house, so it all worked out for me."

"I heard."

"If you still want to take that Dish walk, let me know. If your friend doesn't mind, that is."

I should warn him. Tell him about the bugging device. But then Susan walks out of the bathroom and interrupts us.

Strange. I didn't see her in there.

"It's like old home week around here," she remarks, hovering around us.

"I was just leaving," I say. This isn't the time or place to tell him, I decide. Too many people around. She walks out with me and goes off in a different direction.

As I exit the clubhouse, I spot Mike Tabernaky at one of the cocktail tables. He's standing next to a guy in a black suit and bright red tie who's looking in the other direction. Mike's looking out at the crowd with a menacing glare on his face. I glance over to see where he's looking, and I'm even more perplexed. His death stare is directed at Willa and Susan, huddled together to the right of me.

Something is up with these people, and I wonder once again about Charlie. The dog. All of it. I'm not about to share these thoughts with Ricky though. He already thinks I'm nuts. But there is one person I might like to feel out. Someone who knows them better than I do. If Barnat's still up for it, I think I'll take him up on that Dish walk.

I feel a pang of guilt when I think about Ricky. But although we've kissed, we haven't slept together yet. We're not exclusive—we haven't even broached the subject. Plus, this wouldn't be a date. More like a fact-finding mission. I'll pump him for information about Willa and her fund and see how it goes from there. If I feel I can trust him, I'll tell him about the bugging device. Barnat's standing near the bluff, looking out towards the ocean. I send off a text.

> *Dish walk early tomorrow?*
> *Business to discuss.*

I drop my phone in my purse and head to our table. On the way over, I see that Willa and Susan have joined Mike and his friend at their cocktail table. They all look perfectly at ease, so now I start to reevaluate what I saw a few moments ago. Maybe Mike and Susan had a fight or something, and his expression was the result of something much less sensational than a murder plot, like a marital spat.

The banquet captain announces it's time to get seated for lunch, so Ricky and I head to the clubhouse. As we pass her table, Willa calls out to me and starts to walk over. We meet her halfway.

"It was so kind of you to come." She places her hand on my upper arm and then promptly removes it.

"I hope it's okay. I didn't know your husband very well."

"Of course it's okay. I hope you didn't travel all the way from Wisconsin just for this."

"No. I'm in town for some meetings. I go back and forth," I reply.

"Mike tells me you might be rethinking your decision to leave the valley," she says. "I think that's wise."

"Keep saying things like that to her," Ricky says, flashing her a cheeky smile.

Willa offers him a half smile in return and then excuses herself to go greet the guests. I'm sure he meant to lighten the mood, but he probably came off a bit insensitive with his attempt at humor and his informality, especially considering the occasion.

I see Barnat rush over to Willa as she's about to enter the clubhouse. They talk briefly, and then he heads towards the hotel and the parking garage. I suppose he's not staying for lunch.

We enter the clubhouse and take seats way in the back, away from her close friends, where I can observe the crowd but not engage with anyone. I notice that Mike and Susan aren't sitting with Willa, but the guy he was chatting with at the cocktail table is.

Willa turns to look at the Tabernakys. Her face is kind and cordial, the corners of her mouth slightly upturned—until she sees they're not looking at her. Then her face turns to stone. It wasn't my imagination. Something's up with these people, and I'd love to know what it is.

TWENTY-NINE

Allie

I read Barnat's text once more to make sure I didn't misinterpret it. *Nope.* He said to meet him at the Alpine entrance to the Dish walk at seven. It's fifteen minutes past the hour now, and I wonder if he changed his mind. I arrived a little early, strolled around a bit, and came back to the entrance to meet up with him. It's getting more crowded now, so he could be having a hard time finding parking. I'm about to call him when he comes rushing up to me, a little out of breath.

"Parking was tight. Sorry," he says. "I had to park far away."

"No problem," I reply.

He's wearing black running shorts and a long-sleeved bright blue nylon shirt. I don't think I've ever seen him wear such a vivid color. It changes his entire look. I thought his eyes were hazel, but today they look greenish-blue. He seems lighter. More playful. Not like his brusque, guarded self. Perhaps I'll get something out of him today. I'm wearing a pink tank top with white shorts, under my warm-up jacket. It's chilly still, but I expect we'll heat up soon.

"How long do you want to go for?" he asks.

"An hour?"

"So, about four miles?"

My eyes widen. That's like a fifteen-minute mile. With steep hills, no less.

"How fast do you walk?" I ask.

"Faster than you." He flashes me a smug smile.

I roll my eyes. "I'm not a fitness nut, Barnat. You know that about me. I thought this was supposed to be fun, not a training exercise."

"I thought this was supposed to be business," he replies.

"I, ah…"

"Let's go," he says, and he starts walking ahead of me.

He seems to know the trail well, so I follow his lead. The first part starts out flat but gets steep very quickly. I'm struggling to keep pace with him, while he's like a border collie on a leash, straining to contain himself. He's practically levitating with nowhere to put his energy. My heart is pumping already. I take off my jacket and tie it around my waist. After a few minutes, it's clear we're not a good match.

"Why don't you go on ahead and then circle back to me?"

"Are you sure? I could really use to run off some steam."

"Go ahead," I say.

And with that, he races ahead of me, giving me some time alone to come to my senses. I remind myself that I don't know him very well, and while this European-guy crush is fun to think about in a rom-com kind of way, it's truly ridiculous. I know nothing about his financial situation, but I can't imagine it's very promising.

Ricky has a great job and owns a condo in Menlo Park. It's a two bedroom in a desirable area and probably worth a small fortune. He's well-connected here in Silicon Valley. And he treats me like gold. So, what the hell am I doing here with Barnat Kovaks, who's just literally left me in the dust?

Making the most of my first time here, I take a quick video and post a reel.

Awesome Stanford Dish walk...finally!

After about twenty minutes or so, he comes barreling back down the hill, slows down, and starts walking back up the steep incline with me.

"Thanks," he says, catching his breath. "I hope that wasn't rude of me." He wipes the sweat from his brow with the back of his hand.

"It's fine," I say. As we're walking along, I notice that he's shorter than Ricky. Shorter than I remember. But then we've rarely stood shoulder to shoulder.

"So. What business did you want to discuss?"

I pause, thinking about how best to start. We walk for a while in silence, and that's fine with me. My heart rate's elevated, and it's harder to converse. I'm curious about the Yangs and their background. The fact that they had no family at the service. I'm pretty sure Willa has an accent, but it's hard for me to tell where she's from. With my cochlear implant, all accents sound alike to me, and I can only faintly detect them. Meanwhile, Charlie mentioned he was born in South Korea, but he sounded to me like an American.

"How well do you know Willa Yang?" I ask.

"Not very well."

"Where is Willa from?"

"Portola Valley," he says.

"No. Originally."

"How would I know?"

"Is she American? I think she has an accent, but I'm not sure."

"Allie. Why all the questions about Willa Yang?"

"Because she said that Charlie was interested in my project. And that I should get in touch with her when I had something to present."

"So that's why you went to the service. Smart move. I hate to tell you this, but they said the same thing to me. Before Charlie…passed. They were interested in my project. It will do good for the world."

"And?"

"And nothing happened. I wouldn't get your hopes up. They talk a good story, but I think they're…how do you say it? Full of shit? I'm not sure how much money they even have. He was having financial problems."

"Full of shit. Great."

"Mike too. He talks like he's a big man with a lot of connections, but he's given me nothing useful. Many meetings, but none of his leads went anywhere. My advice is, move on. Forget about them. You moved out of the guest house for a reason. Don't look back."

Barnat tried to get funding from the Yangs too. Interesting. And now he's advising me to move on and not pursue it. He obviously views me as a competitor. Now I'm back to being skeptical about his interest in me. The mild flirtation. The feigned jealousy. I see his game now. He got my apartment, and now he's after my funding. He was at the service too, after all. Sucking up to Willa, just like me.

I decide to play along. "So, you think they're all full of it?"

He nods. "Totally."

Then he steps up his pace. This time, I keep up with him. After about ten minutes, I tell him I need to turn around and head back; I have somewhere I need to be. We continue down the hill for twenty minutes or so, most of it in comfortable silence. With my hearing loss, his language issue, and the wind, it's difficult to talk, and we both know it.

I want to ask him more questions, but I don't know how to start. We walk out to the street together. He sees me to my car and closes the door for me.

I put down the window.

"Thanks for making good on your offer to show me the Dish," I say.

"My pleasure," he says. "Thanks for joining me. I'll see you around, Allie." He turns to leave.

"Hey, Barnat?" I call out the window after him. It's my last chance to get information out of him, and I still haven't told him about the bugging device.

"Yes?" He turns around.

"This might sound like a weird question, but did you see a stray dog in the neighborhood the day I moved out?"

He starts towards me with a stern look on his face, and I instantly regret asking him. He crouches down to my car window. "What kind of stray dog?"

"A big tan one."

Then he leans in closer to me and brushes the stray hairs back from my face. To my total shock, he pulls me in and kisses me softly on the lips. I'm too flabbergasted to protest, so I sink into it. It's steamy, delicate, and re-strained, the kind of kiss that feels more like an end than a beginning.

"Forget the guest house. *Move on*." He accentuates his warning with a firm nod of his head and straightens up. Then he turns from me and walks away.

I recover from the shock and call out to him. "You didn't answer my question."

"Oh, I think I did," he shoots back.

My lips are still tingling as I watch him retreat in my rearview mirror.

THIRTY

Laura

It's been a week since Peter's heart attack, and he's home now. The doctors expect he'll make a full recovery, but he'll need to be on statins and change his diet. Less red meat, more fish and vegetables. I've hounded him about that for years, but there's nothing to be gained by harping on that now.

He's sleeping in the spare room for now. We agreed it would be better that way so I won't bother him if I toss and turn in my sleep while he's recovering. Well, that's the excuse we landed on for the sleeping arrangement. Neither of us is ready to talk about the elephant in the room and the real reason I want separate rooms. At some point, we will need to broach the subject of our marriage. Where we go from here. But I don't want to cause him any more stress right now, so it can wait.

I need to talk to someone about it though, so I'm headed out to meet Sophie for lunch. Peter's mostly self-sufficient. He can drive, he's taking longer walks, and he's going back to work on Monday. Lydia's here, helping him with Kai this weekend so he can rest when he needs to. She's been very helpful. She knows Peter's staying in the guest room, and I hope she doesn't suspect that we're having problems. I don't think she'd take it well if she thought we were splitting up.

I went for a long run, and I'm headed out now. "I'll be back in an hour or so," I tell her. I didn't mention I was meeting Sophie, just that I had to run errands at the mall.

"No rush," she says. "Christopher will be over soon. It's good practice for us." She flashes me a girly grin.

"Lydia? Are you guys already thinking about..."

"Oh, no. Not right now. But maybe after the wedding. I don't want to wait until I'm your age to have a baby. No offense," she adds.

"Right," I say.

No offense.

Sure.

Perhaps she does suspect we're having problems. Or else the thought of having a sibling close in age to the child you're thinking about conceiving is disturbing. I can't say I blame her if she feels that way. I had a storybook childhood, and she didn't. So, as always, I let her little dig go.

—

We're meeting at Stanford Mall, at a sandwich shop Sophie claims she likes. I'm not crazy about it, and I'm not sure she is either. I think it's just an excuse to meet at the mall. She's a power shopper, and I'm certain she's going to try to drag me around to look at clothes and shoes and purses until my feet give out. I don't enjoy shopping much. I love Sophie though, so if she insists, I'll oblige.

She's already grabbed a table, and I join her.

"How's Peter?" she asks.

I fill her in on his recovery and then go order our food. It's the kind of place where you need to go up to the counter and order, and then they bring you the food. I hate that. If I'm going to eat out, I want to be waited on. What's the point if I need to stand in line? It hardly feels like a treat. I order a grilled caprese sandwich and realize I'm quite hungry. I can almost taste the melted cheese and warm tomato as the aroma wafts out from the panini press.

As soon as I sit down, Sophie launches into a story about a client of hers, but I'm not really listening. I'm trying, but my mind is wandering. I can't keep track of all the people she knows. And since I'm in the middle of my own drama, I'm not at all interested in hearing about other people and their messy lives.

She stops midstory. "Laura. What's wrong? You said Peter was doing okay."

I sigh and rest my head in my hands.

"What is it?" She narrows her eyes at me. "Don't tell me. Someone's trying to kill you again!" She flashes me a wry smile, and I can't help but laugh. Only she could get away with saying something like that to me.

I roll my eyes. "You're terrible."

"You love it. So, what is it?"

"It's Peter and me."

"I had a feeling. Let me guess. It has something to do with the talk you had? The one that gave him a heart attack?"

"Yes." I look off to the side, stalling, not really knowing how to start.

She throws up her hands. "And? Are you going to make me guess?"

"You'll never guess."

"Game on. Okay, it's an affair. You're having an affair."

"What? No. Are you crazy? I just had a baby."

"Well, that would give him a heart attack, for sure."

"It's worse than an affair."

"What's worse than an affair? Wait. Did he murder someone? Did you? Don't worry, your secret's safe with me."

I sigh. "Let's stop the twenty questions. I don't like this game anymore."

"Sure. Sorry. I'll stop. I promise." She zips her lips shut as the waiter arrives with our sandwiches.

"Give me a minute," I say. "I want to get something in my stomach."

"Whenever you're ready."

I'm very hungry, so I start on my sandwich, and Sophie follows my lead. I'm afraid this conversation might ruin my appetite, so I want to get some food in me before we begin. We're quiet for a bit as we fill our stomachs.

After a few minutes, I feel ready. I disclose to her most of what Peter told me. How he argued with Jeanine on the side of the road. How she taunted him. And how he ended up with his hands around her neck. I tell her all of it except the part about the blackmail and the payoff. I know Peter's assets were frozen while they investigated Cynthia's death, so I have no idea how he obtained the funds to pay her off. It was probably something illegal. If so, I don't want anyone to know about it. Hell, *I* don't even want to know about it.

"Holy shit, Laura. So that's why she left and never told him about the pregnancy."

"Yes. It finally adds up."

"You must be totally freaked out."

I rest my head in my hands. "I don't know what to do. If Kai wasn't in the picture..."

"Laura, that shouldn't make any difference. You're a wealthy woman now. Do whatever you would do if Kai wasn't in the picture."

I pause for a bit. "What would you do? If you were me?"

"I don't know. I can't even imagine it. Jim isn't like that."

"Peter isn't like that either, Sophie."

"He's got a ton more baggage, Laura. I told you that from the beginning. He's always been a bit cagey about his past. Sure, he blames the failed marriage on Cynthia, but you're only getting one side of the story. And he lied to you. About so many things. And he got physically aggressive with a woman he was romantically involved with. You know the stats on that."

"She provoked him."

"With words, Laura. *Words.* It's not like she pulled a knife on him or hit him in the head with a baseball bat. And he put his hands around her neck. That's... messed up."

"You're right. It is. I know that. But I'm so sad. For Kai. And for Lydia and Carson. For the death of my marriage.

And for Peter too. He loves me, and he's going to be devastated."

"If he'd been honest with you from the beginning, he wouldn't be in this situation."

"But I might not have stayed."

"That was your choice to make, and he robbed you of it. He's not going to get any sympathy from me. I feel for the kids though. Especially his. They've been through so much. Kai has you. Your parents. Me. He'll be fine."

I mull it over as we take a break and make more progress on our sandwiches. I thought that talking about this would ruin my appetite, but it hasn't. It feels healthy to process what happened and to finally get my problems out in the open.

"Sophie?" I hesitate because I'm not sure I want to know the answer to my question. "Do you think Peter's...dangerous? For me? Or for Kai?"

"No. I really don't. I think it was a one-time thing. But I couldn't get past it if I were you. Especially all the deceit. I'd never trust him again. It's up to you though. I mean, how do you feel about him? Take away your history. The fact that he's Kai's father. The inconvenience of blowing it all up. When you look at him, as a man, how do you feel? Not in your heart. In your loins."

I sigh. "I feel...disgusted."

"Well, you have your answer then. Let's concentrate on moving you forward. In my experience, 'disgusted' is not something a woman gets past."

"It's scary, Soph. Starting all over at my age. It's been so long."

"You're a foxy forty, Laura. Not a ninety-year-old woman. You're in the prime of your life. You'll be fighting them off in no time."

Just the thought of being with someone else sends me into a near panic attack. I've been with Peter since I was in my twenties. My lip begins to quiver, and soon tears are rolling down my cheeks.

"Oh no. Too soon for that kind of talk. I'm so sorry."

"I'm just not ready." I cover my face with my hands and try to disappear. I hate falling apart in general, not to mention in public. "What if I'm never ready?"

Sophie's hand rests on mine. "You will be, I promise. Baby steps, okay?"

I look up at her and nod as I choke back the tears.

"I am ready to lay my cards on the table with Peter though. As soon as he's well enough. But I want to keep it under wraps until after Lydia's wedding."

"That sounds reasonable. In the meantime, focus on the foundation. You're doing important work."

"I want to focus on something else too. Something just for me."

"What?"

"I want to race in Kona next October. That's something I can put my energy into. I've put it on the back burner for him. For all of them, for decades. This is something I need to do for me. And I think I can pull it off. I've got a plan to increase my chances of qualifying for it."

"That's an excellent goal." Sophie smiles and puts her hand on mine.

We finish our meals. And as I consider the possibility of a new start, I'm thinking it might not be that bad.

Her eyes light up. "Hey! You know what you need?"

"What?"

"Some new exercise clothes." She smirks. "Good thing we're at the mall."

"Well played, Soph."

"It'll be fine. I promise. I've got you."

"I don't know what I'd do without you," I say.

"You'll never have to find out."

I think about the long road ahead, and it seems insurmountable—until I count my blessings. Sophie. My parents. My brother. Money. She's right. Kai will be fine. I'll be fine. I'm not so sure about Carson and Lydia though. My heart aches for them. How will they handle a divorce? They've been through so much.

Although they're not my biological children, I've grown quite close to them, and with their grandmother gone, I'm the only mother figure they've got. We'll need to keep the split quiet until after the wedding, for Lydia's sake. And I'll do what I can to stay in their lives, If they'll have me, that is. Plus, Lydia and Carson are Kai's half-siblings, and I want him to have a relationship with them.

I pause for a moment to reconsider. Maybe I'm being too hasty, giving up on us too fast. Don't I owe it to my family to try? But then an image flashes in my mind. I visualize the angry look on Peter's face, his hands planted firmly around Jeanine's neck. I think about his illicit scheme to pay her off and cover it all up.

And I know in my heart that it's over.

THIRTY-ONE
Allie

I can't stop thinking about that kiss, not to mention Barnat's cryptic warning to forget about the guest house and move on. I feel so guilty. Not to mention confused. Maybe Barnat's part of whatever Mike's up to, and for some reason, he's trying to protect me. Perhaps he's developed feelings for me, or he's having second thoughts and trying to get out of it. He obviously knows something, and whatever it is, it's not good.

There's nothing to gain from any further involvement with him, and I'm upset with myself for even letting him plant a kiss on me. I'm dating a great guy, and while we haven't talked about exclusivity, at some point it's sort of implied. I don't want to ruin things with Ricky, and I regret going on that walk with Barnat.

As for Willa and her funding, though, I'm not ready to let it go. It's possible that Barnat's trying to deter me so he can have it for himself. I'd like to get something out of my time in the guest house, so I pull out her card, draft an email asking her if she'd like to meet for an update on my progress, and send it off.

Speaking of which, we have our retreat today, and a lot is riding on it. In the morning we're supposed to update Laura and Mina on our progress. In the afternoon we're presenting what we have to the group. Then Laura and Mina will help us form a plan to move forward.

In preparation for my meeting, we've produced three prototypes of the clip-on screen, and while my solution isn't perfect, it's a marketable alternative to the VR options. I've ordered cords in a variety of colors so they can be paired with different outfits, either to blend in or to accent the look.

The prototype looks fine, but I'm freaking out because there's a delay—a long and unacceptable delay—on the captions that appear on the screen. It's taking too long for them to appear. Kevin assures me they can fix it by making the processor a little more robust. That will make the processor slightly heavier and add some expense, but not much. I remind myself that I don't have to solve all my problems right now. I only need to take things to the next stage. Small steps forward. A few steps back. It's never a straight line to success.

———

"I've got some good news and some bad news," I say. "First, the good news." I hold up the prototype and offer Laura a hesitant smile.

Her brow furrows as she holds out her hand. "May I?"

She doesn't wait for my response before plucking it from my fingers. She examines the clip-on screen like a forensic scientist processing a crime scene, gently turning it from side to side for what feels like an eternity.

"Hmm," she says finally.

Hmm?

My stomach sinks. "Ah, do you—"

"Let me see your glasses," she snaps.

I hand my demo glasses to Laura. She clicks the screen into place on the frame and puts the glasses on, turning her head from side to side.

"Not bad." She nods. "A little thicker than I'd expected, but better than what's out there now."

I let out a breath. "It's the best we can do right now."

"So, what's the bad news?" she asks.

"There's a bit of a delay on the captions. But we're working on it."

"How much of a delay?"

"I'll show you."

I pull up the app, connect the caption screen to my cell phone, and start talking.

"It should be working now. Can you see the captions?" I ask.

She nods—a few seconds later. But those few seconds are an eternity in the world of smart glasses. The whole point of the captioning is to make verbal conversations effortless across multiple languages. And this isn't effortless.

"A bit of a lag, but they're crystal clear. Perfect, really."

"You see what I mean though. It's not quite there yet."

She takes off the glasses. "Allie, this is wonderful progress. I'm very impressed. Don't lose heart. You'll get there. And with your social media following, I expect it'll take off quickly once we launch."

"Do you like the cords?" I show her the assortment I've sourced.

"For now," she replies.

And that reminds me not to rest on my laurels. The competition is closing in on me, and a fully wireless all-in-one, the holy grail of smart glasses technology, is on the horizon. I know they'll cost a fortune though, so that's my ace in the hole. I can only hope it's enough to sustain me and get me to the next level of funding.

———

Ricky and I have just finished dinner at a cozy Italian restaurant in Menlo Park, walking distance from his place. Carpaccio, it's called. Our dinner was romantic and comfortable. We sat in the back, in a corner tucked away from the ruckus. He made sure of that so the background noise wouldn't interfere with my hearing.

In subtle ways, he lets me know that he cares about me. I appreciate that he's so tuned into me and my challenges. He's paying attention, making the necessary adjustments to make it easier to communicate with me. I know he's into me. So why hasn't he made a move? Is he waiting for some kind of sign from me? Or is he not ready yet?

We shared a bottle of pinot noir and almost finished it, so I'm a little tipsy. Now we're walking back to his apartment, where my car is. I met him here after the retreat. It's a little chilly, and I'm not wearing a jacket. I wrap my arms around myself as the wind picks up a bit. He takes off his sweater and drapes it around my shoulders. He puts his arm around me and kisses me softly on the top of my head. At six two, he's the perfect height for a taller woman like me, even in heels. I feel safe. Protected. Happy. And I remind myself that Barnat is well under six feet.

Another reason to wipe that kiss from my mind.

When we reach his building, Ricky turns to me and brushes the hair back from my face. "Want to come up?" he says.

Rather than reply, I lean in. Our lips meet. His hands caress my back, then move firmly down my sides. He explores me, gently at first, and then with more intensity. His aftershave is spicy and arousing, even more so up close. All my nerve endings are tingling. Soon we're full-on making out, right there on the street, with an intensity that catches me by surprise. His kisses so far have been tame. Respectful. Timid. *But not this one.*

Maybe this was his plan all along. To throw me off-balance. Keep things PG-13 for the first few dates, and then go in with a full-on triple-X play.

It's working.

I come up for air, nearly breathless. "Let's go," I say.

He takes me by the hand as he buzzes us in the door. We head up the stairs rather than wait for the elevator. When we get to his apartment, he keeps his deep brown eyes glued to mine as he unbuttons my blouse and tosses it aside, and I can see the hunger in them. He runs his hand up my skirt, tickling the inside of my thigh. I'm on pins and needles, and I let out a low moan.

He leads me into the bedroom and whips off his shirt, exposing a sleek and muscular torso with just the right amount of chest hair. Soon, we're in bed, skin to skin, exploring each other. He takes it slow, and by the time we consummate our mutual lust, I'm lost in the powerful release. We settle into each other's arms and drift off, and I feel safer than I have in a long time.

"Good morning, sleepyhead. Hungry?" Ricky's up, wearing boxers and a t-shirt, making breakfast. I threw on his button-down shirt from last night. It's past eight already. I can't believe how long I slept.

"I could eat," I respond.

"Scrambled eggs?"

"Sure. How long have you been up?" I ask as I join him in the kitchen.

"About an hour." We share an intimate kiss, and then he turns from me. I can see his jaw moving, so I know he's still talking. He doesn't know I can't hear him. I tap him on the shoulder and point to my ear.

"My battery is dead, and I don't have a spare with me. I can't hear you."

"Sor-ry," he says, as his mouth exaggerates every syllable. "I was say-ing—"

I shake my head. "No, just talk normally, but look at me." I smile. "You'll get the hang of it."

Most people do that. Distort their mouths and make it impossible for me to lip-read what they're saying in a misguided effort to make it easier for me to understand them. He hands me a coffee with milk and starts on my scrambled eggs and toast.

I head into the living room to chill. He's got a very nice place. I hardly got a glance at it last night. It's a little sparse in terms of personal effects, but his furnishings are stylish and high-end. A midcentury tan leather sofa sits on a dark hardwood floor along with a modern armchair, white with dark wood legs. A marble slab coffee table rests on a white textured area rug. Some well-placed lamps add just the right amount of light. But it lacks character, and I wouldn't be surprised if he'd outsourced it to an interior decorator.

After a bit, he places my breakfast on the table and we eat in comfortable silence. I don't want to eat and run, but I have a meeting. So does he, he says. And he mentions that he's going out of town for a few days, later in the week. I head into the bedroom to get dressed. I feel a bit self-conscious as I don yesterday's outfit.

"Do you want a change of clothes?" he asks, joining me in the bedroom.

"You have women's clothes here?"

"Um, well, they're sort of left over."

"Don't tell me they're from your ex."

He shrugs. "What was I supposed to do with them? Throw them out?"

"Yes!" I bark at him, a little louder than I'd intended, from the look on his face. I can't hear myself.

His eyes widen. "Allie, don't be mad. It doesn't mean anything. You want me to throw them out right now? I'll throw them out right now."

I hesitate for a minute because I know what this means. And I decide I'm ready to commit to him.

"Yes. Throw them out. *Right now.*" I give him a firm nod of my head.

He leaves and returns a few moments later with a garbage bag, opens a dresser drawer, and gets started. "You sure you don't want to…" He's holding a blouse over the bag.

"Yes, I'm sure I don't want to wear your ex-girlfriend's clothes. And don't forget to dump any toiletries too," I command.

He closes the gap between us, caresses my cheek, and smiles. "I think it's cute you're jealous."

"I'm not jealous. It's just…weird."

He tilts his head to the side and looks me up and down. "You can replace them if you want. You look a little conspicuous." He smiles.

I smack him on the butt. "Very funny, you. I need to get going. I'll mark my turf soon. Don't worry."

And with the status of our relationship crystal clear, I tug on my blouse, smooth my skirt a bit, and head out the door.

THIRTY-TWO

Laura

I'm in Kona, putting my plan into action. I'm determined to race in the next Kona Ironman World Championship, which will happen less than a year from now. I'll need to qualify for it, so I'm buying a home here, which will give me an edge. There are slots reserved for in-state residents who do well in the Honu Half Ironman, which happens here in June.

I'll still have to finish with a qualifying time, but only compared to other in-state residents, not the entire racing field. It's a bold move, buying a place, and probably a bit selfish. But conforming to other people's expectations hasn't worked out so well for me in the past. Perhaps it's time for a change.

Peter and I have come to a mutual understanding about our future. He took it better than I anticipated. I think he's even a little relieved, not having to pretend anymore. I was right about the payoff too. He did something illicit to get the money, but he assured me he wasn't in any danger of getting arrested because the statute of limitations has run out. *It's been too long,* he said, *so don't worry about that.*

If that was supposed to make me feel better, it didn't. It made me question our entire relationship and all the time and effort I've put into it. But dwelling on the past won't do me any good, so I choose to move forward.

Sophie's here with me, helping me out with Kai so I can tour properties with a real estate agent. We're staying at the Fairmont Orchid Hotel, the center of the action for the Honu Half Ironman in early June. I've already entered the race. We'll have the wedding somewhere near here, two weeks later.

I found a property that's perfect for me. It's a two-story townhome in a resort community, walking distance to the Fairmont. There's a lovely view of the foothills that sit in front of the massive, brown shield volcano Mauna Kea, and a peekaboo wedge of blue ocean off in the distance. It's fully furnished, and I can rent it out when I'm not here, which makes it a solid investment. With the market stalling a bit, I'm going in with a lowball offer. Hopefully, the sellers will take it.

I don't think Lydia suspects anything's amiss between Peter and me. She's thrilled that we'll have a home base for her wedding and for the future. I'm sure she'll blow a gasket when we divorce and she finds out it's in my name only.

Neither of us wants to keep the Los Altos home with all the trauma we experienced there. Peter will move into the guest room for now, and once Lydia's wedding is behind us, we'll come clean with everyone and sell it. I'll find another place in Silicon Valley, hopefully in Los Altos, and go back and forth. I'm not sure where Peter will live, but we'll stay close for Kai's sake. We're working on finding our way as coparents and friends, and although we're not quite there yet, I'm confident we will be soon.

———

A buzzing sound in my purse alerts me to a voicemail. I feel a little flutter in my stomach. Maybe it's the real estate agent, letting me know they've accepted my offer. It's a little soon to hear back though; I gave them twenty-four hours, and most sellers wouldn't want to seem too eager. Perhaps they accepted another offer, and my agent is calling to tell me it's gone. My stomach sinks at the thought that I may have lost it to someone else.

I fish out my phone to see who called. It wasn't the agent. It was Shep Shackler—and that can't be good. What could he possibly want? I think about ignoring the message. I'm feeling so positive right now, and I don't want to spoil it. I'm due to meet Sophie and Kai for lunch, so it can probably wait. I grab my sunglasses and beach bag then head out of my hotel room and down to the pool area. A host of scenarios flood my mind, all of them terrifying.

Carson in handcuffs.

Peter being hauled away by the Feds.

Chances are it's probably not as bad as what I'm imagining, so I stop at the top of the stairs, step to the side, and listen to the message. Shackler informs me that Mike and Susan Tabernaky have put their home up for sale and that they seemed to have vanished into thin air. Then he asks me to call him back.

What does this have to do with me?

I sigh. Truthfully, I think the guy's a little bored. This isn't the first time he's stuck his nose in where it wasn't wanted. And it seems to me that this is good news. They've left town, and I'm not sure why he would want me to call him back. But even good news from Shackler brings up terrible memories for me. I'm not letting this ruin my day. I'll call him another time. I drop my phone back in my bag and make my way down the stairs to meet Kai and Sophie.

"Hey," Sophie shouts, waving me over to the restaurant near the pool. She's seated at a table with a partial view of the ocean. An oversized white sun hat with a massive ruffly rim dips down and covers half her face. A ginormous, rectangular pair of sunglasses covers what's left of it. So dramatic, just like Sophie.

I'm in a t-shirt, shorts, a baseball cap, and rubber slippers—what those on the continent call flip-flops. I still don't consider myself a tourist. Growing up here as I did, I feel self-conscious about dressing like one at the beach.

Kai squeals and reaches for me as I arrive.

"Hello, my handsome young man." I scoop him into my arms and hold him close. "You smell so fresh and clean. Your godmother's been doing an excellent job."

"Let's not talk about all the diapers I've changed today, okay? I'm starved," she says, "and I don't want to spoil my appetite."

"Me too."

"Here." She hands me a menu. "Take a look. And make it quick. The waiter's a hottie, but he doesn't come by that often."

"What're you having?"

"The grilled mahi-mahi sandwich."

"That sounds perfect."

I place Kai in his holder. The hot waiter finally arrives, and we put in our orders. With that taken care of, I start to tell Sophie my news.

"Wait," Sophie calls out and the waiter comes back. She tap-tap-taps a long fingernail on the rim of her glass. "Can I get a refill? If it's not too much trouble?"

"Sure. Would you like something, ma'am?" he asks me.

"What are you having?" I ask Sophie.

"Iced tea."

"Not a Long Island one, I hope."

"Of course not! What kind of godmother do you think I am?"

"I'll have one too," I say.

"You got it, ladies." He flashes us a movie star smile and goes on his way.

"So, I found a place," I inform her.

"Already?"

"Love at first sight. What can I say?"

"That's what you said about Peter."

"Shh!" My eyes glance down to my son.

"He can't understand me," Sophie says.

"People say they comprehend a lot more than we think."

"Not *that* much more, you loon." She rolls her eyes.

Kai's eyes are fighting to stay open. I brush some hair back from his precious little face, and he smiles at me. His lids flutter a few more times and then gently float down to a close. I wonder if he was waiting until I got back, to feel safe enough to drift off.

I give Sophie the rundown on the townhome. When I disclose that I've already put in an offer, she gets that look on her face. The same expression she had when I got involved with Peter so quickly. But I assure her I know what I'm doing, and then I change the subject. She means well, but she can be a bit of a know-it-all, and that's not what I need right now.

"Guess who left me a message?" I say, changing the subject.

"Scott Carter," she says.

"Who the hell is Scott Carter?" I ask.

"He's the guy you were dating when you met Peter."

"How do you remember things like that?"

She sighs. "That's what I do, Laura. That's why I'm in PR—"

"And I'm not." We smile at the way we can finish each other's sentences.

"So?" she says. "Who called?"

"Shep Shackler."

"The PI?"

"Do you know any other Shep Shackler?" I roll my eyes. "Here. Listen."

I play the message for her, and then our meals arrive. We take a break to doctor up our sandwiches and start on them. She finishes a few mouthfuls, washes them down with a sip of her iced tea, and circles back to the voicemail.

"Why is he even telling you about this?"

"Beats me."

"And why are you still in touch with him?"

I purse my lips, stalling a bit.

She puts down her sandwich and narrows her eyes at me. "Laura? What aren't you telling me?"

And then it all comes tumbling out of me. The entire story. How I hired him to keep tabs on Jeanine Randall. Shackler sending me the video of Carson. The fact that I asked him to do some background research on Allie's bizarre landlord. And that it was a pretense for meeting with him again. I tell her that he looked some more into Jeanine's death.

"And what did he find out?"

"Jeanine died of natural causes." But I also disclose that Carson went to see her that day, to get closure, so that's why he was on the video.

"Holy shit. Well, I can see why you never told me. Anything else you're holding back?"

My body tenses as I think about Peter and his payoff to Jeanine.

"Never mind," she says. From the look on your face, I'm better off not knowing. Anyway, I could have told you it wasn't Carson. He doesn't have it in him. Now, that Lydia, she's another story."

"Stop!" My eyes widen.

She smirks. "Anyway, are you going to call him back?"

"I don't know."

"What does he look like?"

"Mid-fifties. Husky. Virile. A little rumpled, but it works for him. Why?"

"Virile, eh? Maybe he's hitting on you."

"What? No. He knows I'm married."

"Like that would stop a guy. I think you should call him."

"Why? Give me one good reason."

She taps her fingernails on the table and gazes out towards the ocean. Then she turns to me. "Because I'm bored," she says. "Very bored."

I shoot her a sideways glance. She's exasperating sometimes. "You want to live vicariously through my misadventures?"

"Yes."

I roll my eyes.

Sophie puckers her ruby-red lips, closes them around her straw, and takes a long sip of her iced tea. "Now call him. This could be fun."

THIRTY-THREE
Allie

According to Laura Foster's voicemail, the Tabernakys have left town. I have no idea how to interpret this information. She asked me to go over to some private investigator's office and meet with him. She's still out of town. I tried to reach Barnat on his cell, but the number I have for him is no longer working. Willa Yang never answered my email, and I wonder if she knows anything about where they went, or if she's okay. If they did something to her husband, maybe they did something to her, too.

Ricky's on his way to Denver for a tech conference. Lydia's gone to Europe to join her fiancé. Mina and I haven't socialized at all after that dinner when she introduced me to Ricky. I have nobody I can talk to about this.

I think about calling my brother, but I haven't mentioned any of this to him, and bringing him up to speed seems like too much trouble. Plus, he'll probably be upset with me that I've kept it from him for so long. So I text Shep Shackler, and he agrees to meet me later in the afternoon.

The house is dead still without Lydia's footsteps upstairs. Even with my speech processor off, I can feel the vibrations when she's padding around up there. I feel vulnerable now, and I think about asking Ricky if I can stay at his place. But I don't have a key, and I'm not sure how I'd get one since he's traveling. Plus, that might send the wrong message. I moved some of my B-list attire over there and a set of basic toiletries, but I don't want to appear overeager. Things are fine the way they are.

Grabbing my gym bag, I head out the door. I'll get in a workout and then go meet with this PI guy. *Shep Shackler. What kind of name is that?*

———

His waiting area is compact but adequate with sleek modern tables and a pair of comfortable black leather chairs. As I look around, I'm curious as to why the Fosters chose this PI. He seems a bit low budget to me, but then I don't have much experience in this area. Perhaps they're the best kind.

After a few minutes, a tall man with a larger build comes over to greet me, and I stand up to meet him. He's mid-fifties, wearing a navy polo shirt over tan slacks. He's sporting some stubble, but it doesn't seem contrived or manicured. More like he just couldn't be bothered shaving this morning.

"Allie," he says, holding out his hand. "Nice to meet you, finally." His grip is firm and dry.

He's acting as if he's heard a lot about me, which I find strange. "You too," I reply.

He leads me into his office, which is cramped but functional. He gets right to it.

"Laura was concerned about that living arrangement of yours from the beginning. She asked me to keep tabs on your landlords."

"I, um…that was nice of her."

"She's a nice lady," he says flatly. His lack of expression is unnerving.

I nod. "Yes, she is. And what did you want to tell me?"

"As far as I can tell, they've been renting out their guest house to aspiring entrepreneurs for the past ten years or so. I haven't been able to track down most of the tenants because they often ran their rental operation on a cash basis, which is odd for someone with a broker's license.

"I was able to track down one of them though. A young man from Denver who rented from them about four years ago. He was working on some kind of proprietary software for data storage. But a few months into his stay, a competitor launched a similar product ahead of him."

"So you think they've been running this scam for a while now?"

"Looks like it. It may not have been a coincidence that he met you at Starbucks. He could have seen your name in the press. Laura's foundation received a great deal of it with her focus on women entrepreneurs."

"What do you know about the Yangs?" I ask.

"Only what everyone knows. They're a well-respected couple. Or they were, I should say. They funded several successful start-ups. I do know they ran into some financial trouble. Made some bad investments. I heard his widow got a substantial payout from the life insurance though. The fund might be doing better now."

"If he was trying to steal my idea, why would Mike introduce me to Charlie?"

"Maybe that wasn't his only angle. Perhaps he had some kind of arrangement with Charlie Yang to get some kind of finder's fee or a percentage of his share of the venture."

I'm still not sure where this is going or what it has to do with me. "So why did Laura want me to meet with you? I'm afraid I don't understand."

"Laura's had a rough time over the last year or so. Her life was threatened. Now she's concerned about her husband. I'm sure you've heard about his health scare."

"Yes. I drove Lydia to the hospital that night."

"She doesn't want any more surprises. Or any more stress. She wants you to tell me everything you know about the Tabernakys. And she wants to make sure you have no further contact with these people. Even Willa Yang. Laura will help find you some new funding."

I look past Shackler, out the window to the tree-lined street. I don't really want to get any more involved in this than I already am, which may happen if I tell him about Mike dragging the duffel bag and the dog I saw. If only I hadn't told Ricky.

But I did tell Ricky. And if he happens to tell Mina and she tells Laura and they find out I didn't disclose this, it could ruin everything for me.

"There's one thing I haven't told Laura that might be important," I say.

And I go on to tell him about that night, and my assumption that Mike was dragging the dead dog. Then I tell him about the dog I saw, trotting towards the house when I was moving out.

Shackler's eyes widen, a stark contrast to his previous poker face. "You never told Laura about this?"

My stomach sinks. "I, um, no. I told Ricky. My boyfriend. He assured me that Charlie died in a hotel room, days later. And he pointed out that I didn't get a good look at the dog."

"Well, thanks for sharing it with me now." He stands up, indicating our time is up. "I'll see you out. In the meantime, cut all ties with them and their associates. Let me know if one of them contacts you. I'll keep a lookout on my end. And hopefully, this all blows over."

Keep a lookout. *I wonder what he means by that.*

"Will do," I say, and I start to leave. "Thank you, Shep."

He's preoccupied, leaning over his desk, searching for something. "Keep in touch, Allie," he says. Then he darts his eyes towards his office door, indicating that I should see myself out.

I leave his building more confused than ever, left with more questions than answers. On the drive home, I let all the information play over again in my mind.

Was Barnat in on it? Or was he a victim, like me?

I realize that if he was innocent, he'd have been left without a place to live, and his cell would probably not be disconnected. I need to face the fact that he was probably in on it. Playing me the whole time. Good thing I didn't let things go too far between us, and that I never told him about the bugging device.

I pull up to the gate, punch in the code, drive in, and park. I check my phone to see if Ricky's contacted me, but there's no text from him. I check my email. There's nothing from him, but there is one from Willa Yang, asking me for a meeting Monday morning to talk about my progress. *Damn.* Just a few hours too late.

I feel like Laura's being overly paranoid about her, but I just told Shackler I wouldn't pursue her funding. I don't need to respond right away, so I decide to put it on the back burner. I need to think about how to word my email so I leave myself some wiggle room in case I want to circle back to her at a later time. Then I forward her message to Shackler, making good on my promise to him.

I head into the house, realizing that I didn't set the alarm when I left. It's not dark yet, but still. It was an oversight, and I need to be more careful. Once inside, I fully secure the house and settle in for the evening, feeling a bit lonely. Lydia said it's fine to use her kitchen when she's not around, so I head upstairs with some chicken, broccoli, and brown rice that you steam in the bag. I feel my phone vibrate, and I'm comforted by a text from Ricky.

> *Ricky: Hey you. What's up?*
> *Me: Making dinner. Want to FT with me while I cook?*
> *Ricky: That depends. Are you cooking naked?*

I shake my head. *Men.*

He calls, and we connect over FaceTime.

"Sorry to disappoint," I say. "I'm afraid I'm fully clothed."

His smiling face comforts me. "You never disappoint me," he says. "So. What are we having?"

I prop up the phone so I can cook while we talk. He keeps me company as the sun sets over the hills and I prepare my meal. As the darkness settles over the house and the trees cast their long shadows, I decide I'd feel better staying at his house while Lydia's gone.

He's all for it. Except that the only person with a spare key is Mina, and she's in Sonoma this weekend with her wife. An anniversary getaway. I don't want to bother her. She'll be back tomorrow, he says. I assure him I can get through one night here alone. He asks me if I've double-checked the alarm, and I tell him I have. And with that, we proceed to share the details of our respective days. It feels nice and safe and warm.

And I wonder if this is what it feels like to fall in love.

I've just gotten out of the shower when I feel a slight jarring of the floorboards above me. My stomach lurches. My hair is sopping wet, and my speech processor is in the bedroom. It's not waterproof. I throw on my nightshirt and towel dry my hair, trying to stay as still as possible. I put it up in a ponytail so I can grab my processor and put it on, hardly letting myself take a breath.

It's nothing, I tell myself. *Stop.*

But my heart starts to race because I notice more movement overhead, almost imperceptible, that a hearing person might not. I think about what I could use for a weapon if there's an intruder upstairs. There are a few steak knives in my kitchenette, but I'm not sure that would help much. I'd rather have a baseball bat. Something I could swing. Maybe there's one in the supply closet. But that's far. Under the stairs, on the other side of the living area.

My umbrella.

I reach into the corner behind the door and grab it, clutching it in my hand so hard that the metal rods dig into my flesh. I left it in here a few days ago after a rare rain storm, letting it dry out. Not the best weapon, but better than nothing. I stay perfectly still for a few moments. I don't hear anything more. I try and tell myself it was just the house settling. There's an alarm, so why wouldn't it be going off if someone were inside?

But I need to get my processor. And my phone, which I think I left on my nightstand. Or did I leave it upstairs? Ricky's probably asleep, but I'm going to call him anyway. On second thought, I should probably call 9-1-1 first. Even if it's a false alarm, better safe than sorry. My mind isn't firing on all cylinders right now. It's always that way when I start to panic.

Breathe. It's nothing.

I tip-toe out of the bathroom. Why? I don't know. If someone's in the house, I'm sure they know I'm here. My car is right outside, and the lights are on down here. And they would have heard the water running. But if it's a burglar, they'd probably grab Lydia's jewelry and valuables and leave, just like that guy did years ago, if they suspect someone's here. Maybe it's better to make some noise?

Then a jolt of panic runs through me like a lightning bolt. I've been plunged into total darkness.

I can't hear.

I can't see.

I grope around for the walls. A piece of furniture. Anything to orient me, but nothing's within reach. It's like a cave down here, so it's almost pitch black. Maybe we had a minor earthquake which caused the movement I felt upstairs, and now it's knocked out the power? I hold onto that slim shred of hope and try to slow my racing heart. This also means the alarm isn't working now, but I don't want to focus on that. I need to find my phone and get help. I force myself to calm down. I can't fall apart now.

I'll find my phone.

It will all be okay.

My free hand locates the wall. I crawl along it as I make my way to the bedroom from the bathroom. It's not that far, but it feels that way in the dark. I wince as my toe runs straight into the bed leg, but at least now I have my bearings. I feel along the side of the mattress, my throbbing toe distracting me and keeping the panic at bay.

Reaching for the edge of the nightstand, I long for my phone. A beam of light, the feel of it in my hand. I pat around the surface, slowly at first and then frantically, as the realization hits me.

My phone isn't here.

Did someone take my phone?

A sliver of light shines into my bedroom from outside. I glance out the window and my stomach sinks. The neighbor's house, in the distance, has lights. Which means they have power and we don't.

There goes my earthquake theory.

My heart starts to race. Faster and faster. I feel like I might pass out. I stand perfectly still for a bit, and I don't feel any further vibrations. But I sense…something. Someone's down here with me, I know it.

A chill runs up my spine as I brace myself for what's to come, clutching my only weapon in my hand. Sweat beads form at my temples, and my remaining senses are on high alert. I don't move a muscle. Whoever's out there can't see either, and I'm not going to make it easy for them.

Are they in the bedroom with me already?

Or still out in the living area?

A slight puff of breath reaches my neck.

Someone's behind me.

I swing the umbrella around with all my might. It slams into…someone? I still can't see much. I try to pull away, but they're pulling back on my weapon. I shove the umbrella back into them and let go of it. Then I run out of the room, slamming the bedroom door behind me.

My eyes have adjusted ever so slightly, so I can make out a route upstairs. Barely. I don't have time to look behind me, but I'm hoping whoever it is got slowed down by the door. Bolting up the stairs, I make a beeline for Lydia's bedroom.

I trip on a cord and stumble. Grabbing the back of the sofa, I manage to stop from falling on my face. I shift to one knee with my hand on the sofa arm and try to push myself up, but a gloved hand grabs my other foot. I donkey-kick them as hard as I can, but they don't let go. I do it again, harder this time.

It works.

239

Breaking free of their grip, I spring up and run like the wind for Lydia's bedroom. I make it through the doorway and slam the door shut with my right shoulder.

Something blocks it.

A hand?

Hopefully?

I'm facing the wrong way to look, though, and I don't dare turn around. I lean into the door with all my weight, hoping to do some real damage, if it is a hand. The glove would offer some padding, but I'm sure it would still hurt. If it's a foot, though, they could get leverage to open the door. But if I slam it again, I could at least slow them down.

I need to do some damage while I still have my strength. I open the door and slam it shut again, turning myself around in the process.

It's a foot.

And it's still blocking the door. I can see the tip of a dark shoe sticking through the bottom of the door. As I lean as hard as I can on the door, I wonder if they're screaming in pain. Maybe someone will call the police if they are. I can't stay like this forever, though. I need to get this door closed and barricaded.

One more time.

I open and shut it again. This time, it closes. I lock the door and look around for something to secure it. There's more light in here than there was in my bedroom, and I can see well enough to function, but it's still dim.

I don't have time to move anything heavy. There's a vanity and a chair near the door, so I grab the chair and jimmy the back of it under the door handle. I'm lucky. It's a lever-type handle that opens downward, so at least maybe I'll buy myself some time. The handle moves a few times, but then it stills.

Now what?

I look around for a weapon, and all I can find is another umbrella in her closet. My palms are so sweaty, it would probably slip out of my hand. I look around some more.

The window.

I could climb out, jump down, and make a run for it. I look out. The house is on a slope and we're kinda far up. Maybe a story and a half. If I twist an ankle, I'm toast. Plus, if they're fleeing, they will be outside. But then here in this room without a weapon, I'm a sitting duck. There's not much time to make up my mind. And I decide that making a run for it is the right move.

Wait!

Lydia has a gun.

She told me so.

But where?

The bedroom's a good place to keep it. If I were Lydia, where would I hide my gun? I bolt to the closet first, thinking that maybe she has a safe. With a new baby brother, perhaps she'd have it secured. If so, I won't waste my time looking for it. But I don't see a safe. I check up top, in the shoe boxes. Nope. Only shoes there. I rush over to her nightstand and open the top drawer.

It's here.

I can't believe my luck. Like, I seriously can't believe it. I've been lucky too many times tonight. It's bound to run out soon. I'll probably shoot myself with it.

The gun feels smaller in my hand than I would have imagined. But I have no idea how to fire one. I know most of them have some kind of safety device, but it's too dark in here to see it very well. Maybe just having the gun will be a deterrent?

Plus, it's been like five minutes, and nothing more has happened. Maybe I've scared them off. I'm hoping that there was enough noise that someone called the police. I picture them running off as the sirens approach.

Rather than make another move, I sit on the bed with the gun pointed towards the door. I can wait it out. And if nothing happens after a few more minutes, I can tie some bedsheets together and shimmy down.

But then the chair starts to move. They're trying again to get in. I knew my luck would run out. The gun is my only shot.

Unless they have one too.

I crouch down near the window, to the side of the bed, thinking that if I'm not at eye level, I might have an advantage. Then maybe I can get a shot off before they see me. If not, I can jump out the window and take my chances.

I fumble with the gun, trying to find the safety latch in the semi-darkness, if there even is one. The chair pops out from under the handle and the door bursts wide open, startling me. The gun falls from my hand. The outline of a dark figure stands in front of me.

I'm going to die now.

It looks like a man, but I don't think he's noticed me yet. He has a gun, and it's pointed above me, to my left. I think he's wearing night goggles. I turn around in a last-ditch effort to save myself by jumping out the window.

I'm too slow.

A warm wetness washes all over me and my head starts to swirl. I think I've been shot, but I don't feel anything. The blood drains from my head. A tingling sensation creeps up my scalp as the blackness envelopes me.

And then there's nothing.

THIRTY-FOUR

Laura

I'm in my hotel room taking a bath. Kai's asleep, and I'm feeling positive for the first time in a long while. My offer was accepted, much to my surprise. I got a great deal on it. It's exhilarating, being in charge of my life for the first time in decades. I was so young when I met Peter, and he was so much older than me. I've followed his lead for most of my adult life, and it feels empowering to be charting my own course now, making my own decisions.

I met with the banquet director at the Fairmont, took a bunch of photos and some video footage, and sent everything to Lydia. I was planning to check out some other venues tomorrow, but she's very excited about this one. She wants a smaller affair, only about fifty guests, with a view of the ocean for the ceremony and reception. I found the perfect space for both, right here.

We'll have the ceremony on the south lawn of the hotel, a verdant carpet of grass that sits on the edge of the white sand beach with the cobalt sea as a backdrop. It's stunning, and a bit off to the side from the pool area so it feels more private.

Rather than having the reception in the ballroom, which has no view, we decided on a buyout of Brown's Beach House, their fine dining restaurant nestled in front of Pauoa Bay, known for its great food and spectacular sunsets. There's a lanai out in front of the restaurant that we can use for a dance floor. It promises to be an intimate and exquisite affair, which suits my stepdaughter perfectly.

The Fairmont is also command central for the Honu, my qualifying race, so the plan is for me to compete the first weekend in June, and then have the wedding two weeks later. It's perfect. All I need to do is keep our pending divorce under wraps until then.

The bathwater is starting to cool, I've been in here so long. I get out and towel off. Then I hear my phone buzz with another text from Lydia, but it's not about the wedding. She's asking me if anyone is around to go check on her house. She's in Europe, and something is wrong. The power is out at her house, and the security system sent an alert. She's worried about Allie, who isn't answering her texts.

I know Mina's away this weekend on a romantic anniversary getaway, and I don't want to stress out Peter. There's only one person I can think of who might know what to do. I tell her I'll handle it, and I pick up the phone and call Shep Shackler for the second time today.

He picks up right away. "Laura? I'm glad you called." Maybe Sophie's right and he does have a crush on me. It seems a bit odd that he's waiting by the phone at this hour of the night. Either that, or he's very bored and in need of a more exciting profession.

"Hi, Shep. There's something I need you to do." I tell him about Lydia's house, and he mumbles something about things being worse than he thought.

"I don't have time to explain," he says. "I need to call the police. Allie might be in danger. I'm heading over now." He hangs up without saying goodbye.

I'm relieved that Lydia's not there, but I'm terrified for Allie. I should have been more skeptical about that landlord of hers, but I was so preoccupied with my own drama. It's my job to protect my grantees, and I'll never forgive myself if something's happened to her. I pick up the phone and call Sophie.

"Hey. I called Shackler. Be careful what you wish for. We've got trouble." I fill her in on what little I know.

"Oh shit. Me and my big mouth. I'll be right there."

She's in the room right next to me, and soon I hear her tapping at my door.

"I'm sorry, Laura," Sophie says as she enters. "I made light of it, and now look what's happening. Maybe it's bad karma."

"Don't be silly. It's not bad karma."

She shrugs. "Have you tried to reach Allie?"

"Yes. We all have. Nothing yet." My voice starts to tremble. "What if something's happened to her?"

My trauma from last year comes flooding back as a wave of panic hits me. My heart races as I think about staring down the barrel of a gun, wondering if something like that is happening to Allie right now.

"It'll be okay. Power outages happen. Think positive."

"But he said she could be in danger. I have a bad feeling about this."

"I know. I do too," she says.

Breathing through the panic, I send a text off to Lydia, letting her know we're on it. Sophie rubs my back, and we settle in and wait for more news.

THIRTY-FIVE

Allie

Am I dead?

My eyes flutter open. There's light.

A flashlight, I think?

I sit up and see that I'm covered in blood, but I still don't feel anything. I must be dead, with all this blood. Then a face comes into focus.

It's Barnat.

If I'm not dead, he's going to finish me off. I shrink back from him. Then I see his lips move.

You're okay, they say. He places a hand on my shoulder. His face looks soft. Inviting, not threatening. Then he hands me my speech processor.

I put it on. My mind is a swirling mass of confusion.

"Allie. I'm on your side. Steady yourself. It's not your blood," he says.

But it's someone's blood—and it's everywhere. I feel nauseous as the stench fills my nostrils: feces and urine and a sickly metallic smell with a smokey undertone. The sticky substance, globs of it in various shades of red, stuck to me. Covering me. I heave over the side of the bed, adding my vomit to the mix.

Wait. I'm on Lydia's bed? The last thing I remember is trying to climb out the window.

"How did I..." I look around, my mind still numb. Faint sirens wail in the background.

"Steady yourself, Allie. You blacked out for a few minutes, and I lifted you up and put you on the bed. Sorry I had to cut the power. I know you don't like the dark. It was the only way to neutralize her."

"Neutralize who?" I ask.

It starts to sink in, what must have happened. I turn and look to the side. A crumpled body sits on the floor, a river of blood spilling out of its center.

A small body with a silver-gray bob.

My eyes widen in shock and disbelief. "Is that...Willa? He nods.

"Willa Yang tried to kill me?"

"I don't have much time to explain. But yes." Barnat says. "I'm with Interpol." He flashes me a badge. "And I need to leave. The police are coming, and I work under cover. You don't have to worry, though. You're safe now."

"But...Mike and Susan?" I ask, as my mind starts to thaw.

"They were working with the Yangs, to steal technology. They were running that guest house scam for a while. But we flipped them. After Willa killed Charlie."

"She killed her own husband?"

"If he even was her husband. It's very complicated. Even I don't know who she was working for. Just know that it's over. Mike and Susan are cooperating witnesses. They never wanted anyone to get hurt. They flipped on her to protect you, and to protect themselves. They're small-time scam artists, not killers. Do you understand?"

I shrug. "I guess."

"Good," he says. His English seems better now, and I wonder if pretending to be Hungarian was part of his cover.

"Why are you telling me all of this?" I ask.

"Because I don't want you living your whole life looking over your shoulder. You're safe, Allie. I made sure of it. I need you to tell me that you believe me. Do you believe me?"

"I...um. Yes. I believe you."

Because you saved my life.

The sirens are getting closer now.

"I have to go," he says.

He vanishes into the night, leaving me sitting in darkness, covered in Willa's blood. I still have no idea where my phone is.

———

Shep Shackler arrived just in time to keep me from having a nervous breakdown. I still can't keep track of all the people hurling questions at me, but he's been running interference. One of the officers knows him from his time on the force, so that helped. He seemed to know exactly what to say to get them to back off me without sounding like an asshole and pissing them off more. We're upstairs in the living room now, thankfully, and I'm on the sofa. Shackler's wrapping up a conversation with an FBI agent, and I'm sitting here waiting, trying to make sense of it all.

They finally let me take a shower, but I still don't have my phone. It was in Willa's pocket, and they need to examine it. Take fingerprints or whatever it is that they do. I told them it was fine. I have nothing to hide. Shackler said that we'll get a burner for me, on the way to the Fosters' house. Peter Foster's in town, so I'm going to stay at their place as a temporary solution. I can't imagine living here anymore. I suppose I need to find a new place to live, but I can't worry about that now.

The local police arrived first, a few minutes after Barnat took off. I hadn't moved a muscle and was still sitting on Lydia's bed in the dark, curled up in a ball. They grilled me about the shooter, shining their flashlights in my eyes, and it almost felt like they were going to arrest me, as if I wasn't freaked out enough with the near-death experience. I feel like suing them.

I think when they saw the syringe lying next to Willa's body, they realized this was a bit out of their league. It seems like she was going to shoot me up with something to knock me out then move me somewhere and kill me, maybe make it look like I disappeared. I wonder if that's what they did to Charlie Yang: drugged him at the house and then staged his suicide in the hotel room later. Barnat flipped off the main circuit breaker so he could trip up Willa. Shackler's the one who figured that out and got the lights back on.

When the two FBI agents arrived, they were a bit more congenial. They seemed to know something about the Tabernakys and the Yangs, but everyone insisted that Interpol wasn't involved in this investigation. That was confirmed by the woman from Homeland Security who arrived a short time later. I overheard someone say that Willa might be some foreign agent they've been after for a while now. It's crazy, really. And what's even more crazy? I feel surprisingly calm. Shackler says I'm probably in shock and it will hit me later.

I gave everyone my description of Barnat, like four times, and explained that we'd both rented units at the Tabernaky residence. I'm sure they can verify his existence. His cell number is in my phone. Maybe they can trace it. If he is some kind of undercover agent, either they don't know or the Feds don't want me to know.

I'm starting to think he lied to me though. It seems more likely that he was in on the scam and had a change of heart. That's probably why he had to disappear. If he turned on whomever they were working for to save me, his life is in danger. I suppose either way I owe him my life.

Shackler comes over and places a hand on my shoulder. "How are you holding up?"

"I'm okay," I say.

But I'm not.

He nods.

"Wait," I say. "How did Willa get in the house? I'm positive I set the alarm."

"She hacked in and jammed the sensor at the back door," he says.

"That happens?"

"Not often. But she was a pro."

I shake my head, still trying to get my brain around all of it.

"We can go, if you're ready," he says.

"I'm ready," I reply. I can't wait to get the hell out of here.

"Okay, Allie, let's get you over to the Fosters," Shackler says.

I stand up and wobble a bit; I'm still a little woozy. He puts an arm around me and guides me through a maze of detectives and agents and crime scene investigators. They told me I'll need to make myself available for questioning later. Right now, I'm exhausted. We've been up most of the night, and I need sleep.

"Thank you," I say to him.

He seems to be going above and beyond for the family, and I wonder if he and the Fosters are more than just business associates. Right now, I'm grateful for his help. He opens the passenger door of his Range Rover for me. I climb in, drop my overnight bag on the floor, and strap myself in.

I knew when I took this opportunity that my life would change. That I was taking a risk. That I would face obstacles and challenges along the way. But in my wildest dreams, I didn't expect to get mixed up in some kind of life-threatening spy ring.

I think about leaving. Going back to Wisconsin. But then I remember that bad things can happen anywhere, even when you're safe in your bed with your mom in the next room. In some ways, that's a liberating realization, and I'm not going to let fear drive me anymore. I faced death and lived to tell about it. It's a compelling story for a successful entrepreneur, and I'm determined to make it my own.

THIRTY-SIX

Allie

The first week after Willa tried to kill me was the hardest, but I got through it by throwing myself into my work. Ethan fixed the delay on the captions by compressing the data so that it flows faster, so we didn't need to waste time and money trying to make the processor more powerful. It works as well as the VR glasses on the market now. We don't have a wireless option yet, but with my clear, lightweight solution, I now have a shot at securing more funding—and I need it.

I have only enough money to sustain me for two more months if I want to keep Ethan on and try to get it to work wirelessly. It's better to wait until we have the screen in production rather than pitch with a prototype, but the competition is nipping at my heels, so I want to start pitching now.

Ricky's been helping me compile a list of VCs who can get me to my seed round. Moving in with him was supposed to be a temporary solution, but it's been two weeks, and neither of us seems to be in any rush to end it.

"Morning," he says.

"Hey," I say, and give him a peck on the lips.

"Hungry?"

I shake my head.

"Coffee?"

"Yes. Please."

He reaches for a mug, but I put my hand on his.

"You don't have to wait on me, you know." I grab a mug from the holder.

He shrugs. "I like to be a good host."

My stomach sinks.

If I'm a guest here, I don't want to overstay my welcome. I understand where he's coming from, and it's not like I'm going to fall apart emotionally because he's not ready to make that kind of commitment. Our relationship isn't in a move-in-together kind of place. But after what I went through, the thought of scrambling to find another apartment gets my pulse racing.

I don't want him to let me stay here out of pity though, so I'm going to start looking for a new place. Immediately. And save him the awkward task of having to gently nudge me out the door. But without steady income and with my funding dwindling, it's not going to be easy. It's a rough time for start-ups, and every day I read about more of them folding.

"What's on your agenda for the day?" he asks.

I fill my cup with coffee, then head over to the fridge for the milk. "I'm meeting with Laura to update her on my progress."

"Have you contacted any of those VCs yet?" he asks.

255

"Not yet. But I will soon. Thanks again for that."

He comes over and brushes my cheek with his hand. "My pleasure." He kisses me softly.

I force a smile. "And you? What's your day look like?" I ask.

"I have a meeting in the city," he says. "And I need to get dressed."

He heads into the bedroom, and I get on the computer to put the finishing touches on my slide deck and elevator pitch. Then I can start to contact the VCs and see if I can get some appointments lined up.

I've been ignoring my influencer business, but now that I've got the prototype working, I will try to give it more attention. I have two product managers asking me for promos. One is a new type of visual fire alarm, and the other is a cosmetics company. It's always been a sideline for me, and I've never tried very hard to make money at it. But maybe I should. I need the money, so I quickly DM the product managers and tell them that I'd like to move forward.

Before I start looking for a new apartment, I locate the website of the therapist Laura Foster recommended. Oddly, I haven't been feeling panicky or anxious about that night, and that could mean that I'm still in shock. How could I not be affected by what happened?

And I usually have very vivid dreams. But for the past two weeks, I can't remember any of them. When I wake though, something is hovering on the edge of my consciousness. Something unsettling. I feel like this is the calm before the storm, and I'd like to get ahead of it, especially since I'll soon be living alone again. It will probably hit me when I least expect it, like when I'm about to go pitch a VC. I find a slot for two weeks from now, which is the earliest she has, and schedule an intake appointment.

"I'm headed out," Ricky says.

He blows me a kiss, and I wave at him. As soon as the door closes behind him, I pull up some apartment listings and start combing through them.

—

Laura Foster is giving off a different vibe. Not a bad vibe, but something's up. She seems like herself but on steroids. Her expressions are slightly more animated, her gestures a tad gustier. She seems…happy.

And that makes no sense to me at all. Her husband had a heart attack. I was nearly killed at her stepdaughter's home, which is now a crime scene. What could she possibly have to be happy about? This is, for sure, a strange family.

I'm in her home office along with Mina, and I wonder if Ricky's said anything to her about the living situation. I fill them in on the new prototype and the fact that we fixed the delay in the captioning.

"Do you want to give it a try?" I ask Laura.

"Sure," she says with a genuine smile.

She puts on the demo frames, clips on my screen, and then connects it to my cell phone. I start talking about trying to find some funding.

Her eyes widen, and I'm hoping that's a good sign.

"Is it working better?" I ask.

"It's…perfect. Mina, give it a try."

She hands it over to Mina, and her reaction is just as positive. I'm beaming. Then I run through the new slide deck and elevator pitch, and we all agree that I'm ready to move forward and line up some appointments. Decisions are made in the first sixty seconds, I've been told. My pitch can't just be good. It needs to be phenomenal.

I hear a voice out in the living room, but I can't place it.

"Lydia's here," Laura says. "I need to go talk to her for a bit."

She heads out, leaving me alone with Mina. It feels a little awkward between us, since I've been dating Ricky, like we don't know where the boundaries are.

"How's things with my cuz?" she asks. Her directness catches me off guard.

"Oh, fine."

"Fine?" she asks, her head tilted to one side.

"Great. He's been so supportive. But I need to find a new place soon. I don't want to overstay my welcome."

Mina's jaw stiffens, ever so slightly. "Well, that's between the two of you," she says.

Laura comes back, thankfully, ending our uncomfortable interaction. She tells us she needs to wrap things up, and we head out. Peter and Lydia are seated in the living room. I only stayed one night at their house, and I hardly spoke to him that night. He seemed like a nice enough guy. I haven't seen Lydia since she got back from Europe.

"Allie!" Lydia rushes over and hugs me.

"I'm so sorry about everything," I say.

"You have nothing to be sorry about," she assures me. "I'm just glad you're okay. We were all frantic."

"I'm…fine. Or I will be. Thanks for all you've done, Lydia. You're amazing."

"Of course, Allie. That's what friends are for."

I didn't realize that she thinks of me as her friend. It feels a bit awkward because I have so little to offer her in return for all she's done for me. But I'm glad to have her on my side.

"I appreciate it."

"I've put the house on the market," Lydia says.

"But it's your family home." I shake my head. "This is all my fault."

"No, Allie. It's time. I need to move on. It holds dark memories for me. I'm ready to start a new life with Christopher. It's a good thing. Trust me. Being out of that place for the last two weeks made me see how it's been holding me back."

"Okay. I'm…happy for you."

"Thanks."

"So you're living with Christopher now?" I ask.

"Yes. And you're living with Ricky, right?"

"Yes, but—"

"We should double-date! That would be so much fun. But not before we have a girl's lunch. I need the inside scoop on how things are going with him."

"Sure," I reply. "That would be fun."

I'm a little wary of getting too friendly with my bene-factor's stepdaughter, but it's not like I have much choice. I can't very well turn her down. And I really do enjoy her company. But now I'm even more motivated to secure fund-ing and move on from this phase of my business venture.

As supportive as they all are, it would be better to have my personal and business worlds separate.

"Send me some dates for both, and we'll get it on the calendar," Lydia says.

I thank Peter and Laura again for letting me stay at their place, and we say our goodbyes.

Mina and I walk out together. Her eyes narrow on me. "Ricky's like a brother to me," she says. "And he's the kind of guy who will be there for you no matter what. He was there for me during the most difficult time of my life. And he's all I have now."

My stomach tenses, and I'm momentarily speechless. I have no idea what time in her life she's referring to, or why she's so upset with me.

"He's a great guy," I reply, shrugging my shoulders.

"Yes, he is. Don't hurt him, Allie," she says. Then she turns and walks away.

I call out to her, but she waves me off, leaving me totally confused. He's the one who made me think he wanted me to move out. We obviously need to talk.

I pull out my phone to text him and notice a message from the product manager at the company with the visual alarm, the one I'm promoting on my Instagram page. She says the CEO is asking for a meeting with me this week.

Why would the CEO want to meet with me?

Of course, I immediately say yes. He probably wants to offer me a marketing job, and although that doesn't interest me right now, it might be wise to have it on the back burner in case I get desperate. She says his assistant will be in touch with me soon. I send one last text asking what it's about. Her reply leaves me filled with anticipation.

> *No idea.*

I sit in the driver's seat staring at my phone, wondering what the CEO might want. The Fosters' front door opens, so I start up my car and pull away from the curb. I've had enough of them for one day.

THIRTY-SEVEN
Laura

N ow that I've made a commitment to qualify for the Ironman, I've stepped up my training. It's the perfect way for me to process all that's happened, and I'm finally feeling like myself again. With the baby and my career vying for my attention, I can't train with my former team very often, but I joined back up with them anyway.

We did a long run today. A half marathon length. It's been a while since I've run that distance, and it went much better than I expected. I felt strong. Focused. It was motivating to have the support of the group.

But as I arrive back home and head for the front door, I feel my stomach sink. Seven months is a long time to be in limbo, and it's wearing on me. Acting polite. Dancing around our issues. Pretending things are normal when they're not.

Peter's sitting in the living room when I arrive. He springs up to greet me.

"How was your run?" he asks.

"Just what I needed," I reply.

He gives me a tentative smile. I know he's still holding out hope that if we fake it for a while, things will go back to normal and I'll change my mind. It's a strange mix of emotions I'm feeling. Excited to finally be moving my life in the direction I want it to go. Fearful of how it will all turn out. And crushingly sad about the breakup of my family and what it will mean for my son.

Our marriage has always been congenial. We've never been the kind of couple to have plate-throwing blow-ups. We genuinely like each other, and that hasn't changed. I'm not angry, but I'm not in love with him anymore.

I know that we'll be fine as coparents of Kai, but I'm still concerned about how this will affect Lydia and Carson. Will they want nothing to do with me because I've hurt their father? I could live with that for myself, but they're Kai's siblings, and since I don't see myself having another child, I want Kai to have them in his life.

"How was your time?" he asks.

"Best ever." I smile. "One forty-one."

An hour and forty-one minutes for a half marathon. That's faster than I ran it in my twenties. I won't be able to do that in a triathlon, but it gives me confidence that I'm back.

"I'm happy for you," he says.

And I know that he is.

"Thanks."

"You're going to qualify this summer. I can feel it." His eyes widen. "Need a foot massage?"

I sigh. He's been putting out these kinds of feelers every so often, trying to be more intimate. He asked me out to dinner last weekend, but I turned him down. The last thing I want is to hurt him any more than I already have, but giving him false hope isn't good for either of us.

"Peter. You know that's not appropriate."

"No strings attached, Laura. Consider me your personal trainer. At your disposal."

He smiles.

I don't.

And then he hangs his head and turns from me.

I walk over and tap him on the shoulder. He turns around and falls into my arms. We stand there for a while, locked in an embrace, and then I pull back and look him in the eye.

"Peter. I'm sorry. But I'm not going to change my mind. It's over."

His eyes start to well up, but he bats back the tears. I hug him again, and then it's my turn to cry. Sobs rack my body as I think back on all the good times we've had and how tragic all of this is. Peter's traumatic childhood. Cynthia's mental illness. Peter losing me, the love of his life, all because of that horrible Jeanine Randall. But I remind myself that nothing excuses his behavior that day, never mind all the deception over the years.

So I straighten up and dry my eyes.

He brushes the hair back from my face. "I'll love you until the day I take my last breath, Laura," he says. "And nothing you can do can change that."

I nod. "I know, Peter. I love you too. Just not in the same way anymore."

His eyes look heavy and full of pain, and I'm sure I just made it worse. If I'd said I hated him, it would have probably hurt less. Hatred implies some level of passion, and that's clearly gone, at least for me. What I feel for him is more like pity, and that's way worse, especially for a man like Peter. I know I'll be fine, but I'm not so sure about my husband. But I can't change the way I feel, although I've tried.

He turns away and heads upstairs with a lumbering gait, as if his legs have grown too heavy to lift. And I'm starting to think we won't be able to keep up this ruse for very much longer.

THIRTY-EIGHT

Allie

*I*t's a good problem to have, I tell myself. But I still don't know what to do.

That CEO? He didn't want to offer me a marketing job. He wanted to acquire my fledgling business. The company makes a host of assistive devices. They've been trying to develop a captioning device, but mine is further along and much better than what they were working on.

And they want it.

My caption screen could be a game changer for their company, he said, because it has the potential to reach a larger market with its capacity for language translation. They see the potential of offering a device that focuses only on captioning, rather than the entire suite of VR capabilities. Working together, we can offer it at a lower price point and get it to market more quickly. They have a substantial R&D budget, and with their ample resources, we're much more likely to get it to work wirelessly.

It's a miracle, really. And something that will leapfrog my product along in the process. But I'd be giving up control. And, I'd be giving up on the opportunity to lead my own company. It's a boatload of money though, and I'm going to run out of funding very soon.

My brother and mother think I should take the deal. Ricky's not so sure. He's more entrepreneurial than I am, so I think he views it as settling. I ran it past Lydia, and much to my surprise, she offered to fund my seed round if I want to take it to the next level on my own. It's a generous offer, but I'm somewhat wary. There's something off about that family, and I'm not too thrilled at the idea of being dependent on the Fosters to bring my product to market.

I reached out to Shep Shackler to get a recommendation for an attorney. I wasn't sure if he was the right person to ask as he seems to deal mostly with criminal matters, but he's the only neutral person I could turn to. He gave me the name of a financial attorney, and she gave me valuable advice. We worked up a counteroffer that would allow me to retain some measure of control—along with a lot more money. Now it's well before dawn, and I'm on a plane to Chicago to meet with the CEO to try to strike a deal. He might laugh in my face.

But then again, he might not.

"So how did it go?" Ricky asks.

I got back from Chicago late this afternoon. We're having a romantic dinner, tucked away in a quiet area of

Carpaccio, where we had the date that finally propelled our relationship into high gear. Turns out I was completely misreading him. He wanted me to move in, but he thought I'd feel he was rushing things if he asked me.

We've been living together for over a month now, and it's going well. I insisted on contributing to the mortgage, over his protests. I don't want to be a freeloader, and I like to be able to take care of myself. But it's nice to know I won't be out on the street if I run out of funding.

"I made him a counteroffer," I say.

I didn't tell anyone about meeting with the attorney or my plans to negotiate. I wanted this to be my decision and mine only.

He nods in approval. "Nice move. And?"

"I told him I wanted double the amount he offered. And that I wanted to retain some control by coming on as part of the executive leadership team. In exchange, I'll sign over my patent, but I want stock in the wider company and a bonus structure tied to the development of my product."

"Wow. That was bold. How did he react?"

"I was worried I might get laughed out of his office... but I didn't." I flash him a smug smile. "He's running it past his team and the board. He seemed open to it, but then you never know with someone on his level. They tend to play their cards close to the vest. Oh, and I told him he needed to make Ethan an offer too. I'm not sure he would even be interested in coming on board, but I didn't want to leave him out in the cold."

"So, what will you do if he says yes?" Ricky asks. "And what about Lydia's offer? She's giving you an opportunity to take this to the next level on your own. Do you really want to give up on your dream?"

I was afraid of this. I know how he thinks. How everyone here thinks. But I don't view this as giving up. My dream was never to be the leader of my own empire. My dream was to bring a device to market that would make verbal communication easier for D/deaf and hard of hearing people. And in the process, to find my passion. Plus, I don't want to be in business with the Foster family. I'd rather take my chances with a veteran CEO and the board of a publicly traded company. But I'll keep that to myself.

"Ricky. We're different. This *is* my dream. And we both know it's a terrible time for start-ups."

He takes my hand, brings it to his lips, and kisses it. "Then I'm happy for you. I hope he says yes."

"Oh, and one more thing. I told him I'd need to have a flexible work situation, not be tied to a desk in Chicago."

He smiles. "I see. And where do you see yourself... flexing?"

"Well, as you know, Silicon Valley's where it's at, in terms of innovation. I'm sure he can see the value of having someone here. You know, networking and all." I wink at him.

"If that's what the kids are calling it these days."

I put my hands on top of his. "Look, I'm happy here with you. Even with all the insanity that's happened. That's really saying something."

"I'm happy that you're happy. Now let's eat."

THIRTY-NINE

I'm not looking forward to turning Lydia down, but I need to get it out of the way. They countered my counter, not in terms of the money, but in terms of the job. They want me to head up an entire division and oversee all the assistive devices for D/deaf and hard of hearing people. I'd keep some control over the captioning device, but the day-to-day would be handled by someone with an engineering background, which makes sense. They want me to work on marketing, promotions, and R&D for new products.

Of course, I said yes. It means I'll have to be in Chicago more often, but I'll be able to afford it. Ricky understands, and we can manage a long-distance relationship.

This is our second get-together since I moved out of her place, and we've been growing closer. We're doing a quick power walk near downtown Los Altos. We're both too busy today to do a sit-down lunch or get to the gym, so this seemed like a good solution.

"I've got some news," I tell her, launching right in. I explain everything except the part about having already accepted the deal.

Her face lights up. "Allie! This is fantastic news. I'm so happy for you. Of course, you're going to take the deal. Right?"

"Well, I want to. You're not...upset?" I wince a little.

"Upset about what?"

"That I'm not taking you up on your generous offer," I say.

"No. Don't be silly. This is so much better for you. Anyone can see that."

She's being so understanding about this. "Thanks for being so supportive," I say.

"That's what friends are for. I'm a bit relieved, to tell you the truth. I value our friendship, and I was worried it might complicate things. Mixing business and pleasure is never a great idea."

"True."

We cross over to the other side of the street, stopping to let a cyclist go by.

"And your timing is fantastic," she says as we continue our walk.

"My timing?" I ask.

"Yes. You know we're having a small wedding party. Only two other people. Carson's the best man, and Christopher's sister was supposed to be the maid of honor."

"I remember."

"Well, we just found out that his sister's pregnant. And the baby is due in early June, a few weeks before our wedding. She needs to back out. I thought about asking you, but with my being a possible investor…" She shrugs.

I nod. "Right."

"But now that's not an issue! I hate to put you on the spot. I know it's a big ask. But will you think about it?" She places a hand on my arm. "No pressure."

I'm flattered, but surprised. I figured I'd be invited, but to be in the wedding party seems a bit much. I guess Laura wasn't exaggerating when she said Lydia doesn't have many female friends. But then neither do I. I don't have any sisters, and although I was a bridesmaid at my brother's wedding, this might be my only chance to be a maid of honor.

"Of course, Lydia. I'd be honored."

"It means a lot to me, Allie. Thanks."

"Thanks for asking me."

We come to the end of Los Altos Avenue, where it meets up with downtown. As we head to where our cars are parked, Lydia points out a shop she likes. Cranberry Scoop.

"Can we pop in for a minute?" she asks.

It's so cute. I'll need to come back and get some holiday decorations when I have more time. She heads for their selection of travel purses.

"I could have used this in Europe. Aren't they great? I'll get one for my honeymoon. We're going to Thailand."

"I, um…" I glance towards the door.

"Another time. I know you need to get going." She puts back the purse and we head out.

"How are the plans coming along? Are you getting excited?" I ask.

As we walk to our cars, she fills me in on the wedding plans. I notice that she never talks much about Christopher or their relationship. I've met him only once, when we went out to dinner. They seem happy and compatible, and it appears to be working for them. But they appeared a bit restrained for a couple that is engaged to be married. No PDA. Not much heat. Polite dinner conversation with the occasional round of banter. If I didn't know better, I'd think they were close business associates, not newlyweds waiting to happen.

She fills the space between us with talk of plumeria lei ceremonies, white sand beaches, azure waters, and her perfect beachfront wedding. She's obviously ready to marry him. I'm getting excited to be a part of it. I've never been to Hawai'i, and now I can afford to do it in style.

As I get in my car and drive off, I reflect on myself and my relationship with Ricky. I still feel a bit guilty about Barnat, and not only about the kiss. I've dreamt about him a few times, waking up breathless and brimming with desire. I suppose it doesn't mean anything. The guy saved my life, so it's natural that he'd be on my mind.

It's such a trope too. The handsome stranger. The bad boy who's only good for you. I know I'll never see him again, and that's fine with me. He's a harmless fantasy I can keep to myself. I wonder if it's that way for Lydia. Does she have some other guy lurking in the recesses of her mind? But we're not really at a fantasy-sharing place yet in our friendship, so I keep this to myself.

And although my Silicon Valley adventure didn't play out exactly like I'd expected, I'm happy with where my life is now. My mother and I are doing better. I offered Kevin a substantial cut of what I got for the business, but he wouldn't take nearly as much as I offered. I'm planning to move my mother into a nicer home and set up a college fund for my nephew. Ricky and I are going strong, and so far, I love where things are headed with my career.

The best part is the encouragement from my followers, many of whom are D/deaf or hard of hearing. I'm chronicling the journey for them, allowing them to be part of the development process. It's motivating me, and I can't let them down. They remind me why I started this in the first place. Not to get rich, but to make a difference in the world.

Funny. That's exactly what Willa Yang said. She wanted to fund products that could make a difference in the world. I wonder who she was working for and why she felt compelled to take things as far as she did. I remember her saying something about all the greed and excess in the world. And for some reason, I believe she meant what she said.

I doubt my technology was the reason she came after me. That wouldn't make any sense. I'm sure it was because of what I saw that night. And whatever she was after, it was important enough for her to kill over—and die for. My guess is she was a true believer. A zealot, working for a cause or a country she believed in.

But what about Barnat? Did he save me out of duty as an undercover agent? Or because of his feelings for me, risking his own life in the process? I suppose I'll never know, and that's okay. It's all starting to fade, like the plot of some spy novel I read. I'm focused on the future, and it's looking brighter than ever.

EPILOGUE
Laura

Seven months later

The feeling was electrifying. As soon as I hit the water, I knew it was going to be a great day. I'd trained and prepared, not excessively but steadily. And the strategy worked. I learned the hard way. In the past, I've overtrained and then ran out of steam in the race.

But not this time.

The swim felt wonderful in the warm, clear waters fronting the Fairmont, a stark contrast to the Bay Area with its frigid temperatures. I was home, in my element, and my body responded. I did the swim in thirty-six minutes, getting kicked in the face only once.

I wasn't looking forward to the bike race, my Santa Cruz crash still fresh in my mind. But I pushed through it. It's the most important leg of the triathlon, and I had to fight the urge to slow down when I was sailing down the hills after my climb up to Hawi, the farthest point on the ride.

Unlike the swim, the heat is not your friend in this part of the race. The course winds up and back down the main highway along the Kohala Coast: hot, dry, and covered in black lava and asphalt that absorbs the heat and serves it back to the riders.

My bike time was adequate but not great, a little over three hours. At first, I beat myself up for my weak bike time. But I soon realized that it left me with more energy, and as I started the run, I knew I'd finish strong.

Running is my best event. It's where I shine. The course meanders around the golf course near the hotel, and although it was later in the day, there was a slight breeze coming off the ocean that invigorated me. I finished with a time of 1:50 for the run, my best time as part of a triathlon. I was hopeful that I'd qualify, but I held my breath until the results were in.

And I did it!

I accepted my spot in the October Ironman World Championship, feeling a tinge of melancholy that Peter wasn't there to share it with me, but still thrilled. Then I put it all on the back burner. From that moment on, it was all about Lydia.

I see her now, coming down the makeshift aisle that runs down the grassy area in front of the beach, my father's arm linked with hers. It's a bittersweet visual. I can see the sadness in her eyes from here. Peter had another heart attack five months ago, and this time he didn't make it. I offered to drop out of the race, but she wouldn't have it.

My heart aches as I think about how proud he would be right now. She's radiant, her clear blue eyes matching the sea behind her. A simple white lace strapless dress hugs her body and floats along the grass, a sprinkle of baby's breath threaded through her long dark hair.

Our eyes meet as she walks by. We share a bond few people would understand, and in a way, I'm relieved that I didn't have to damage my relationship with her by divorcing her father, although I wouldn't mind distancing myself from their past.

When Shep Shackler called about a month ago, I felt he was fishing for a reason to see me again. Turns out Sophie was right. He did want to date me, but he didn't start with that. First, he asked me, hypothetically, if I'd want to know if something new were to surface regarding Jeanine Randall and her death. I told him no—because I don't. That part of my life is over, and I want nothing more than to forget about it and move on.

I figure it was a pretense to call me because he asked me out to dinner after that. I told him I was headed to the Big Island for a month, for the Honu race and the wedding. And I'm still not sure what I want to do regarding his offer. He's not handsome in the classic sense like Peter was, but there is a certain masculine energy about him that I find attractive. A rugged manliness that's kind of intriguing. Plus, he's the only person I can date who already knows all my secrets.

Shep's also the one who figured out that Willa Yang was not who she appeared to be, the day Allie told him about Mike and the duffel bag. He did a search and matched her to a photo on Interpol's most wanted list. The photo was over twenty years old, and he wasn't sure it was her.

But once I called and told him about the power being out at Lydia's house, he alerted the FBI and headed right over.

It seems she was some kind of spy, playing the long game. I don't know if Charlie even knew who she really was. The Feds aren't telling us much, and I have no idea who she was working for. Still, it's impressive that he was able to get to the bottom of it so quickly, and I feel safer with him in my life.

But my life is my own now, and I like it that way. So I told him I'd think about it. And that's as far as I can take it at the moment.

—

Allie

The wedding was magical. Now we're finishing up a post-wedding breakfast at an open-air venue at the Fairmont that sits near the beach, where the dance floor was last night. It's a massive veranda that now houses tables and chairs and a self-serve buffet. Lydia asked me to go for a walk after we finish. It's good timing because I need to talk to someone. I've got a big decision to make, and I'd like to talk through it.

"Let's bail," she says. "I need a break from all these people."

"Sure," I say. "Let me grab another coffee."

After I get my coffee, we stroll past the pool and enter the beachfront pathway that leads from the hotel to the petroglyph park adjacent to it. The walkway is sprinkled in a polka-dot pattern with bits of white and black lava that crunch under my feet. It's a lovely walk with the waves gently lapping at the shore and the birds chirping overhead.

"How's it going with your job?" she asks.

"Couldn't be better. We're launching our product this summer, and it never would have happened this fast if I hadn't taken the deal."

She rests her hand on my forearm. "I'm so happy for you, Allie."

"I'm happy for you too. The ceremony was so moving. But I'm sorry your dad wasn't here to give you away." I sigh. "I suppose I'll be in the same situation."

"Wait. Are you telling me that Ricky...? You and Ricky?" Her eyes widen.

I smile. "Well, not officially. He sort of pre-proposed to me, two nights ago. He didn't want to steal your thunder. It was more of a feeling-me-out kind of conversation."

"That's so exciting!"

"He still has to get a ring and make it official."

"Well? What did you say?"

"I said I'd be very open to the idea. You know, if he happened to ask me." I smile.

We come upon a picnic table.

"Let's sit for a bit," she says. She pats the bench, inviting me to join her.

I sit next to her, both of us facing the ocean. It's very peaceful. My eyes focus on the horizon where white, fluffy clouds hover over a tranquil, turquoise sea.

"That's wonderful. How do you feel?"

"Um, you know. I feel...excited."

"What is it, Allie? Something's bothering you. I can tell."

I turn to her. "It's just, how do I know for sure? That Ricky's 'the one'?"

"I don't think anyone knows for sure."

"Did you have doubts?" I ask. "About Christopher?"

"No. I didn't have any doubts. I knew I wanted to marry him. But that doesn't mean that I knew he was 'the one.' I don't believe in soulmates and all that fairy-tale stuff. I think you find someone you love, and then you work at it. My parents stopped working at it, and they let other people come between them. I'm not going to let that happen."

I nod. "It's just that I've been having this dream. About someone else. It's sort of turned into a fantasy, and I feel guilty about it."

"Fantasies are totally normal, Allie. What's it about? You simply must tell me, now that you brought it up."

"I'll tell you mine if you tell me yours." I flash her a sly smile.

"Ooh, I like that. You first."

"Well, you know Barnat? The guy who saved my life?"

"Yes. The mysterious European guy."

"That's the one. Well, I never told anyone, but we kissed once. Before Ricky and I were serious. And I've been having these dreams. Steamy dreams, where we give in to the sexual tension. And it's amazing. Do you think it means anything? I love Ricky, and I want to marry him. So why am I having these dreams?"

"Oh, that means nothing. I dream about other guys from time to time. And I love Christopher. He's the perfect husband for me. We work. We make sense. There's a certain rhythm we have with each other that's hard to describe unless you've experienced it. I know it will stand the test of time."

That makes sense to me. "I know what you mean. I have that with Ricky."

"Then it will be fine. Trust me. And you know, if you ever got to really know that Barnat guy, he'd probably end up being a total douchebag. You'd dump him inside of a month. Keep him as a fantasy. It's better that way. And nobody needs to know about it. Your secret's safe with me." She winks, and I feel my face flush a little.

"Thanks. I feel better. That's solid advice."

And I really do feel better. I want a life with Ricky. And she's right. Barnat would be a total nightmare in a real relationship. He's probably not even capable of having one.

"Now it's your turn," I say. "Who's your dark stranger fantasy guy?"

"I have a dark fantasy," she says. "But it's not about a guy."

My eyes widen. "Okay then...what?"

She's got a faraway look in her eye, and now I'm not sure I want to know. *How weird will this get?* But she starts, and I can't very well stop her.

"I'm in a nurse's uniform, and I'm looking down at Jeanine Randall, the woman who destroyed my family. I grab a pillow, hold it over her face, and press down. Not long enough to leave any evidence, but long enough to stress out her weakened body. I do this several times until I see her eyes flutter and close. When I'm sure I've done enough damage, I leave and let nature take its course. As I'm exiting her floor and entering the stairwell, I hear the code blue announcement. And I know that monster will never be able to ruin anyone's life again."

I swallow. *Hard.* And try not to appear too shocked.

"That's...wow, Lydia."

She snaps out of her stupor. An oddly cheerful smile replaces her blank stare as I struggle to look nonchalant— and fail miserably.

"Ha! It's only a fantasy, Allie." She bats me on the arm. "Goodness. Look at your face!" "You've gone pale. Don't worry. I wouldn't be stupid enough to actually do something like that, let alone tell someone about it. But you see, family means everything to me. And I'd do *almost* anything to protect the people I love."

"I...yes. I get that, Lydia. I really do," I lie.

"I knew you would! You're like a sister to me now, Allie. I feel like I can tell you anything."

She reaches over and hugs me. I wonder if she can feel me shudder as an icy chill runs through my veins.

"Welcome to the family," she says.

"Thanks," I reply.

"Let's head back," she says. "I'm sure everyone's wondering where I am."

"Sure," I say, trying not to sound too eager.

As we're walking back, it dawns on me that my caption app has been on the whole time, recording our conversation. I was testing it out this morning and forgot to turn it off. She's a good person to have in my camp, and I'm clearly in her good graces right now. But things can change at any moment, I sense. So just in case, I'll save that transcript for a rainy day.

I always said there was something strange about the Foster family.

Turns out I was right.

AUTHOR'S NOTE

My daughter, like Allie Dawson, is deaf with a cochlear implant. Like Allie, she was also in the first wave of children to take a chance on what was, at the time, a very new technology. Cochlear implants are somewhat controversial, although not as much as they were twenty-five years ago when I made the most difficult and gut-wrenching decision of my life and scheduled her surgery.

In this novel, "Deaf" refers to people fluent in ASL who identify as culturally Deaf and do not consider it to be a disability, while "deaf" refers to the physiological condition of not hearing. D/deaf is an inclusive term that refers to both groups. I've tried as best I can to get this right at press time, although I know conventions change over time.

As far as the technology, smart glasses are a reality, and some of the information I included was factual. XRAI Glass, for example, is an app that's available now and can pair with VR glasses or be used on a smart phone. XRAI is also working on speech-to-ASL technology, which would be a welcome addition to their product line. There are other options in various stages of development, including waveguide glasses. These promising and potentially life-changing technologies need funding though, so if there are some investors out there, have a look at these companies.

This is a work of fiction, but I have attempted to portray an accurate picture of what life's been like for my daughter Erica. I know it's been hard for her, not being able to communicate effortlessly in the hearing or Deaf world, and it's remarkable how well she handles it. There are challenges that most people don't think about. When she first lived on her own after college, for example, I bought portable visual fire alarms for her apartment, but we still worried that she would sleep through the flashing lights in the event of a fire, and that kept me up many nights. Verbal communication has never been effortless for her, and even with her implant, she relies on lipreading to fully comprehend people. The masking during the pandemic made it even harder and more alienating for people who need to rely on lipreading, something that likely didn't register with most people.

I've often wondered if I made the right decisions and whether she would have been better off in the Deaf community, using ASL. She learned ASL as a second language and taught it to her hearing husband, although she predominately communicates in spoken English. I've tried my best, but like many parents, I ruminate sometimes about the choices I've made, second-guessing myself. I wasn't a passed-out drunk like Allie's mom. But at times, I wanted to be. I can only hope that she knows I tried my best.

I'm happy to report that Erica married a wonderful man a few months ago in a fairy-tale wedding nestled in the mountains near her hometown of Kailua. It was spectacular, and many people from near and far came to celebrate with her. Lifelong friends, new ones, and everyone in between. So, I suppose as moms go, given the outcome, I'm not the worst one on the planet. For now, I'll focus on our happy ending and, like my characters, try to think positive about the future. Thanks for sharing in my journey.

ACKNOWLEDGMENTS

This book would not have been possible without the many people who helped shape it along the way. First, I'd like to thank my daughter Erica for inspiring me every day. Thanks to my husband who once again read countless drafts and helped me when I hit roadblocks. Thanks to my alpha readers Susan, Donna, and Robin who gave me valuable feedback on my early draft. Thanks to my beta readers for their thorough and professional beta reads which helped me fine tune the plot, especially fellow thriller author Leslie Lutz. And thanks to my editor Julie McKenzie for her meticulous attention to detail.

My gratitude goes out to Dan Scarfe, CEO and Founder of XRAI, for taking time out of his extremely busy life to help me understand and accurately portray the technology as it exists today and as it could be in the future. I shared the XRAI Glass app with my daughter, and she now uses it regularly. My sincere thanks to Bella Hughes, my former student and phenomenally successful entrepreneur, who helped me accurately portray Laura Foster's foundation and the process of taking a start-up to exit. In addition to successfully launching two start-ups, Shaka Tea and

Better Sour, Bella also co-founded FoundHer, an accelerator serving Native Hawaiian, Pacific Islander, and/or Asian women, which was the inspiration for Laura Foster's fictional foundation in my novel. Sadly, the statistics I used in the series about women and access to venture capital were accurate at press time. Hopefully, that will start to change. My sincere thanks also goes to Jon Jacobs, Honolulu attorney and former Honolulu prosecutor, who helped me accurately portray interagency relations and interactions between state, federal, and international law enforcement.

As always, thanks to my readers. I am so grateful for the time you take to read my books as well as rate and review them. I read all my reviews and it helps me to improve, so please keep them coming. I really appreciate it. I'm presently working on a new mystery set on Lake Michigan, revolving around a neighborhood feud that turns deadly. It should be out sometime in 2024. For information on new releases, special deals, and book recommendations, sign up for my mailing list at www.bonnietraymore.com.

Please enjoy a sample of
Head Case: A Psychological Thriller

PROLOGUE

Kimi

Kimi knows what the other teachers call her behind her back. She's heard them before, although she's pretty sure they don't know she knows.

Here comes the mole.

It's not like she signed some formal agreement. And it's not like she had much of a choice. It had all started pretty innocently. Her boss befriending her and then subtly starting to pump her for information.

Then it became an unstated directive. A quick promotion to English department chair in exchange for some hints about who might be plotting behind the woman's back. Getting her preferred chaperoning duties in exchange for a few tidbits about who might be holding up her latest initiatives.

And then it became even more complicated.

She wonders how Brooke will take the resignation letter she left in her mailbox yesterday afternoon. It's a terrible career move to leave now, just two weeks before winter break. But Kimi feels that she doesn't have much choice.

It's not just the strained relationship with the other teachers, although that's part of it. It's that she's pretty sure her boss doesn't know what she overheard, and it needs to stay that way. She'll go back to North Carolina and re-group, then come back for the rest of her belongings some other time.

As she enters the deserted Cortlandt train station and starts walking towards the tracks, she feels a chill run up her spine. It's dead still on a frigid Saturday morning. No commuters. Not another passenger in sight. But she has a nagging sensation that she's not alone.

Is someone following me?

She stops for a moment and turns to look behind her. Nobody's there. She glances out the window to the parking lot, but the view is obstructed by a thin layer of ice. Then she takes a deep breath, steadies herself, and makes her way over to the staircase that leads down to the train tracks.

The hairs on the back of her neck are standing up, but she reminds herself there's a good chance she's overreact-ing—to all of it. And for a moment, she considers that she might be making the biggest mistake of her entire career.

Too late to second-guess myself now.

When she lifts her foot to start down the stairs, she freezes, reacting a split second too late to the sensation of a presence behind her. In an instant, she's flying headfirst in the air looking down at the cold, menacing metal stairs.

She closes her eyes and braces herself, incapable of emit-ting the terrifying scream that's welling up inside her.

ONE

Cassie

I accepted this position last summer, in the wake of a gut-wrenching breakup. You'd think after he broke my heart, he would at least have been gentlemanly enough to offer to move out of our apartment and let me stay put.

But that's not how it happened. He reminded me that it was his apartment first, which is true. Then he offered me a small sum of money. And then he gave me a deadline to find a new place. It was all very businesslike.

"There's someone else?" I asked.

"Does it really matter?" he replied. "What's the point in doing this to yourself, Cassie?"

He tried to deny it at first, to spare me the sordid details. But I eventually got most of the story out of him. We'd been living together for over a year. Dating for over two. I thought we were "going somewhere." Our sex life had never been electrifying, but it was satisfying and comfortable, and that was enough for me.

When things cooled off a bit, about six months before he dropped the bomb on me, I figured that was just how it was in a long-term relationship. I'd never lived with anyone before, so I had no frame of reference.

Then our silly little arguments stopped. He began to act polite—the way you interact with a relative stranger—like he didn't care enough to fight back. I felt something was up. Something had changed, but I didn't dare bring it up. I held my breath and waited to see if things would go back to normal.

I guess on some level a woman can sense when she's losing a guy, I just wasn't ready to face it. Because for me, getting involved with someone is a lot more complicated than it is for the average person. In hindsight, I suppose I can see that the relationship was never all that great. He probably did me a favor by ending it.

But it was all I had at the time, and I wasn't ready to let go. So when he told me that, yes, there was someone else, I felt like I'd been punched in the stomach. I have my pride, most of the time, but it seemed to be eluding me that day.

I'd like to say I held my head high and stormed out when he fessed up, but that's not what happened.

"You better be sure about this," I offered. "I don't give second chances."

"I'm in love with another woman. I'm sorry. It's over."

Then he turned from me and walked out the door.

So when I went to a conference in New York City the following week and learned about a teaching position at a boarding school thousands of miles from my California home that offered faculty housing, it seemed like it was meant to be. I could pocket my payoff from Evan, regroup, start over, and live happily ever after, following a proper but brief mourning period. I had just turned thirty so I didn't plan to pine away for too long.

Obviously, I wasn't thinking straight. I've stranded myself on top of a mountain in rural upstate New York, surrounded by acres of woods. A two-hour trek to New York City on a good day.

What was I thinking? Who am I going to meet here?

One thing I've learned from this experience is never make a major life decision in the midst of emotional turmoil.

I moved here from San Diego, totally unprepared for the insane winter weather we've been having here. Falcon Ridge Academy sits near the top of a medium-high peak of the Catskill Mountains on a plateau overlooking the Hudson River far in the distance.

It all looked so beautiful when I came to interview back in June. The day was clear and breezy, the setting a bucolic wonderland. I imagined long walks in the woods surrounded by vibrant fall colors where I would clear my head and heal my heart. A respite from the rat race. I'd write. I'd think. I'd grow stronger.

Now it's December, and the campus feels more like a minimum-security prison: isolated, creepy, and desolate. The walls of my four-hundred-square-foot apartment feel like they're closing in on me as the bare branches of the tree outside my bedroom window scrape at it with each gust of wind. Long, craggy fingers trying to claw their way inside.

From a distance, the structure I'm housed in seems to teeter on its foundation, threatening to tumble down the steep mountainside with every gust of wind. It's perilously close to the drop-off behind it. I was surprised that there's no real barrier there, aside from a row of stubby, round sage green shrubs that dot the perimeter of the grounds behind my building.

Winter arrived early, with a vengeance. And although the weather warmed up a bit today, there's still snow piled up outside from a "squall" last week. At least I'm learning some new vocabulary words. That's a blinding snowstorm that comes out of nowhere and makes it impossible to drive, see, or basically do anything, including walk from my apartment to the dining commons. I have no sense of direction. I'm sure I'll get lost and freeze to death or fall down the mountain before this winter is over. And it's just getting started.

Could this possibly get any worse?

But as I stare down at the alert on my phone, I realize I shouldn't have asked that question. They've called an emergency meeting of all faculty and staff that starts in twenty minutes. On a Sunday. And it's supposed to be my weekend off.

I thought we outlawed indentured servitude, but apparently not. For nine months of the year, they own me, and they know it. I forgo the primping—there's nobody to impress anyway—throw on some clothes, grab my jacket, and head out the door.

―――

Kimi Choy is dead.

I heard our head of school say it, but it's not registering. I feel detached, like I'm watching a movie. I'm not sure if that's because I'm in shock or because I'm simply a terrible person. I was pretty close to her, at least until recently. Shouldn't I be feeling something?

Other people are reacting. I see a few eyes tearing up, but I can't seem to get my brain around it. The fact that this happened out of the blue. The fact that she was totally fine when I saw her Friday afternoon—and now she's gone. The fact that she died from a fall down the stairs at the Cortlandt train station.

Why did she go there, one of the most deserted stations around, and one that's at least twenty miles south of us? There are busier ones closer to our school she could have used.

And then I realize I'm probably in shock. I think back to when I arrived last August. Kimi was my department chair, and she went out of her way to make me feel welcome.

I'd never worked at a boarding school before, but she was a veteran. She was really friendly and offered some tips about where to get my hair cut and how to stay sane. She warned me that I would need to get some distance from the place on my weekends off. And she was really supportive when I told her about my break up and what a hard time I was having.

"I've got the perfect solution!" she said.

"What?"

"Let's go to the city for a night. Hit some of the trendy spots. Get you out there again."

"I don't think I'm ready to be 'out there,' Kimi."

"Oh, come on. It doesn't have to go anywhere. We'll get dressed up. Flirt a little. I could use some attention, too."

She had a point. Proximity to Manhattan was part of the reason I took this job. I love it there, but I didn't realize how hard it would be to get into the city.

"Okay. Let's do it," I said. What did I have to lose?

We had a great time. Shopping. Bar-hopping. Most of it by ourselves, but we did mingle with a pair of older banker-type guys who seemed to enjoy the company of two "hot teachers." It didn't go anywhere, and I suppose we could have been offended by the comment. I needed an ego boost, though, and it worked to lift my spirits.

Our friendship cooled off a bit over the semester, and that's on me. Other teachers warned me off her, saying she was a sycophant, in tight with Brooke Baxter, the Dean of Faculty and our supervisor. Anything I told Kimi would get back to her, and Brooke is the type of administrator you need to vent about on a daily basis.

And now I feel guilty for going along with the crowd, for not giving Kimi the benefit of the doubt. It's possible she didn't have a choice.

Because the other teachers were right. Brooke Baxter is, at best, a power-hungry narcissist who'll stop at nothing to get ahead. At worst, she's a full-on manipulative psychopath. The woman hasn't bothered me much yet, but then I stay as far away from her as possible, and I hardly present as the weakest member of the herd. I'll do my time, save some money, and leave.

If Brooke got her hooks into Kimi, though, she may have felt her only option was to go along. It's possible she sought Kimi out because of her diffident demeanor. Like all mean girls, she preys on the weak ones.

I abandoned Kimi and left Baxter free to feast on her. And now I feel terrible about it. Kimi reached out to me the other day, in fact. She said she wanted to tell me something important. I told her I'd check my schedule and get back to her, but I never got around to it. I could have made time, but I didn't.

I feel truly horrible. I was weak, but it's like *Lord of the Flies* around here. The isolation of this place combined with the close proximity to a limited number of other adults who were strangers to me just a few months before creates a surreal atmosphere. Fitting in matters more here than in any setting I've been in since middle school. Alliances form out of necessity, like a nine-month-long season of *Survivor*.

Thinking back on my behavior and the way I cooled to Kimi, I finally start to feel something. Tears erupt and stream down my face as I admit to myself that I was a coward and a total shithead to her. And now I can never make amends because she's gone forever.

My tender moment comes to a halt when two police officers enter the auditorium and walk up to our new head of school, Doug Walker. He seems just as surprised to see them as I am. My stomach lurches and I sit up straight. I feel a tingling in the back of my scalp as I struggle to process what's happening.

I turn to the person next to me, an older cafeteria worker named Sharon who always calls me "dear." Her eyebrows rise as we lift our hands and shrug at one another.

What are police officers doing here? This was an accident.

Wasn't it?

I've been hiding in my apartment all day. I'm about to venture out to the gym, but I don't want to run into anyone. Our boarding population is pretty small, only about sixty students. They dine with us for lunch during the week, but they eat in their building on the weekends. Unless I'm on duty, I pretty much have the weekend to myself, and I don't see too many students, but it's impossible to avoid my coworkers unless I hibernate.

I know the gossip mill will be churning today. I'm not in the mood to engage, so I've been avoiding the other faculty members, which means I have nothing to eat besides cheese and crackers, the only food in my mini-fridge. I decide I might as well get a workout in before grabbing an early dinner, and I head out.

The school campus itself is fairly compact, less than a hundred acres, and houses several buildings. There's the dilapidated faculty apartment building where I live; the state-of-the-art student dorm and center on the opposite side of campus; the central, two-story building that contains the classrooms, gym, and faculty dining commons; and the executive residences adjacent to the central building.

Calling the architecture eclectic would be a euphemism. The central building is old-school Gothic, made of brick and stone, the student center is modern and sleek, and the faculty dorm sits on the edge of campus like an afterthought: shabby, not chic, and fit only for the help.

As I'm walking to the gym, my mind is reeling. Is it possible that Kimi's death was foul play? Why else would the police come to the school? It's not like it happened here on campus.

The administration offered no explanation for the police officers. They simply wrapped up the meeting and dismissed us, so we are all left to speculate. And what people dream up on their own is usually so much worse than the truth. I wish they would level with us, although they might have their reasons for keeping things quiet. Maybe the police tied their hands.

I start to consider the implications, and I feel like my blood pressure is a little elevated. There's an energy in the air that wasn't here before—morbid curiosity mixed with fear—and an undercurrent of grief for those with a heart. Nothing happens here most of the time. It's not like living in a city where sensational news bombards people on a daily basis. The thought of a murderer in the area is terrifying yet titillating for some people but not for me.

I don't like being in the limelight. I like to keep a low profile, and not just because I feel out of place here. If they open up a murder investigation and question us, they might start prying into people's pasts. That's not good because I have something to hide.

And it needs to stay hidden.

———

My attempt to avoid other faculty members failed miserably, but it ended up being okay. After my workout, I shared a dinner table with some other faculty members. The mood was pretty somber. Even the two biggest Kimi-bashers looked remorseful.

It was surprisingly comforting to experience a shared sense of grief, and I decide to stop being so negative. My attitude is probably part of the problem. A major reason why I'm having such a hard time adjusting to this place.

I vow that I'll try to give people around here more of a chance. It's too late to make amends to Kimi, but at least I can learn something from the way I treated her.

The wind has picked up again and the temperature has plummeted. I can see my breath as I approach my building. I pull my collar tight around my neck. I'll be happy to get back into my room, even if it's not that warm.

It's dark already although it's not very late, and I long for the California sun as I enter the deteriorating structure, walk up the creaky steps, and get safely into my apartment.

Once inside, I hear the scraping of the tree branches on my window. I make a mental note to email the facilities team tomorrow to ask them to cut back the trees, but I'm not going to hold my breath. Falcon Ridge Academy is in a death spiral in terms of student enrollment, and I feel like it's on its last legs.

The boarding program relied a great deal on international students, and although that market has bounced back a bit, it's nothing like it was years ago. Even before the pandemic, they'd started to accept day students in an effort to fill seats, but that only kept things at a subsistence level.

The campus is in Ulster County, on the opposite side of the Hudson River from the train line to Grand Central

Station, in an unincorporated hamlet with the same name as the school. A hamlet is a small village with no governing structure. The closest town is Plattekill. We rely on them as well as other nearby towns for our municipal services.

I'd never heard of a hamlet before I moved here. Most people outside the state of New York probably haven't either. There are hundreds of them peppered throughout the vicinity. And it's apparently difficult to determine where many of them begin and end.

It seems very medieval to me, and I wonder what the implications are. What happens when we have an emergency? Do the various towns we rely on for ambulance or police service flip a coin for who comes? Most people don't seem to give it a second thought, so I keep these concerns to myself.

Although there are some pockets of wealth in the area, generally speaking, this isn't a very affluent area. Not many families around here can afford our tuition. As a consequence, we're struggling to stay afloat. That's probably why they keep it so freaking cold; I doubt there's much of a budget for tree pruning. I turn on the television, my only companion, get ready for bed, and count the days to winter break.

TWO

Cassie

I drag myself out of bed and into the bathroom after a fitful slumber that seems to have left me even more tired than I was last night. I should wash my hair, but I don't have the time.

Instead, I pin up my shoulder-length dark waves, enter the shower, and let the hot water run over me, trying to exorcise the chill that's nestled in my bones. I wash and exfoliate my face and scrub with citrus body wash to try to perk up my limbs. Letting the steam from the shower waft out into my bedroom, I towel off, hoping to warm up my apartment a bit.

I smooth some moisturizer on my perpetually dry face and take a good look at myself. I always thought I had an olive complexion, but maybe it was just the California sun. I have never been so pale. It's a stark contrast with my dark hair and eyes, so I apply some tinted foundation and stop to add a touch of mascara, which I haven't used since I've been here. If I'm going to be more social, I may as well look halfway presentable. I don't get carried away, though. Like I said, who am I going to meet on top of this godforsaken mountain?

———

"Hi, Cassie."

Ed Roberts, the tall, geeky, white-haired patriarch of the science department, waves me over to the empty chair next to him near the front of the auditorium, which can hold about two hundred people. With fewer than forty faculty and staff employed at the school, the space appears cavernous. I would rather have sat farther back, but I head over to him.

He's starting to feel like a friend, although he's old enough to be my father. They've called another meeting before school today, and I'm wondering if they are going to tell us anything more about what happened to Kimi.

"Hey, Ed."

"You look nice," he says as I settle in next to him. I feel maybe I should tell him that comments like that date him. I don't take offense or anything. It's just that younger guys seem to know instinctively not to give those kinds of compliments at work. Still, it's nice that my efforts are appreciated, even if it's by someone nearly twice my age.

"Thanks," I reply.

I take off my scarf and place it on my lap.

"How are you holding up? Weren't you close friends with her?"

307

This catches me off guard. I didn't realize people thought I was close with Kimi. I don't feel like I'm close friends with anyone at this place.

"I, um…" I clear my throat.

And now I feel like I'm being put to the test, like the ghost of Kimi is hovering over me, waiting to see if I'll throw her under the bus again.

"Yes." I give my head a nod. "She was a good friend."

Ed places his large hand on my shoulder and gives it a rub, and I look over at him. I heard his wife died about a year ago, and he's been having a hard time. His hazel eyes seem perpetually filled with grief, like a light behind them went out. I noticed it right away, although I didn't know the reason. He's always been kind to me, and I wonder if perhaps we bonded due to our shared sense of loss, although I can hardly compare my breakup to the death of his wife.

Doug Walker, our new head of school, is about to take the stage when Judy Prather sits next to me. She's the last person I want to see. She's the math department chair and perhaps the only woman at the school who could go toe to toe with Brooke Baxter.

She dresses like a secretary from the fifties: ridiculously high heels, body-hugging dresses that fall just below the knee, and poofy hair that looks sprayed into place. Judging from her face, she can't be more than late forties, but her outfits age her. And I don't know how she doesn't break her neck on the icy pathways that meander around campus.

Judy turns to me, leans in, and places a hand on my forearm. "Cassie. How are you holding up?"

I pull away from her, and my right shoulder bumps up against Ed's.

"How am I holding up?" My tone is sharper than I intended. I don't like her, but I shouldn't be so obvious about it.

"I mean, I know that you and Kimi were...close."

I narrow my eyes at her because she's the one who initially gave me the heads-up about Kimi being tight with our boss and suggested I cool off the friendship. She's playing a game with me.

She folds her arms, leans back, and shoots me a sideways glance.

I don't really want to make an enemy out of her, though, so I try to soften our interaction. "I'm shocked, like all of us. But thanks for asking, Judy. It means a lot."

The corners of her mouth lift up to a half-smile and she nods. Perhaps it's genuine. Then she looks off to the side, fiddling with a stray strand of hair. Maybe she feels like an even bigger piece of crap for bad-mouthing Kimi than I do for abandoning her. I certainly hope so.

We focus our attention forward as Doug Walker takes the podium. He's a tall, striking man in his early fifties with just enough gray popping through his dark hair to make him look distinguished but not old. The previous head of school was dressed down when I met him last summer during the interview process, as I've heard he was most of the time, but Walker is always in a suit and tie.

He seems well-liked by almost everyone, although it's only been a few months. Most people are on their best behavior the first months after they start a new job, so it's hard to tell. There are rumors about a health problem. I have no idea if they're true. He looks pretty healthy to me.

"I want to thank everyone for the outpouring of support we've received and give you an update on the situation."

He goes on to tell us that the police being here yesterday was routine. At present, there's no reason to suspect that Kimi's death was anything more than a tragic accident. I feel relieved, and I'm happy to go back to my biggest worry being the fact that I was a shitty friend.

After a bit, he gives the floor to Brooke Baxter, Dean of Faculty, and our second in command. She looks harmless enough, but we all know better.

She's a smaller woman with a formidable stance. She wears her dark hair in a blunt cut that curls in towards her collarbone. The outfit she's wearing—slacks and wedge shoes with a white cardigan—makes her look a few years older than her actual age, which is somewhere around early forties. I sense that's intentional. She's a bit insecure about her youth and about managing so many people with more experience than she has.

I'm surprised when she takes the podium and announces that she's already found a replacement for Kimi. Who on earth would be available this late in the year for a position this undesirable?

Some guy named Dan Moralis, that's who. She gives us some background on him. He comes to us from an international school. He's returned to the area because of a sick grandparent in the vicinity. It's just before winter break, and the semester's not over yet, but he didn't want to wait a few more weeks to come home. I suppose it's touch-and-go with his grandmother and, lucky for us, he's available to stay through the academic year.

She continues with his credentials, and she's borderline gushing, which is weird. He has a master's degree, she says, but some of the faculty here have doctorates. A master's is sort of a given at an independent school. Especially in the humanities.

But then I guess in this job market, she's feeling fortunate to have any warm body to put in front of the students, never mind a qualified one. I take some comfort in that thought, and I hope it continues to be a teacher's market for a few more months until jobs for next year are posted. Then I can secure a new position and get out of here.

"I'm pleased to introduce you to Dan Moralis. Please give him a warm welcome."

Someone in the front row stands and walks up to the stage, and I suddenly feel grateful that I've brushed out my hair and slapped on some mascara for the first time in months. I can't believe my eyes. Dan Moralis is a total hunk. It's like a Christmas miracle.

I look down at myself. I'm wearing a navy sweater dress that flatters my curvy figure, with stylish yet practical waterproof boots, and I'm thankful this is the first day I don't look like a lumberjack. This guy could be a lumberjack though. He's wearing a long-sleeved black thermal shirt, almost the same color as his ebony hair. I can see his biceps and delts straining against the fabric.

Then I realize how totally inappropriate this is. First, I ice out Kimi, and now I'm swooning over her replacement. I'm not planning to act on these feelings. But I take it as a good sign that my heart is starting to heal, as well as some other parts of my anatomy. I'll do my time here, keep a low profile, save money, and go back to San Diego in June ready to put myself out there again. In the meantime, I have to say, the arrival of a hot guy on campus makes things a little more tolerable for me.

We all start to get up, like we're about to be dismissed. We're going to be late for first period if it doesn't happen soon. But then she starts again.

"Oh, and I have one more announcement. I've decided to promote Cassie Romano to English department chair. Although I must apologize if this comes as a surprise to everyone. Including Cassie herself. Hopefully, it's a pleasant one."

She gets some compulsory chuckles out of the crowd and dismisses us.

I look over in disbelief at Ed, and he flashes me a smirk. I've confided in him that I'm planning to leave, so I'm sure he knows this is the last thing I want. *So much for keeping a low profile.* I also realize that now my hands are tied in terms of Dan. I'll be his department chair, so he's somewhat off-limits. I know I just said I wasn't going to act on my attraction, but it was nice to have the option. Any fantasies I have of a steamy romance to keep me warm at night during this long, cold winter can stay safely tucked inside my head.

Brooke Baxter is divorced, and I wonder for a moment if she planned it that way. Promoting me to department chair so I'd be less likely to go for him, and she could have him to herself. I don't think she's stupid enough to hit on him, but then you never know. Smart people do stupid things for love all the time.

——

After an abrupt beginning, the rest of my day was pretty uneventful. It was busy though, and I didn't even have time to be introduced to Dan because the faculty meeting ran late and I had to rush to class. Brooke Baxter popped in on my first break to let me know we'd meet more formally tomorrow. And to make sure I was up for the job. And that I actually wanted it.

What could I say? Of course, I said I was fine with it. And I even pretended to be a bit grateful for the opportunity. I know I'm acting like a suck-up, but all I want is to get out of here. All schools want a recommendation from your previous supervisor. Brooke holds my life in her hands, and she relishes that fact, I'm sure.

After that, I got on with my day, taught my classes, and kept to myself. I didn't see Dan at all. Not at lunch, and not just now when I grabbed an early dinner. Most people eat later, and it was more deserted than usual this evening. I ate alone, which was fine with me.

On my way to my apartment, I stop to grab my mail from my cubby in the admin building. In with the junk mail and an issue of *Education Weekly*, there's a letter in a plain white envelope with "Cassie Romano" and the school address printed in block letters. There's no return address.

I find this a bit unsettling, and one step away from those bizarre letters you see in crime shows, with cut-out words pasted together to form a chilling message. But then I remember getting a few letters from religious groups back in San Diego. They were always addressed by hand. Maybe that's all this is. Still, how would they know to call me Cassie? My legal name is Cassandra.

I have a sinking feeling in my stomach, so I bury the letter inside my magazine and walk a little faster, enter my building, and head up the stairs. It seems strange that somebody would use snail mail these days to reach me if this letter is somehow important.

Continuing down the hallway to my studio, I check my phone to see if there are any text messages or voicemails I missed. But I see no new communications. I'll check my email when I get inside, and I make a mental note to check my spam folder too.

Then a blood-curdling scream fills the air—and it's coming from me. I've nearly run smack into someone. My keys and mail fall onto the worn beige carpet. Whoever it is seems about a foot taller than me, so I can't see whose face it is. I step back and look up. Of course, it's Dan the Hunk. And I just stand there.

Dumbfounded.

There are two studio apartments on this wing of the second floor, but the one next to me has been vacant all year. The presence of another human being near my apartment caught me totally off guard.

"I'm so sorry I startled you," he says.

Then he bends down and starts picking up my mail. The mystery letter is peeking out from inside the magazine, so I quickly crouch down and stuff it back in. But as I do, my hand lands clumsily on top of his, and things get even more awkward. It's like an electric shock goes through me. A delightful electric shock, and I wonder if he can tell.

Meanwhile, I still haven't said anything, and it feels like it's been way too long. I pull my hand away, grab my mail, and smile, but it's more of a clowny grin, not sexy at all. As we start to stand, I finally find some words to use.

"No, *I'm* sorry. I wasn't looking where I was going. But there's been nobody on this floor all year."

"Right. Sorry to invade your space."

He smiles, and of course he's got a totally sexy smile. Not blindingly white like a pretty boy, but white enough. If his teeth were yellow or chipped or missing, perhaps I'd have a fighting chance here.

"Not at all," I say.

"I just moved in. I guess I'm your next-door neighbor. I'm Dan." He pauses while I stare at him, still somewhat in shock. "Dan Moralis?" One brow lifts, like he's wondering if I even know who he is.

"Right! The new English teacher. I'm Cassie Romano," I say.

"You're the new English department chair. I suppose you're my...boss?" He holds out his hand and smiles.

We shake hands, and I try not to feel anything, but it's useless. He's even better up close than he was on stage. There's a faint manly smell emanating from him. I'm guessing it's shaving cream or deodorant because he doesn't look like the kind of guy who would bother with cologne.

Or maybe it's just a man scent, something I haven't been around in a while. Although as I recall, Evan never smelled like this.

"Oh, no." I shake my head and let out an awkward, honking laugh. "Brooke Baxter's your boss. I'm just a paper pusher."

"If you say so."

There's another agonizing silence. I search for something clever to say, but I fail miserably. "Well, I'll let you get on your way."

"Nice to meet you, Cassie Romano. Have a good night."

"You too, Dan."

When I get inside my quarters, I close the door, bolt it behind me, and take a deep breath. After that painful interaction, at least I don't have to worry about the consequences of an illicit campus romance. I'm sure I've effectively ruined my chances. I'm totally out of practice after being in a relationship for so long.

I wonder for a moment why they didn't give him Kimi's apartment. Hers is much bigger. But then I remind myself that she's only been dead for two days. It's probably still got all her stuff in it. She was single, and I think about who will come to gather her belongings. Probably her parents. I decide I'll offer to help pack up her things. It's the least I can do.

In all the chaos, I totally forgot about the letter. I sit down on my tiny green loveseat, holding it between my thumb and forefinger. It's postmarked Plattekill, the closest post office to the school. I feel like I'm holding Pandora's box. I should just rip it up and throw it away.

But of course, I don't. I stare at it for a bit longer. Then I open it. I scan down to the bottom, and my fingers start to tremble.

It's Kimi Choy, talking to me from beyond the grave.

I read it carefully, twice, and I'm still not sure what to make of it. The letter is vague and fairly brief, expressing concerns that "something strange" is going on at the school and asserting that Brooke Baxter is out to get the new head of school, Doug Walker. She tells me that Brooke is angry that she didn't get the head of school job, something I already know. Everyone knows that. Why would she tell me that in a letter?

Then Kimi informs me she's going to resign. She warns me to be careful of Baxter and to watch my back. I wonder if she was planning to leave town that morning and never return. Maybe this is her way of saying goodbye to me.

I know the right thing to do is to give it to the police, but I don't want to call attention to myself. Besides, she didn't say I should go to the police if she was found dead. And there's nothing at all earth-shattering in this letter. Doug Walker said there's nothing to worry about in terms of foul play, and I don't want them poking around in my business. I have no reason to think this was anything more than a tragic slip and fall.

Right?

We all know about the feud over the head of school position. It even spread to the board of directors. A board member even resigned in protest about the decision, one of only two women in the group of seven. Brooke expected to be promoted to head of school when the last one retired, and she and Doug were finalists for the position. It's common knowledge that she blew a gasket when they gave it to outsider Doug Walker. She threatened to file a lawsuit, claiming gender discrimination.

Doug Walker is the school's first African American head of school, but he's still a man, she pointed out, and then she gave the board a bunch of statistics trying to show that gender discrimination is more of an issue in private school administration than race. Which might be true—the stats on women in independent school leadership are terrible—but that's not the reason she didn't get the job.

She didn't get the job because she's a toxic administrator, and one of the least popular leaders I've ever worked for. She bullies people and plays favorites. Pits people against each other. And nobody wants to work for her. I'm frankly shocked they kept her on after her little tirade. I'm assuming it's because they're afraid of a lawsuit, and they're hoping she finds something else soon and moves on, as we all are.

I care less than most people because I'm out of here in a few long months. I sometimes fantasize that they fire me so I don't even have to finish out the school year. But they won't. And I need a good recommendation, so I'll stay on and do a decent job. And just in case there's some truth to Kimi's warning, I'll stay out of all the drama. Which brings me back to the letter and what I should do with it. What if it's important in some way? Is it fair to Kimi to rip it up and forget about it?

Then a thought occurs to me. I could send it to the police, anonymously. My fingerprints are all over it though, so I'll use gloves, cut off the part with my name on it, make a copy on my computer printer, and send it off to the police. Then, I'll have officially made amends to Kimi, and I can get on with my life.

THREE

Miles

"What the fuck is going on over there, Brooke?" I realize a split-second too late that if I want information from her, this probably isn't the best way to get it. But she's been avoiding me, and I don't like being ignored. But I'm in my study, just a few rooms away from my wife and daughter, so I remind myself to keep my voice down.

"What do you mean?" she replies, with a hint of sarcasm.

"You know what I mean. I have to hear it on the news that this teacher of yours died? Why didn't you call me? And why didn't you return my phone call last night?"

"I didn't even know about it myself until early Sunday morning. I figured Doug Walker would call and tell you about it. Isn't that *his* job?"

Here we go again.

I made her all kinds of promises about the head of school position, promises on which I failed to deliver. But then I hadn't expected so much pushback from the other board members. I'm board chair at Falcon Ridge Academy, but I'm not a king. We hire by committee, and there were legitimate concerns about her management style.

I could throw that in her face right now, but I've got more to lose than she does at this point, and if she's becoming unhinged, she could even be dangerous to me. She knows too much, so I'm stuck having to play nice. I hate that she has something on me. But then I have something on her too, so I need to keep that top of mind.

Plus, she has a point. It's Doug Walker's job to inform me about the teacher's death, not her job. And if there's any chance Brooke's mixed up in it, I need to tread carefully. But I need to see her, to read her facial expressions and her body language.

I find it a strange coincidence that she voiced concerns about Kimi Choy being on to us just a few days earlier while I sat in this very chair using this very same burner phone—and two days after that call, the woman turned up dead. I'm losing patience, but I need to try and play it cool. Not let on that I'm harboring doubts about her.

"Doug did call me, Brooke. That's not what I mean, and you know it. But we need to talk. Are they doing an investigation? Did she say anything to anyone? Do we need to be concerned?"

"We shouldn't be talking on the phone," she says.

"It's my burner."

"Well, it's not *my* burner."

I realize that she's right about that too. Maybe I'm the one who's becoming unhinged. My back is against the wall and I'm running out of time, so I'm not thinking straight. We settle on a face-to-face meeting the following day at our usual spot: a clean, low budget chain motel just outside town. And then we sign off.

———

I come out of my study and make my way through the hallway, the foyer, and the living room. I stop when I spy my family in the dining area. I can smell something pungent coming from the kitchen, and I realize I'm hungry.

Garlic and ginger maybe?

But I see my wife Madeline helping our sixteen-year-old daughter with her homework at the dining table, so I assume the meal will take a bit longer. Our dog Max, an aging golden retriever, is curled up near my wife's feet.

Madeline gives our daughter a hint, but doesn't solve the math problem for her. Erin has a pained look on her face, and I watch as Madeline places her hand on our daughter's shoulder and gives it a rub. She looks over at her mother. What passes between them is timeless and precious and beautiful. There are no words exchanged, but I'm confident that Erin knows she's supported, and that her mother has her back. Erin takes a deep breath and goes back to work, and I see a smile light up her face when she comes up with the correct answer. But even if she hadn't, I'm sure she knows she'd be loved just the same.

Madeline makes it all look so effortless. Keeping our family on a steady course. And it puts my stomach in knots to know that it's all in jeopardy.

My wife's face is clean and bare today. I can spot the faint row of freckles that dot her nose and cheeks. I've always loved them on her, even more so now because I see them mirrored in our daughter, and I don't understand why she covers them with make-up. They make her look young. Fresh. Innocent. Like when we first met.

I've tried my best to be a caring husband and father. And up until recently, a solid provider. It's Madeline who keeps the family unit together, though. I love my wife and daughter very much. And as I take in the sight of the two of them, I'm thankful that they have no idea that their world is in danger of being blown apart—and I'd like to keep it that way.

There's still a way out, so I don't want to let on about any of it until the last possible moment. And even then, I'll do what I can to protect them.

Madeline finally notices me.

"How long have you been standing there?"

"Long. But not long enough." I walk over and give my wife a kiss. "How's the schoolwork coming?" I give Erin's head a rub but she bats my hand away.

"Fine, Dad."

She's been a little distant lately, and I worry for a split second that maybe rumors are circulating at school about me and Brooke Baxter. But I have enough to worry about, so I push that thought from my mind.

It's probably just a phase she's going through. It was so much easier when she was younger. I wonder, again, what it would be like to have a son. Would we relate better to each other? We tried for more kids, but Madeline wasn't able to get pregnant again. It was putting a strain on our marriage, so we both decided to quit while we were ahead rather than resort to fertility treatments.

"When's dinner?" I ask.

"Twenty minutes."

"It smells good."

"Dad. *Shh.* I'm trying to concentrate."

I can't see her face because I'm standing behind her, but I sense there's more to this than an eagerness to do math homework. My eyes meet Madeline's and I shrug. Then she mouths *guy problems.* I nod and decide to take Max for a walk, my one male companion in this female-dominated household. I pat the dog's head rather than disturbing Erin again. Max's hearing isn't what it used to be so I'd have to almost yell to get his attention. The dog springs up and follows me to the door.

"Let's go boy."

I relish the eager look on Max's face as I snap on the leash and head out the door, the only member of the family who'll continue to look up to me no matter how this mess plays out.

If you enjoyed this sample, please go to www.bonnietraymore. com for current retail availability.

Made in United States
North Haven, CT
23 June 2024